W9-BAW-054

FRANCINE TOON

Pine

doubleday

TRANSWORLD PUBLISHERS
61–63 Uxbridge Road, London W5 5SA
www.penguin.co.uk

Transworld is part of the Penguin Random House group of companies
whose addresses can be found at global.penguinrandomhouse.com

Penguin
Random House
UK

First published in Great Britain in 2020 by Doubleday
an imprint of Transworld Publishers

Lyrics on p.vii from 'Every River' written by Calum MacDonald

A CIP catalogue record for this book
is available from the British Library.

ISBNs 9780857526700 (hb)
9781781620526 (tpb)

Typeset in 12.5/16.5pt Sabon LT Std
by Integra Software Services Pvt. Ltd, Pondicherry

Printed an   f S.p.A.

Penguin R   ure for
our bus   nade
    fr

For Yassine

Little girl, little girl, don't lie to me,
Tell me, where'd you stay last night?
I stayed in the pines where the sun never shines
And I shivered when the cold winds blew.

'In the Pines', traditional American folk song

You ask me to believe in magic.

'Every River', Runrig

1

They are driving out for guising when they see her. It is the narrow part of the road that cuts through the hem of the forest. Some firs arch so densely here they block the night sky. Lauren sits high in the passenger seat, her elasticated gym shoes swinging over cans of Kick and a chewed-up tennis ball. She has braided her hair and wears it in a circle like a garland. Niall, her father, is steering their dented pickup and listening to Aerosmith. It smells of dog fur even though Jameson isn't in the truck.

'Is that lipstick?' her father asks.

'No, it's face paint,' Lauren says, lying. It is the one time of year she can wear something of her mother's. It feels precious. Clandestine.

She holds a pumpkin-shaped bucket on her knees. Her face is powdered white except for the deep-red trickle at the corner of her mouth. There is no reason it can't be face paint. Her dress is black with a cream lace collar. They bought it for her grand-mother's funeral eleven months ago, when she was nine and a half. Her arms stick out of their sleeves, reminding her that next year the dress might be too small. Her father says next year maybe they'll stop. But for now, she is a vampire. She likes this outfit and because they live in a tiny village no one can tease her, unlike at school. In her pocket, there's a piece of antler that folds out into a knife.

The headlights cast two white beams into the black. Up ahead there is a kink in the single-track lane, a passing place, its diamond sign growing luminous as they approach. Lauren sees a skinny figure standing in the scrub of the verge, enveloped in a large white dressing gown.

'Jesus,' her father says as they bump past.

'Who's that?' Lauren cranes back at the dark road. The trees are thinning out.

'Who's what?' replies her father and turns up the music.

Lauren puts her hand in the dress pocket and runs a finger across the ridged antler, then along the metal strip that is the edge of the blade. She has been doing this recently. Soon they break out of the forest altogether and speed down the hill to Clavanmore: four houses dotted along the road; a constellation of lights among the dark fields. Niall parks near her friend Billy Matheson's house, at the disused phone box. Its bare bulb is still working, illuminating one corner of the pavement. Weeds are growing through the cracked tarmac and up under the glass.

Lauren watches the wing mirror for several minutes, until she sees the small figure of Billy and his frost-coloured shorts. His mother Kirsty and little brother Lewis follow behind, walking downhill from their home along the narrow edge of the road.

Billy has fake blood smeared over his face and down the front of his long-sleeved goalie's jersey, under his coat. His hair stands up in gory spikes. 'What've you been doing to that football strip?' Lauren's father says flatly, slamming the pickup door.

'He's a zombie.' Kirsty's voice catches in the iced air. She is wearing a yellow and navy Puffa jacket that reminds Lauren of a bumblebee. Her cornflake-blonde hair is mostly tucked under a bobble hat. It looks cosy. 'Red food colouring,' Kirsty says, smiling at Lauren, her eyes small and bright. 'Lewis here is a little monster, aren't you?' The toddler is wearing a dinosaur onesie over some bulky under-clothes, his chubby cheeks flushed.

'You can say that again,' says Niall, with a sting of humour in his near-expressionless face.

Lewis looks up at him and says something urgently that they can't understand.

'He's excited,' says Kirsty. The wind howls in the distant trees.

'What are you?' Billy asks Lauren, as if it isn't obvious. He's growing taller than her.

'Vampire,' says Lauren. She tries not to sound too excited about it. The supermarket had sold out

3

of glow-in-the-dark fangs, so she had to make do with the lipstick-blood.

They leave Niall in the pickup, the muffle of Moray Firth Radio fading as Lauren and Billy make their way further down the sloping road, Kirsty and Lewis ambling behind. The dark is broken by the light of windows shining through the cotton backing of curtains, and two streetlights, like orange boiled sweets. They walk towards the homes of people they have known their whole lives.

Alan Mackie's is the first house on the road. The cottage smells of paint stripper and sawdust. Lauren trips over a stepladder folded in the hallway as she shuffles into Alan's beige lounge. Kirsty picks up Lewis, who begins to grumble, his plump fingers reaching towards a screwdriver on the hall table. Lauren takes her place next to Billy, in front of the roaring football with its green glare. Sun-bleached photographs balance on top of the television. They are of Alan and his wife, much younger and stockier, on red bikes in the Aviemore hills. There is a picture of his wife in later years, pallid and close to the end, sitting in a pink dressing gown with a large ginger cat curled on her lap. Billy's mother sits with Alan now on the same toffee-coloured sofa. It squeaks when she crosses her legs. He mutes the wide television. The smell in this room is sour and musty, like a pub. Lauren hardly visits Alan or notices him around. There is something about him that gives her the creeps, and seeing the inside of his house is rare. Once in a blue moon, Niall will bring her by to pick up a piece of hardware he needs to borrow. He's comfortable when socializing has a practical purpose. One time they were there, Alan took Lauren through his trophy collection that shines now along the back wall. He stood closer to her than she liked, and she could smell his body odour. He told her he used to be her father's PE teacher and showed her his awards for shot-put, discus and stone-put at the Highland Games, turning them over in his crêpey, speckled hands. She likes the crystal trophy the best, and second best the trophy with the little gold man holding a tiny gold stone at his neck.

'So,' Alan says, 'what's your party piece?'

Billy says, all in one breath, 'Why could the skeleton not go to the dance?'

'I don't know,' Alan says, with a nod. He looks at Kirsty, then back at the children. His teeth are yellow when he grins. 'Why *could* the skeleton not go to the dance?'

Billy pauses. 'Be*cause* he had nobody . . . to go with.'

Alan bursts into a wheeze. 'Ach, no *body*, very good, son.'

For her party piece Lauren sings 'Bat Out Of Hell'. She's rehearsed this several times in her bedroom, but when she starts to sing, her throat feels as though it is trying to close up. 'Bat Out Of Hell' is a song her dad puts on in the pickup or when he is frying bacon on a Sunday morning. One summer he opened the windows and blasted it at Jehovah's Witnesses walking up their empty stretch of road. She wishes he was here to listen to her. He doesn't like being polite if he doesn't have to be, unlike Kirsty or her husband Craig. He's the kind of man who slips away, unnoticed, any chance he gets. People in Strath Horne, their closest town, raise their eyebrows at this sort of thing.

Alan Mackie reaches down and hands Lauren one of the Mars bars laid out on the low glass-topped table between them. He puts his hand on his back as he leans forward to do so. There is a large chip on the coffee table's wooden frame, as if something heavy has fallen on it. Alan's cardigan looks itchy and a button is missing, exposing his off-white polo shirt. He wheezes to Billy's mum, 'We'll be seeing her on the telly, eh? *X Factor.*' He ruffles Billy's hair and gives him a Mars bar, too, as they get ready to leave. He says, leaning towards Billy in his football kit, 'And this one'll be the next Billy Dodds, eh? Billy Matheson.' His laugh takes all of his breath. Lauren doesn't see what's funny.

She runs as fast as she can down the cottage drive-way until she is warm. It makes her cape, a split bin bag, float in the air. She laughs a pantomime laugh.

'*I'm your arch-nemesis!*' she says in an American voice.

'What's that?' Billy is not far behind.

'It's me!' Lauren swirls around. 'Can we go guising to Diane's?' she asks his mother.

'It's a bit too far, love,' says Kirsty. 'We'd have to walk a couple of fields in the dark. Anyway, I expect she'll be busy looking after her mum. We'd best not disturb.'

'I never see her though,' Lauren says in a sing-song voice, knowing she shouldn't.

'Do you not see her on the bus, with the older kids?' asks Kirsty, brisk and dismissive.

'Not really,' Lauren says in a quiet voice. She wraps her foot around the back of her left leg to scratch it, like a flamingo. It's true that when Diane gets on the school bus, with her slouchy black hoody, she will sometimes touch Lauren's hair as she passes, like a blessing. On those days the girls her age will leave Lauren alone, although they still whisper. It's an unspoken rule that the seats at the back of the bus are for the older kids, who go to the high school next to their primary. Diane is the kind of teenage girl who takes the middle seat of the very last row and doesn't care if her throaty laugh travels down the aisle. One time their bus driver, Roy, threw her off for smoking. Lauren remembers looking down at the stony verge as they drove away. Diane stood giving the bus the middle finger, the wide purple heathland stretching behind her into wide white sky.

Lauren wishes Diane could see her Halloween costume. She's someone who enjoys old films with vampires. Lauren thinks she would too; if she was allowed to go to Diane's to watch them, they wouldn't scare her.

There are lots of times when Lauren does feel scared: at school, on the bus, even at home when her father yells at her for asking too many questions. But Diane gives her a little thrill of fear that can feel good. She once dared Lauren to touch an electric fence for as long as she could, which was just a few seconds in the end. A week later, Diane gave her a bottle of glittery nail polish called Electric Eel. She showed Lauren where she had ripped off the security tag, so the alarm wouldn't be triggered when she took it out of the shop. 'The name reminded me of you . . . though you're more of a prawn,' Diane said, smiling with dark lipstick. It was still one of Lauren's best memories.

'If she told you to jump off a bridge would you do it?' Niall had asked at the time, when he heard about the electric fence. Lauren had shaken her head, but deep down, she knew she probably would.

When the small vampire and zombie go down to Vairi Grant's cottage they hear her tiny dogs start yowling like monkeys. Gingerly, Lauren tries to open the door of the white plastic porch just as Billy's mum and baby brother amble up behind them. The door is unlocked as usual. From inside the house, they hear Vairi Grant shouting a hoarse '*Wheesht!*' at the yapping. *That auld wifey*, Lauren's dad sometimes calls her. A little taller than Lauren, she has a powerful voice and a fragile gait. They find her balancing on a kickstool, rummaging through a dark top cupboard in her foosty kitchen. The main light has blown, and the room is illuminated by a lamp on the table.

'You all right there, Vairi?' asks Kirsty. She looks at the children with raised eyebrows and sets Lewis down in the hallway. He stomps his small foot forward at the dogs, who begin barking again. Vairi doesn't reply. She fishes a clear, open bag of monkey nuts from the cupboard and places it on the table. It looks identical to last year's.

'And how's this little laddie? So much bigger every day!' Vairi grins toothily down at Lewis, who toddles behind his mother's legs. 'Have you no got a party piece?' she asks.

'He's a wee bit young yet,' Kirsty replies.

When Lauren sings 'Bat Out Of Hell', Vairi frowns at Kirsty and then at Lauren, with wrinkled eyes like a chicken. Lauren looks at the woman's veiny hands, free of rings. On the window ledge she sees a pair of binoculars and a spider plant.

'Oh, I don't think I know that one,' Vairi says, wiping the olive-green countertop. One dog barks and stands on its hind legs. Vairi hums tunelessly. 'How's your dad keeping?' Before Lauren can reply, Vairi turns to Kirsty. 'I never see them on a Sunday.' The other dog yaps, as if in agreement. Kirsty's smile doesn't reach her eyes.

When they are back outside Billy asks his mother, 'Why is Vairi weird?'

'She's just an old lady – she's getting on a bit. Sometimes people go a bit doolally, you know. And let's be honest, she likes to talk, like everyone else round here.'

Billy has stopped listening and runs across the empty road but Lauren makes sure she overtakes him. He throws monkey nuts at her caped back. She picks up the nuts from the cold ground and hurls them over her shoulder as she runs. Kirsty, now some way behind, tells them to stop. 'He's just a zombie!' Lauren says.

'She's my arch-nemesis,' Billy replies.

Lewis begins to wail. His dinosaur costume has become grimy and snot-streaked. 'C'mon,' says Kirsty. 'It isn't that bad a joke.' The wailing grows into a scream and she looks uphill towards Niall's parked truck in the distant smudge of the phone-box light. 'Look, you guys go on ahead. He doesn't like the cold, so we'll go and sit a while with Niall. C'mon, you. No sweeties.'

Lauren chews her lip.

'On you two go to Angela's. It's not that far.'

'Is Dad coming?' asks Lauren.

'You know he's not her biggest fan. C'mon. She won't bite.'

Now alone, Lauren and Billy approach the third house, tucked away on a narrow side road, guarded by trees. They walk through its open black gates and up its curved drive, their feet sinking into tiny pebbles stolen from the local beach. Either side, scrawny birches bend back in the wind.

Angela and Malcolm Walker answer the door in soft Tattersall shirts, each leaning against a heavy stone wall. They look over their shoulders in tandem and call 'Ann-Marie!' into the gloomy hall. Ann-Marie Walker is home from boarding school. She appears, sixteen and pale with dark eyes like her father, hair the colour of school shoes. A silver stud catches the light in the left side of her nose.

'Your hair's so short now,' says Lauren, stepping in from the cold and standing by the overloaded coat stand. She didn't know boys' hair could look good on girls. When Ann-Marie turns her head, Lauren counts the piercings on her right ear, unwittingly touching her own.

'She takes them out during term time,' Angela Walker says. Her accent is threaded with English vowels, though she has never lived there.

Ann-Marie gives her mother a look and shakes her head.

'Came home full of metal,' says Malcolm Walker in his Lowlands accent. 'I said she's to be careful she doesn't end up with an ear like a Swiss cheese!'

'Dad.' With a backward glance, Ann-Marie slips back down into the cellar that is now a kitchen. Lauren has opened her mouth to sing but watches her disappear, crestfallen.

After 'Bat Out Of Hell', Angela and Malcolm Walker clap their hands and nod. Angela passes a flowery plate of toffee apples from the hall table, her auburn hair escaping its tortoiseshell clip. 'They're from the orchard,' she says.

Lauren picks one up. It feels unwieldy on its thin stick. She tries to bite into it, but the amber glaze is solid and her teeth scrape against the sugar. She asks to see their Irish wolfhounds, big as bears, kept in the converted kitchen cellar.

Billy follows her down. It smells of damp and saddle-soaped horse tack. He says, 'No one found my joke funny.' Classical music murmurs from a scuffed stereo in the corner. Ann-Marie Walker is sitting at the broad oak table, her teenage head bent as she carves a jack-o'-lantern from a turnip. The sleeve of her grey turtleneck is rolled up past her elbow and Lauren can see her muscles flex under the material. A small pile of silver bracelets and rings lie on the knotted surface. She shows the children how much she has carved out of the middle of the vegetable. 'It's hard going,' she says. 'How's school?'

Billy shrugs and kicks a ball towards one of the dogs, who bombs out from its basket.

'Fine,' says Lauren, absently, as the other dog comes close to her, sniffing for attention. Its coarse hair moves like rough seas.

'Sure?' Ann-Marie asks.

'Yeah.' Lauren looks back down at the dog, who is more interested in Billy's ball game.

Ann-Marie props her head on one elbow. 'You'll tell me if that girl bothers you again, won't you?'

'Yeah.' Lauren tries to pull the lace cuff of her sleeve over her wrist.

'I love your hair, by the way.' The brightness pops back into Ann-Marie's voice as she carries on with her carving. 'I think my mum's got some sweets for you guys.'

On cue, they hear Angela on the creaky stairs, a little breathless as she bears her weight carefully. 'Ann-Marie, have you shown them the turnip? Last time we were in Inverness, we bought this book on Halloween traditions.'

Ann-Marie flicks her eyes up and says, 'It's called Samhain,' and goes back to work.

Lauren leans on the Aga, avoiding the Hunter wellies that are drying in front of it. 'Are you off school?' she asks Ann-Marie, who is looking at her strangely. 'We had our tattie holidays already.' She wonders then if Ann-Marie's older brother Fraser is here too, before remembering he set off for university last month.

Before Ann-Marie can reply, her mother cuts in from the foot of the stairs. 'That school is *use*less. They don't know *what* they're doing. Sometimes,' she says, as if talking to an adult, 'I think we should have sent her to school in Strath Horne with you, Lauren, not Edinburgh.' A dog bounds up to Angela, its breath heavy and wet. 'Get,' she says, thrusting her arm towards its basket. 'You're not making a mess of me this time.' In the kitchen light, her face looks bare except for a shade of autumnal lipstick and the chunky purple glasses that frame her eyes. Angela has the kind of eyes that like to peer into other people's business. 'Remember, wash your hands now before eating sweeties,' she says to the children as they go to pet the retreating dog. 'And it says, that book, they used to use turnips, so,' she continues, nodding at the turnip, 'bloody difficult, let me tell you. A lot of elbow grease.' She moves over to the cherry-red kettle. 'Who's for tea?'

Billy is in his own world with the dogs and doesn't respond.

'Can I have a cup, please? Angela, why did they do that?' asks Lauren, quietly.

'The turnips? Oh, this is before we grew pumpkins. Hang on. I've made some other treats.' She makes her way over to the larder like a blustery wind.

'So,' says Lauren, 'you back for long?'

'Um. A few days.' Ann-Marie does not look up as she carves.

Angela returns to the table with ice-cream boxes repurposed as Tupperware. She adjusts her glasses and prises off the lids, revealing marshmallow top hats and meringues. 'Happy Halloween!'

Lauren takes a bite of a top hat, smudging the lipstick trickle on her cheek.

Without Billy's mum in sight, the children make their way back across the main road and uphill past Vairi's. Niall's truck is no longer by the phone box. As they reach Billy's house with its fat stone walls, Lauren sees the pickup in the driveway. Its engine is rumbling and the headlamps throw an impatient light on the gravel. She walks up to the truck and presses her face against the cold window. Lewis, no longer wailing, is sitting next to Kirsty in the passenger seat. Lewis tugs at his mother's arm. She catches sight of Lauren and scrambles to open the door. 'Oh, here,' she says, getting out. 'Never mind, Niall,' she calls back. 'And thanks.' She hurries inside, dragging Lewis.

'Come in for a sec,' she says to Lauren. Lauren steps into the bright hallway of Billy's home. 'I suppose you can have some too,' Kirsty says to Billy and grabs handfuls of Freddo chocolates and Swizzels Matlow sweets from multi-buy packages.

'Thanks, Kirsty,' says Lauren, emptying her hands into her bucket.

'See ya tomorrow then!' Billy says, turning towards the stairs. 'Are you wanting to work on the hut again?'

'Yeah, I think so,' says Lauren. 'Bye, Kirsty.'

Lauren passes the sycamores outside, their dry leaves chattering. A whiny guitar riff slithers from the truck and she catches the shadow of her father, waiting.

As Niall drives his daughter home, he says, 'What did Angela give you?', his chin jutting up like a question mark.

'Top hats.'

He wiggles the back of his free hand by his cheek. '*Ooh.*'

'*Dad!* It's not that fancy!' He always moans about Angela. *At least she made me something,* she thinks.

''S only kiddin'. Trying to make you smile. You're like a teenager already.' Her dad's face is stony, as it often is, looking ahead at the road, but she can read the tiny margin of difference between anger and irony, like now.

They listen to rock radio without speaking. The headlights track the monotonous black road, spotlighting potholes and rubble. The glowing white sign of the passing place jolts into view again.

Then there is more white, moving this time, as the blurred shape of a woman runs into the road. '*Fuck*.' Niall pulls on the steering wheel, but they lurch towards a ditch. The pines jump close and Lauren's scream seems to come from a different girl's mouth. For a moment she only knows branches on glass, the squeal of tyres and Steven Tyler's voice.

In the stillness that follows, she notices the pumpkin bucket has fallen to the floor and lollipops are rolling between cans and dog hair on the shredded carpet. Lauren looks up, past the cut-out air freshener ticking back and forth like a metronome. The woman on her hands and knees comes back into view as Niall restarts the engine. 'I Don't Want To Miss A Thing' blares as he swings back on to the road and the headlights catch her, crouching still as a hare, her face bleached out.

'It's that lady again,' Lauren says. Looking more closely at her, *lady* sounds wrong. She's too young. *Girl* isn't quite right either. She might be the same age as Ann-Marie and Diane, or a few years older, it's hard to tell.

Her father doesn't seem to be listening, but then in a distant voice he says, 'I know who it is.'

He dips the lights and Lauren can make out fair hair, hanging in a clump. The girl-woman rises and takes a shaky step towards them. Her dressing gown has been made for a man and is gaping. She's skinny and her feet are bare. There are dark marks on her legs. 'What's wrong with her?' Lauren asks.

Niall frowns into his large palm as if trying to cover his whole face.

'She . . . can't walk properly,' Lauren says. The young woman wears nothing but the dressing gown that slides down one shoulder. Lauren has never seen someone so naked before. Fear pulls close around her. She draws her feet up on the seat and sticks her woollen knees against her chin. 'Dad?' They should help; she knows they should.

The woman has reached the bonnet, her shadow in the headlights stretching over the small stones of the road. The black pines are thick on either side.

'It's OK, love, it's—' Niall's heavy jacket rustles as he shifts in his seat. 'Stay here.'

Lauren pulls her vampire cape over her head. She feels her father touch her shoulder, then the spring of suspension as he opens the door to leave the truck. Her cape lifts when the door slams. '*Dad*,' she whispers, her tongue parched as a leaf. She hears his workman's boots, heavy on the ground. Then there is no sound except her breath against the plastic of her cape. She opens her eyes, then closes them and it is the same black. She imagines she is shrinking smaller, very small, and the cape spreads into bat wings, growing from her back. She needs to fly out of the window, the same colour as the night.

This does not happen. She listens to her own breathing as her skin grows clammy, then lifts the cape to see her father standing in front of the bonnet, holding the strange woman's body to his. The woman is so much smaller than him, her shoulders narrow. Her girlish face is turned towards the wind-proof fabric of his chest and he looks straight down at her, pulling in his chin, running his rough hand over her wild hair, his own ponytail trailing from his ski hat. Lauren fidgets in her seat and makes a quiet sound that is not the same as crying.

Niall leads the woman by a thin arm to Lauren's side of the truck. She looks in at the passenger window and right through Lauren, her face gaunt and moon-coloured. Lauren's bones feel cold. Niall moves his hand, signalling that Lauren should shift over to the driver's seat. He opens the passenger door and the woman climbs in with the cold air, shaking, but her expression does not show it. For the ride home, Lauren sits on Niall's knee, behind the steering wheel. It is cramped and quiet. The fan heater covers the windows in steam.

'Not far from home,' Niall says as the headlamps search the road in front of them. 'We'll get you home. Up the road.' He taps the sides of the steering wheel and drives slowly up the wooded hill to their house.

Behind her father's padded arm, Lauren can only see parts of the woman. She can see parts of the dressing gown and parts of her hair. The parts are shuddering. Lauren doesn't see how her father might know this woman, whose face looks so young but whose expression is old.

Time seems to still. Lauren's dad smells of sweat and air from the woods. His beard and chin are touching the circle of Lauren's braided hair. He makes her lean to his right side and she feels nauseous. 'We'll get you home,' he says again. 'Get us all home.' The woman remains silent and Lauren looks ahead. They could be driving into nothing but the lit-up claws of trees, strange gestures. Lauren imagines the pickup eating the road as they drive, sucking it like a tarry soup, the trees trying to wave it down with their bony wooden limbs. 'Stop wriggling,' says her dad.

Lauren begins to say the words to 'Bat Out Of Hell' inside her head. She repeats the verses without thinking of their meaning, just the shape of the words and their sounds.

They reach their own stone house in minutes. Niall shovels coal from the outside bunker into an iron bucket while Lauren fiddles with the key in the lock. She can feel the woman standing behind her. Yet when she looks over her shoulder, as she opens the front door, there is only the dark rustling of trees. Lauren looks around. The woman is standing behind her father at the bunker. She has a strangely crooked body and her dressing gown is so white it almost glows in the starlight.

As they enter, the woman drifts silently into the house behind Niall. Now they are inside, her eyes remind Lauren of puddles, frozen over. The hollowed skin beneath them is the shade of bruises as she takes a seat on the pleather sofa of their back room, the place they spend time eating and watching TV. The woman looks straight ahead, almost unblinking, at the painting on the wall of a wolf in the snow.

It is hard to stop watching the woman, but Lauren has to go to the kitchen and creak open the boiler door for her father. She jerks her head round as Niall shakes the coal out of the scuttle.

'How do you know her?' Lauren asks. Despite the boiler starting, she still feels cold.

'Did I say that? It's late now; I'll explain to you in the morning.' His voice is distant, dreamy, like when she tries to wake him up from the sofa, the times she takes herself to bed.

Once he has finished shaking out the coal, he passes Lauren, looking straight ahead, before kneeling by the hearth. His glassy eyes dart between the woman's blank face and his twists of newspaper, ready to burn. Above him, on the mantelpiece, stand a Himalayan salt lamp and two chunky amethysts, halved like purple fruit, their insides catching the light. Crystals hang over the sliding doors to the overgrown garden. These are objects that belonged to Lauren's mother, before she slipped out of their lives, when Lauren was a baby. Lauren's father doesn't like her asking questions too often. Their house is still filled with these salt lamps and candles. Niall says they belong to him, but Lauren knows they are her mother's. The only times Niall will speak of her, *your mother*, is when he has drunk four glasses or more. *Your mother*. Two words that sound soft together. He never says too much though, only that her mother was a healer and different to anyone else. They met when she was eighteen and had moved to Strath Horne after a stint in Edinburgh. If Lauren tries to ask where she might be now, Niall says she must have gone on to better things. This makes Lauren scared to ask any more, scared that this means she, as a daughter, was not a good thing and her mother was looking for something better. Maybe her father doesn't like to talk because he knows she won't like to hear what he has to say.

There is only one photo in the house, taken by Lauren's granny, who has now passed, where her mother is so young she looks as though she could be Lauren's classmate. Sometimes if Lauren is browsing in a shop in Strath Horne, which is only a little bigger than a village, she will notice women looking at her out of the corner of their eyes. Children have made strange comments in the cloakrooms at school, before talking among themselves.

Lauren hopes one day she'll be able to overhear a hushed conversation long enough to understand.

From her seat on the sofa, the woman is looking at Lauren on the floor. She doesn't seem happy or sad, but empty. Lauren wonders what she is thinking, if she is thinking anything at all.

'Would you like . . . ?' says Lauren in a quiet voice. 'Would you like . . .' She bites her lip and looks away. She thinks maybe the woman needs a hug, the way she would hug Ann-Marie when she's sad, but something stops her. There is a long pause while Niall scrunches a ball of magazine pages to add to the fire. She takes a breath and looks back. '. . . something to drink?'

The woman sits motionless, staring at the painting. Her thin body under the dressing gown makes her look like a bundle of laundry. Her legs remind Lauren of a chicken's and her skin of eggshell. There is a crookedness to her nose. It has a bruise at the bridge.

Lauren's dad breaks white chunks of firelighters with mechanical movements. Firelighters remind Lauren of the foam casing from the internet packages he picks up at the post office. She gets them confused sometimes, but her dad says you shouldn't burn plastic. The room is heavy, as though invisible smoke is clogging up the air.

Lauren remembers the time she rescued a bird from a cat. The bird was so sick it was tame, and sat on her shoulder, and she hoped it could be her pet. She fed it food and made a bed for it in her clothes drawer with cotton wool. But the next day, the bird was lifeless. Her father told her cats' teeth are like poison and the bird never stood a chance. He is scrunching more newspaper and stacking kindling in an upward point, adding blocks of peat like thick slices of dark cake. He lights the fire and it burns into the silence. The white-green moss on the kindling starts to crackle and curl. Niall pulls the heavy blue curtain across the door frame. He pokes the fire again, goes over to the other side of the room and takes a bottle of whisky, nearly empty, from inside the hatch. He glugs it, slouching on the sofa. Jameson pads in and lies down by the fire. Lauren kneels and gives the spaniel's tummy a rub. He comforts her, more than she comforts him.

Can I ask you something? Are you a vampire? Are you a kelpie?

She doesn't say these words aloud, but instead looks over to her dad and says to the woman: 'It's OK. We'll look after you.'

The pale young woman is still staring at the wall, making Lauren wonder if she is deaf or speaks any English at all. As if reading her thoughts, the woman looks her in the eyes and smiles.

Lauren looks away. 'Dad, I'm hungry.' She can't help but glance back. There is something unearthly about the fabric of this woman's dressing gown and the colour of her hair. Unearthly and yet familiar. Perhaps it is the way she smelled when she was sitting close to Lauren in the pickup truck. Musky, warm blood and soil, like a nocturnal animal that has come out from its den. The woman sits still but shifts around in Lauren's mind. Her eyes are huge and black. When Lauren turns away, she can feel the eyes burying into her back.

'Dad, what are we eating the night?' She wants things to be normal.

Her father takes a moment to respond, tight-lipped through his teeth. 'All these questions, Lauren, you're doin' ma heid in.'

'I just—'

'*Gies peace*, all right? Christ *sakes*.' When he speaks like this, a blade in his voice, Lauren knows she shouldn't ask any more. He sits down in the armchair with a sigh and begins peeling a small stump of wood with a knife, shaping it like an owl. Lauren knows then that he can't be too annoyed, because this owl will be for her. Vairi once told her that the Gaelic name for owl translates as 'night-hag'. This is what she imagines when she hears them hooting in the dark. She will find this wooden night-hag sitting on her pillow when it's finished.

'There's stew in the freezer. That rabbit.' His eyes are sad. This is how he looks when he isn't talking or listening, when he is in his own thoughts.

The young woman rises, followed by her shadow. Lauren's father gets up to face her. His eyes still have a dreamy, glazed look in the firelight.

'Look at you,' he says to the woman. She doesn't reply, but sits back down on the sofa, as silent as a moth. Niall shakes his head and goes into the leaking utility room to take the stew from the freezer. He begins to heat the icy lump in the metal saucepan. Usually they eat easy things: mashed potatoes, scrambled eggs, sausages. Sundays he might roast a chicken or stew a rabbit in the big pot. He calls this a batch. Through the hatch, Lauren watches him take another whisky bottle out of the cupboard.

Lauren's dad's rifle is propped outside the kitchen doorway. He uses it to shoot rabbit, pheasant and foxes. She has never seen the deaths herself, but she has heard the shot in the woods. She has seen the rabbit pelts and their unskinned bodies hanging in the garden and laid in the kitchen. She has touched their matted fur. *Careful*, her dad always tells her, *ticks*. Jameson eats their insides, the bad parts. He likes them, the same way that if he finds a dead animal in the forest he will roll on his back in it. Watching this woman, Lauren thinks of those animals and their bad parts.

Lauren's father kneels in front of the woman, who does not meet his gaze. He tries to make her eat from a steaming bowl, holding the steel spoon to her mouth. He blows on the food and holds it to her again. The woman keeps her mouth shut. He tries a third time, the spoon at her closed mouth, her closed face.

'I'm so hungry,' he says. He places the bowl by the armchair and sits with Lauren at the wooden table in the kitchen and they eat together without speaking. There is comfort in the stew. Lauren looks up. The grey bristle of her father's jaw is working away, while his shoulders and head, with its blond and white ponytail, tower over the bowl. His hands are big and coarse from making things, mending fences and hewing posts, hitting them into the earth, unrolling chicken wire. He builds things for inside the house too. Chairs, boxes and shelves made from wood from a further part of the forest, which he collects from the sawmill. On his forearm is a tattoo of a blue rose.

When the fire starts to take, he holds the woman's hand and leads her up to the chest of drawers in his bedroom. The temperature is colder up here. He takes out his black Motörhead T-shirt with flames on the back and tucks it under his arm. Lauren watches the woman shake with cold. Lauren pulls the tartan blanket from her father's bed and wraps it around herself. He has not switched on a light.

Niall leads the woman to the bathroom and locks the door. They are in the bathroom for a long time.

Lauren hears water running. She wants hot water too and the lounge fire. She presses her ear to the bathroom door and hears her father's low voice, singing something.

'Dad, can I help?'

'No, love. Out in a sec.'

Lauren walks slowly along the dingy landing clutching the blanket like a toga. Her pumpkin bucket bangs against her knee. The house is never fully bright apart from the skylight over the staircase. A royal-blue carpet covers the floors throughout, including the damp bathroom. Net curtains veil the small windows and heavy velvet covers the entrance to the back room. Unopened letters clutter the spindly table in the hallway. The walls are clad in a deep-yellow pine. There are a few pictures of hilly landscapes, icy rivers and wild animals painted in soft, fantasy colours.

Lauren listens hard but only hears the drip downstairs in the utility room, nothing more. Droplets of water are falling from the roof into a red bucket that her dad put out the day before. He says he will fix it tomorrow. Outside the wind grows thick and it starts to rain. In her bedroom, there are outlines of horses on the walls, pages carefully torn from magazines. Dreamcatchers hang on her curtain rail, their feathers heavy.

When she gets into bed, she reaches down into the gap by the corner of the wall and brings out a small drawstring bag and an old battered notebook. The bag is printed with gold stars on midnight-blue velvet. There is a tarot deck inside. In the evenings she will often shuffle the cards, unwieldy in her small hands. She tries to read and learn the cards as best she can, but sometimes she dreams up the meanings when she doesn't understand. On the first page of the leather-bound notebook it says *SPAEWIFE'S BEUK*. This is a book she found in the bottom compartment of her mother's vanity case. She soon learned it tells secrets and explains powers.

Some of its yellowed pages are covered in scrawls made by her grandmother, her mother's mother, who wrote her name inside the front cover. Others are written in a more old-fashioned script. Others again are written in bold, curvy letters that look friendlier to her, like a teacher's writing. Some of the pages have been taken from jotters and glued or Sellotaped into the book. Many are dedicated to the reading of cards, with illustrations and diagrams.

She is too tired to try and concentrate on the deck, so she flicks through the pages of the book to see what she might find. Someone has sketched out pentangles, clubs, wands, an overflowing goblet and a dove and, in one beautiful illustration, a blind-folded woman crossing sharp swords.

Next to the notebook on her pillow is a thumb-sized box of worry dolls that she talks to each night.

She has given them names. She takes them out of the box and lines them up against one side of her pillow. *Stacey. Crystal. Spencer. Kendall.* Silently, she communicates to each, asking them to keep her and her father safe as she places them under her pillow.

Her breathing is shallow against the heavy rain outside. She remembers she is wearing her mother's lipstick and goes back along the landing to the bathroom. It is empty. 'Dad?' she calls out. There is no answer. She feels cold, so she runs the hot tap over her palms and wrists and touches her neck with her warm hands. In the dim light she sees tiny smears of blood in the sink. She is not sure for a moment whether there was a lot more and she has been washing it away. Sometimes when Lauren brushes her teeth she spits out blood, but this is not the same. She tries to wipe the smears away and, in the gloom, wonders if they were ever there to begin with.

She scrunches up her eyes at the mirror. A cold draught blows. There is a flicker and she glances at the bottom corner of the mirror to look at the room behind her. She once heard older girls talking about a woman who would appear in a mirror at night if you said her name three times. She looks back at her face to check it is unchanged. The damp has worked its way into her hair and the black kohl has spread around her eyes. She undoes the plait circling her head and her hair springs out in a shock. She looks stranger now than when she was guising. She rubs her blotchy eyes while the rain batters the frosted window. The wind sounds like a dog whose owners have been away too long.

2

Sunlight has broken through the curtains. The back garden outside is made of three concrete levels, giant steps that are covered in flowerbeds and gravel and now overgrown with brambles. In the summer, Lauren hits a tennis ball against this side of the house with a warped racket. In winter, she keeps indoors and looks at the miles of forest that rise beyond the garden on the hillside.

Waking up, Lauren notices how messy her bedroom is, crumpled clothes and books with splayed pages scattered around the edge of her divan in the dingy light. The house has grown cold again. As she makes her way down the staircase her stomach chews at itself. The previous evening swims back to her and she pauses at the blue curtain to the back living room. She is hungry again and thirsty and there is no sound in the house except the drip from the leaking roof of the utility room.

She pulls back the edge of the curtain and slips through, letting the velvet slide from her fingers. The room is empty and smells of ash. There are no blankets on the sofa and no signs of a bed. The Himalayan salt lamp is illuminated. She doesn't remember it ever being used, and goes to turn it off. She inspects the kitchen and the utility room, which lead off from the sofa-dining area, for some sign that the woman stayed over, but they are empty too. Bowls and plates are all stacked in the cupboard. She peers out of the back room's sliding glass door, hoping to see her father outside chopping wood in the grey light, but he is not there. She does not know what time it is. There is a sharpness in the sky and the bushes look dark and slick from the rain.

The chill of the kitchen tiles rises through the cable knit of her socks. She pours milk over a snapping bowl of Rice Krispies on the tiled work surface and fills her favourite puffin mug with water. At the clink of crockery, Jameson appears and offers his paw. She shakes it, his wet nose brushing the tips of her fingers. She can feel the bones of his claws under the tough fur.

She turns to the window, the stoneware bowl freezing her palms as she eats. She finishes her cereal and sees patterns in the milky dregs: the shape of a bird, the shape of a house. The clock on the wall says ten thirty. She never lies in this late and neither does her father, except for the days when he doesn't get up at all.

'Dad?' she calls. She vaults back upstairs and knocks on his door. Silence. She enters slowly, squinting at the mound of lumpy blankets in the half-light. 'Dad?'

'What is it, Lauren?' His voice sounds swollen and cracked.

'Where's that lady?'

'What lady?'

'The one from last night.'

There is a long silence. Just as Lauren thinks he is falling back asleep, he says, 'What?'

'The lady in the dressing gown.'

'I dinna ken what you're on about.' His voice snaps into Scots when he's frustrated.

The silence ebbs back. 'Lauren, leave me be the now. I'm not feeling well.'

As she turns to leave, he speaks again from beneath the covers. 'Have you made yourself something to eat?'

'Yes.'

'I'll be down in wee while . . . and I'll cook us a fry-up. OK?'

'Can you get the boiler going?'

'In a bit.'

Standing by the bedside table she can see the back of his head and his long mess of hair, the colour of lightning. He turns towards her with his eyes closed. His chin is light-grey stubble.

'Dad, do you not remember that lady?' She hovers in the doorway, knowing that the more she asks, the more she will wind him up.

Sure enough, his tone changes to a warning. 'Lauren. Away and read your book. See Billy. Please, now, on you go. I've got the cold this morning.' His eyes stay shut.

Lauren shakes her head, slumps back to her room and pulls back the curtains. The dim morning light feels strange. From a nest of T-shirts on the floor, she picks up a Jacqueline Wilson novel that she has borrowed from the library bus and drinks her water. A damp spot is spreading quickly across one corner of her ceiling.

Their orange Bakelite phone rings like a musical drill. When she doesn't hear her father creaking, she runs downstairs to answer it.

'Hi, Lauren. It's Billy.'

'Hi.' She knew it would be.

'My mum says she's making apple scones today. She was wondering if you want to come around.'

'Yes please.'

Lauren can hear Billy's mother, Kirsty, in the background.

'She says we're going on holiday the day after tomorrow and she's clearing out the fridge.' Billy pauses as Kirsty says something else. 'She's got some food that you might want to take home.'

'Thanks.'

'I'm going up to the woods now. To work on the hut some more. Are you coming?'

'Yeah, OK, I'll just get ready.'

'I'll wait for you.'

She dresses quickly, taking another T-shirt – with white horses galloping across a shore – and jeans from the colourful pile of laundry under her windowsill. The sill itself is strewn with the little wooden animals her father has carved for her: owls, cats and fishes. She knocks quietly on his door again.

'Dad. I'm going to the woods with Billy.'

There is no answer.

'How are you feeling?'

'Be fine in a bit.'

'I'll bring you back some scones from theirs. Maybe some other food. I'm taking Jameson.'

'Sorry about the fry-up, love. I'm just not feeling great.'

'No bother.' She just wants to be with Billy and the trees.

Lauren scoots down the creaking stairs, whistling for her dog and grabbing her zip-up jacket as she runs.

To get to Billy's, Lauren takes a shortcut, climbing over a gaping wire fence at the back of the garden that Jameson can scramble through. From there, she cuts diagonally across the edge of the forest and four fields, her wellies sucking against the mud. Three pheasants take flight ahead of her like a gust of autumn leaves. She thinks about the emptiness of the house and her father. She knows she didn't dream up the previous evening. Sometimes when her father drinks too much he gets very sad or angry, so keeps on drinking until he sleeps and forgets. She can imagine the young woman feeling scared and slipping away, but that was the wrong decision. They live in the middle of nowhere, in northern Scotland. What if she needed their help?

Billy is waiting at the lichened back gate of his garden. He ruffles Jameson's soft, rust-coloured ears. 'How are you today, Jameson? How are you?'

Jameson tries to put his paw in Billy's hand.

They walk up the stony track towards the forest, bordered by spiky whin bushes and birches tangled with old man's beard. The hilly land stretches into yellows, deep greens and deciduous orange. Jameson is well camouflaged as he sniffs the hedgerow for rabbit holes and badger setts. Lauren jabs around in her pocket among old tissues and the bumpy shell of her pocketknife. She found the knife in her father's work shed a few weeks ago, a place that had always been forbidden, just like the room by the front door. Her father says it's a living room 'for best', but on the odd occasion someone comes round, they never use it.

When her father isn't in there, the work shed is locked up, but if he is, she creeps up to the draughty entrance and looks at the sharp metal tools hanging from the walls, both frightening and alluring. If he catches her standing there, he'll yell at her to get back inside. A few weeks ago, when he had been out working at someone's house, she saw the shed keys, glinting, dropped accidentally on the ground. Certain he would not be back for a couple of hours, she opened the shed padlock with a clunk. Inside, she studied the bow saws of different sizes on the walls and the rope and electrical leads that coiled around giant cotton reels. They were all precious, simply because they were forbidden. It made her heart race to know she had been here and touched these surfaces, one by one, and that no one would have to know and she wouldn't get shouted at.

She looked along the shelves and in boxes, as if trying to find something as yet unknown to her. A clue that Niall was not just her father, but also a human being, with parts to his life she didn't know about. The table in the middle of the shed was made of thick, battered wood that, like everything around it, was spattered with paint. Next to a couple of sandbags and a roll of carpet mesh, Lauren found a rusty blue tool box with two sides that folded out like bug's wings. Among the screwdrivers and nails she found this sleek piece of antler with a wide steel blade about as long as her foot. This was her treasure, her trophy. The thing that had made the adventure worthwhile. She holds it now and enjoys its weight in her hand.

On the path to the forest, she finds the dog biscuit she is looking for and throws it to Jameson. He leaps in the air, twisting like a salmon.

'Dare you to eat one of them,' Billy says.

'Don't think so,' says Lauren, trudging on, her hands clenched in her pockets.

After stealing the knife, she was careful to leave everything in the shed as she had found it, and locked the door behind her as she left. Just before her father walked into the room, she put the keys down the side of the sofa. She still wished she could tell someone this story and how quick-thinking she had been.

Billy tries to keep up with her. 'Mind when Grant MacBride ate they dog biscuits, that time on the bus.'

Lauren doesn't reply. They walk some more in the November air. The juniper bushes and giant hogweed thicken at the sides of the path as they go. Billy takes some foil-wrapped chocolates from his pocket, left over from guising. 'One for one?'

'What, a dog biscuit?'

'No-o! Have you got any more *gummies*? You know, the ones Angela Walker had.'

'No.' She remembers them stuck to the rubber mat on the pickup's floor. She tries to shake the woman in the dressing gown out of her head;

perhaps it is better that she left. People in Strath Horne love to talk about her and her dad, she knows that. And the incident feels too strange a thing to say out loud.

'I don't have any more, I ate them all,' Lauren says. 'Ya pie.'

'Billy!' She tries to hit him but he dodges her arm and, like this, they weave up the stony track. They stop bickering when they reach the mouth of the forest where the fields disappear and the mottled trees turn to miles of pine.

The sprawling forest is the same size as their hamlet, fields, farms and small town put together; the wild inverse to their man-made space. They take the path known by locals as the Loop, which cuts into a section of forest for a couple of miles and back again. The only people to do this now are children and the occasional dog-walker. The children know this path by heart, making it easy to forget that they are surrounded by large swathes of parts unknown.

'I'm only at school tomorrow then I'm away to Disneyland Paris,' Billy says, trying to sound casual. 'My mum got permission.'

Lauren looks at him. Her ideas of 'Disneyland' and 'Paris' are a fuzzy mixture of the photos Billy brings back every year and the film *Ratatouille*. 'I've never been on an aeroplane before,' she says.

'I canna believe that. Seriously?'

Lauren ignores him.

'Anyway, we're only flying from Inverness to London, then we're taking the Eurostar.' He stops and looks at Lauren. 'It's this train that goes under the sea.'

'You've told me before.' She rolls her eyes.

'What's that?' He grabs her arm and points to where someone is walking in the trees to the left of the path. There are flashes of white material among dark-green branches. She looks straight into his sky-blue eyes and then back. The person is walking away from them, deeper into the forest.

Billy has already started walking further up the path, but Lauren stays standing and lets out her breath. 'She's gone.' She's sure the figure was the young woman from the road.

'Who?' Billy says as he continues to trudge on up the path.

'That person. The one we just saw there.'

'Didn't see anyone.'

'Yeah, you did. You grabbed my arm. Two seconds ago. And now they've gone.' He has to be winding her up.

'Did I? I didn't mean to . . . I've got a bit of a sore head.'

'We both saw them. *Her.*'

'Her?'

'How can you not remember?' She hasn't moved from her spot on the path, but now he is far enough ahead that she has to raise her voice, her eyes darting to the empty trees. He shrugs in reply. She wants to go home now. But the idea of walking back alone feels wrong. She runs to catch him up.

'You probably saw Stuart or Maisie,' he says. Stuart and Maisie MacAllister live on the neighbouring farm, whose land stops at the edge of the forest. They occasionally come up to play in the trees and at school they claim that the land is theirs. Billy usually tells Lauren to keep a lookout for them. In the summer, someone kicked Lauren's stick hut to pieces and stole the tarpaulin roof, as well as a huge cake tin that contained a bottle of lemon Fanta and five back issues of *The Beano*.

'If I saw them, so did you.'

'I'm not remembering this at all,' he replies, as if he's talking to a much younger kid.

Banks of beech ferns bow either side. Their leaves are changing from bright green to a rusty brown, with many at the in-between stages of deep orange and golden yellow, spreading sunset colours across the forest. Lauren likes to turn the fern fronds over and pick off the bright spores underneath.

On the path, the children reach the old water tank, a shed of browning corrugated iron, and pick through the marshy reeds to peek inside for frogs.

'Hel-looo, froggies, you seen anyone?' Billy's voice reverberates across the dark metal walls of the tank, but only their reflections stare back at them from the deep black water. Billy runs away but Lauren stays and watches. There are times like this when a feeling comes over her and the world stands still for a few moments. There is a rippling in one corner of the water, which spreads out in circles, suggesting something is moving beneath the surface.

Soon the children reach the towering pines and the mossy stone foundations of an old bothy, close to the path, where they have started to build their hut. It is made of carefully placed sticks fitted around a stray cluster of birch trees that grow close together, mottled with reindeer lichen. They start to walk around, searching for fallen branches. The springy moss underfoot and the layers of pine needles soak up any sound.

As they stand making sure the walls of the hut are still sturdy, Lauren begins to lop off stray twigs from the outer walls with her pocketknife. She keeps turning round as she works, with the crawling feeling someone might be watching her. Someone could live out in these woods, easily.

Billy sits his rucksack down at the base of a tree trunk. He loosens the drawstring and pulls out a packet of Golden Grahams.

'Hungry?' He offers her the box.

Lauren grabs a handful and tries to cram them in her mouth, smiling slightly as she does so.

'You're like a hamster,' Billy says.

'Shut it,' she says through crunching teeth. She runs her hand over a part of the hut that is a little spindly and will let in rain and snow. 'We need more sticks.' She takes another handful of cereal and tips back her head.

'We need to turn this area into a fully operational military zone,' says Billy. 'I'm planning on building in some spy holes here. And an embrasure over there.'

Lauren sighs. She doesn't know what an embrasure is, but it sounds boring. 'I think this is more of a house,' she says. 'Like a secret cabin.' It's hard to concentrate on the game, because she can't shake the discomfort of last night. It has seeped into the daylight. She wonders if she really did just see the same woman as last night. She tries to focus on what Billy is saying.

'We've got to protect ourselves, though,' he explains, rootling further into his rucksack. He is becoming less fun to play with.

The urge to tell him keeps bubbling up. She wants to feel safer, but not in the way he means. She looks at the soft bloom of fungus growing on the side of the trunk. When she starts to talk, it comes out in a ribbon of story, unspooling. 'When Dad and me were driving home, we saw this woman standing in the passing place and so Dad picked her up and we took her home.'

'Who was she?'

'I don't know. She didn't speak.'

Billy is readjusting some of the branches on the hut roof. 'What?'

'We took her home. I didn't see her in the morning.'

'Where is she now?'

'I don't know.'

'Did your dad fancy her?'

Lauren sighs. 'Get tae France.' She walks away down a small hill of bracken and sits on the wet verge. She puts her arms on her knees and plucks a reed. Her fingernail splits a line down the middle and she scoops out the spongy white insides like the stuffing of a tiny cushion.

'Lauren! I was only *kid*ding.' His voice is muffled by the trees.

Jameson snuffles up to her, pushing his nose between her arms and head. She gives him another dog biscuit and walks further down to find more branches, her feet squelching as she tries to get a hold in the mud.

She can hear Billy wandering off somewhere in the tall ferns, so she returns to fix the hut. She takes some scissors and string that Billy has brought and starts tying crooked sticks together. At that moment Billy bolts out of the trees, snatches a branch like a rifle and makes the sound of gunfire.

'Gonna get my own one day. I asked Dad for one but he wouldna let me.'

They hear Jameson growling, his head inside a rabbit hole.

'Lauren, you're in a mood today.'

'You're the one who's acting weird.' Lauren imagines the woman walking back through the trees. Her shoulders tighten, but the forest stays still.

'How am I?'

'You keep forgetting stuff.'

'Like what?'

'That person, the girl.'

'Lauren, I swear, I didna see anything. Sorry.'

'You don't get it.' She wishes she could move through the world like Billy, the way a duck crosses a pond, without thinking what's beneath it.

'Good thing I brought these too.' He pulls out a pair of walkie-talkies like giant black insects from his rucksack. Lauren begged her father for a pair two months ago, but he said there was no point when she could use Billy's. Niall has bought her a mobile phone instead. When she points out that the phone rarely works in the village and never in the woods, he just shakes his head and mutters about batteries.

Lauren clutches a heavy radio and runs further out into the trees. When she switches it on, static crackles through the air. She sneaks towards a large tree and crouches, her back against the bark. 'I feel like someone is watching us,' she says.

'I have an idea.' Billy's voice scrapes through the radio grill. She's not sure at this point whether he is in character. 'I need you for reconnaissance.'

'What?'

'Go and do a recce – try and find Stuart and Maisie.'

'Nah, I'm OK.' Lauren looks through the trunks between her and the hut, but she can't see Billy. Jameson's ginger tail waggles out of the bushes on her left.

She runs deeper into the woods, skidding sideways down a mossy slope and into a patch of crackling bracken, then denser trees. The only paths here are narrow cuts into the undergrowth, made by deer. She wants large sticks, which can only be found a little way off, where bigger birches and oaks grow, nearer the edge. She feels the silky bark of a birch tree. Birches, she understands, are protective, the same as rowans, which cleanse the air in their own fiercer way. She edges her thumb under some of the peeling bark and pulls it off gently; she takes a couple of small birch branches that have fallen on the floor and breaks them up into little pieces. She picks the leaves of twinflower and primrose.

Billy's voice crackles over the radio again: 'See anything?'

'No. I'm finding more sticks.'

She follows grey stones sunk deep in a line, the remains of a cottage or outhouse at some point in history. The forest used to belong to the local estate and in the Victorian era it was used for shooting game. But the trees grew too quickly and spread out in the intervening years, making the land unmanageable.

Lauren hears a fluttering behind her and stops. She switches off the radio and turns, but there are only more trees. If she listens hard she can hear them creak. She is thinking about her father's lined face and whether he lies or if he does things and doesn't remember. She moves closer to one broad trunk. Of course he does. Both. She's seen him almost forget her altogether, sometimes, although those days are rare. She's seen him lie to the neighbours when they ask too many questions. He keeps her out of the wood shed and the posh living room she can't remember using. He keeps parts of himself locked and secret. It annoys her that she isn't allowed to lie. He still doesn't realize she puts on her mum's lipstick in the bathroom sometimes.

At that moment, her footsteps squeeze water from the moss like a sponge and it runs over her wellies. She imagines how strong his hands must be when they haul logs into the back of the pickup. He can still lift her up over his shoulder and she will hang like a dead weight. A cool damp lingers from the rain. She once overheard him telling Kirsty how you strangle a chicken. She walks down a ridge of ferns to a fallen oak and hears the sound again. She spreads her hand against the trunk and notices the tarry puddles of black witch's butter mushrooming near the roots. There is a tawny blur in the trees ahead. A deer, now still, with its neck bent downwards, has its eyes on her. They stand facing each other until the deer leaps and vanishes into the bracken.

When Lauren makes her way back to their den, Billy has gone. She starts to weave more sticks into the walls. There on the ground is something she didn't notice earlier. Someone has placed large pebbles and stones in a neat ring around the hut. She counts them. Twelve in total. Each stone is of a similar size and placed the same distance apart.

Lauren steps out of the circle and holds the radio to her mouth. It fuzzes with static. 'Billy?' she says.

Piercing feedback screams out of the machine.

Lauren drops it on the ground, screwing up her eyes.

When she is sure it's quiet, she picks the radio up by the antenna like a dead fish.

'Jameson? Jameson, home time.'

Billy walks out of the trees instead. He's smiling.

'Where'd you go?' she says.

'I was just up that way.' He is out of breath and she wonders if he has been looking for her.

'Did you hear my radio? It's broken.'

'No?'

'It was so loud! Here you go. I was on my way home.'

'Hey, it's not finished yet, come on and do a bit more.'

She looks up at him and notices his freckles and blue eyes. She keeps noticing them, these days, and the fact he is now a bit taller than her. She turns back to the ground. 'Have you seen these stones?'

'You're such a girl,' says Billy.

She shoots him a look. 'I didn't put them there.'

'Sure you didn't.'

It starts to rain. A few heavy drops, widely spaced, then more, falling quickly through the branches. Billy shrugs. 'Fine then.' They pull up their hoods and start back to Billy's, with Jameson following, covered in mud.

'Maybe we should get a tarp for the roof. It's gonna get wet,' Billy says.

Lauren doesn't answer. The sky grows too dark for the afternoon. The rain is so thick and loud that Billy, too, is quiet. There is a faint, deep sound of thunder beyond the fields.

When they reach Billy's house, water has seeped up their denim jeans to their knees. The Mathesons live in an old steading with a slate roof and untidy brambles. There is a football net in the paddock-sized garden, edged with dry stone. Billy's mother Kirsty is taking her horse Pepper to his stable in the far corner of the adjoining field.

The children walk through the back door and shriek as Jameson shakes his wet coat in the passageway. The kitchen smells of fresh baking. They take their wellies off, one foot helping the other, and lean against the radiator. Jameson begins to smell of wet dog drying. Lauren can feel her hair slimy on her skull. The house is brighter than hers in lots of small ways. They stand warming themselves, looking at the plate of apple scones on the waterproof tablecloth. A couple of leftover Braeburns have been placed in the centre for decoration.

'Can we eat them?' Lauren asks, picking up an apple.

Billy pauses. 'Mum'll have to say.'

He starts to make two glasses of Robinsons orange squash when Lauren puts the apple in her pocket and says, 'I think your aura is blue.'

'My what?'

'Your aura.'

'Oh aye. What's that?'

'It's a kind of colour that comes out of you.'

'Like . . . blood?'

'Don't be daft.'

'Lauren the auren.'

'Aura.'

Billy's mother comes through the back door, peeling off her bumblebee jacket and taking a seat at the table as she rubs her arms. 'How's that den coming on?'

'Fine. Lauren says she can see my aura and it's blue.'

Billy's mum laughs. 'Is that right?'

Lauren doesn't look at either of them.

'Billy,' says his mother, 'have you packed yet?'

'I will in a bit.'

'Well, you'd better do it soon – you've got school tomorrow, then we're off.'

'Lauren saw a wifey on the road.'

'She wasna a wifey,' says Lauren too quickly.

Lauren loves the television at Billy's. She sits alone watching it, huge and colourful in the living room, and it takes her into a world of Nickelodeon animation and American reality shows. She loves the strangeness of Americans. People who live in a universe of lie detectors and drug addiction and paternity tests. She likes watching shows about women with puffed, frozen faces who talk to similar women in restaurants about other women. There are large mansions and tiny dogs.

She doesn't know how much time has passed when she turns around to see Kirsty sitting behind her on the sofa, laughing too, with Lewis on her lap.

'Oh, she is not a happy bunny, is she?'

'She found out that her sister lost her memory when they were skiing and has been keeping it a secret.'

'Aye, that's what she's saying.'

'I think she really did. Uh-oh. The mum's not happy . . .' They laugh, and toddler Lewis tries to laugh along too, not understanding.

Kirsty says, 'Lauren. Are you going to be all right while we're away?'

'I'll be fine, of course.'

'Do you want us to bring you back some Minnie Mouse ears like last time?'

Lauren tries to suppress a smile. She looks down at her crossed legs and nods.

'OK, I'll add those to the list. You think your dad'll want something? Maybe some Mickey Mouse ears for him?'

Lauren giggles.

'Your dad knows you're here, doesn't he?'

'*Uh*-huh.'

'OK, just checking. We've got quite a few things left in the fridge unopened that'll be going off while we're away. Do you want to tell him to come round and pick them up maybe?' She says this as Lewis tries to grab her hair and she brushes his small hands away.

'OK.'

'I found Billy upstairs playing *FIFA*, but I think he's almost packed now. And I'm going to be making us tea soon. Would you like some?'

Lauren remembers her father lying up in his bed seeming as though he'd had too much to drink.

'I think I should check my dad's OK. He didn't seem so well this morning.'

'Oh, is that right?'

'Yeah.'

'Will he be making something for you to eat?'

'Think so. Yeah.'

'I'm going to make you a sandwich to take away home with you. In case you get hungry on the way, eh?'

'Thanks.'

'Is your dad keeping all right these days?'

'Seems . . . fine.'

'You'll be OK while we're away, won't you?'

Lauren tries to brighten. 'I'll be just fine, Kirsty.'

3

When Niall wakes up again, the house seems to be floating on water. Varnished pine planks edge the walls like a fence. It was a previous owner's idea, a woman from the Lowlands, before his uncle bought the house. He remembers his wife Christine's face the first day they moved in. She called it 'perfect'. Perfect seemed something simple to attain back then. Niall didn't think it was perfect, though, and didn't like the walls, but within a few years of living here they became invisible to him. He sees them now anew, and closes his eyes. He tries to lie still against the nauseous fog rolling in. He will not be working today. A song is turning around in his head, a music without words that he cannot place.

One day he will make big changes. He likes to sit with a tin of beer in the evenings and tell Lauren he's going to paint the walls another colour or reclad them or build an extension. He asks her what she wants him to build and she will say *a turret, a swimming pool, a library with a hidden door, a dog bedroom for Jameson.* Once she asked him to build a slide from her window into the garden. He said he would build her a tree house, but he never has. Now he buries thoughts of the workshop and carpentry, sandpaper, drills, hammers. He buries all thoughts and all potential for thoughts. He has become quite skilled at this over the years.

The lady from the Lowlands made one alteration he approved of: she changed the name of the house to Dunscaith. Before that it was home to Alan Mackie's uncle and known as Trapper's Cottage.

Alan's uncle, the trapper, had been a drinker. Alan says that the outhouse that's now Niall's workshop was once full of traps and carcases of poached animals and barrels of home brew. Alan says his uncle's fingernails were always black from dried blood and earth. One night the trapper took an axe to the bare staircase and hacked it to pieces, which he then burned on the fire.

But the circumstances of the trapper's death are unclear. One evening, in the pub, Niall asked Alan what happened to him but Alan just drank the last of his ale and set the empty glass on the small round table and wiped his mouth. A silence passed between the two men. Then Alan got out of his chair and started putting his coat on. He said, just before he left for the night, that some stories are better left buried. Niall thought of bodies in the ground.

Cherie, who owns the petrol station, once told Niall that the trapper passed away soon after he cut up the staircase. She leaned forward over the cash register patched with lottery advertisements and mouthed 'hanged himself' with her hand lying lightly on the base of her neck. Christine was horrified at the story and tried to clutter the house with New Age crystals to 'dissipate bad energy'.

Niall was told this same fact by Hamish Murray at the Black Horse Inn, who said that Alan found the trapper in the outhouse. Bruce Dunbar the egg man also told this story, sticking his head inside Niall's truck window, his breath smelling of Golden Virginia. He said the body was hanging with the dead animals for two weeks. Local children used to ask Christine if her house was cursed. It explained some of the looks he got when he told people where he lived.

Niall remembers the fate of the old staircase occasionally when he climbs its replacement. It is happening more often now. 'I've had my moments,' he said to his friend Sandy a few weeks ago at the pub, 'but can you imagine? No way. Never.'

Sandy Ross just smiled at him. Niall knew it was a smile of sympathy, but in these moments he felt it was insincere, that his friend could not truly understand how he felt. When he had had a few drinks, he felt a growing paranoia that he was being mocked. They both watched Diane, a teenager who worked weekends, carry a stack of foamy glasses. Niall said then, 'How much more do we need to drink before we start throwing these bar stools on that fire?'

Sandy Ross was calm and when he spoke sounded as if he thought himself full of wisdom. 'You canna be doing with they thoughts. I'm calling it a night. For me and you, pal.'

Sometimes, more and more, Niall stops dead in the middle of sawing wood or hammering nails and looks down at the metal object he is holding in his hands. He will straighten his back and touch the points of the blade or weigh the heaviness of the iron hammer, maybe take a swing at a post in his workshop, and carry on.

In the past few days he has been thinking of how Christine would have made them call Halloween 'Samhain' or 'Oidhche Shamhna', the start of the Celtic year and the beginning of the time when the dead can pass to the realm of the living. He remembers how she would make a ritual bonfire, late at night, outside the house. He was never able to live her strange habits down. Once an old man outside a pub told him she was a witch. Everyone else was too polite to say it to his face.

Somewhere and some time before she moved to Strath Horne, she decided to learn the art of building bonfires, of filling the sky with smoke. He always assumed she had learned in Edinburgh, the same time – in her teens – when she had started to learn reiki and EFT. She used to work at Napier's, an old herbalist, and the Forest Café. She began to make friends with students who studied in the Georgian university buildings near by and she became more than friends with some, he guesses now, kissing rich English boys with lip piercings who volunteered for People and Planet.

He bases this idea on a few small details she told him in passing. He remembers it made his skin flush with jealousy and a quiet, heavy anger that surprised him. He prefers to think of her alone at seventeen, spending the long summer evenings on a wide expanse of grass called the Meadows. He imagines her among the drumming circles and poi dancers and tightrope walkers, reading palms, eating apples and getting high as the shadows lengthen, her blunt Highland vowels changing.

From Edinburgh, she moved to Strath Horne, to work at the Castle Hotel and, as she always said, for a change of scene. The town was a wild, unknown place to her. He heard later her mother Lillith was from the west coast and part gypsy, but maybe that was after Christine started telling people's fortunes. She said she had the sight. People in Strath Horne didn't act like that. He had always thought Edinburgh was the place that formed her, but maybe she learned it from her mother.

He opens his eyes in his bed and, keeping his head still on the pillow, reaches out and switches on the radio. He turns the volume down and listens to the wind rise up, the sound growing louder than the football phone-in. The window is a light-grey square. The spare bed sheets pegged out in the garden will be wet now.

The radio hisses with static and cuts into a squeal, like a faulty microphone. An electric pain hits him behind the eyes and screws itself into his head. He slams his hand on the radio and it topples off the table, but the noise is unrelenting. He swears and props himself up on one arm to lean over and unplug it from the wall.

Niall falls back on his pillows, clammy with sweat, and folds a third pillow behind his back. The room tilts slightly. He sees the mug of tea Lauren has brought him and looks at the time. Nearly noon. Now the tea is cold and grey, but he sips it all the same and appreciates its sweetness.

He sinks back down and falls into a light, uncomfortable sleep, his brain like padded, lumpy bedding. He is in the work shed and there is a hand on his shoulder. He hears a creaking and the sound of a gun being cocked. He wakes again and realizes he is hungry and shivering. Some of the sick feeling rolls back and he lies still for a while, cold air on his face from a gap in the window. He wants to get up and eat but his body is a grey sack of coal. He can hear Lauren still bumping around downstairs, then walking up and closing her bedroom door.

'Lauren?' There is no answer, just a crash.

He puts on his dressing gown but as he stands, the room spins, and he heads to the bathroom, touching the walls for balance. He kneels on the damp blue carpet. Nothing comes. It doesn't any more. He rests his head against the edge of the bath for a while. 'Lauren?' He listens carefully and hears another bump. He picks himself up slowly and slumps under the shower.

He calls Lauren again, but the house stays silent. He knocks on her door and, when there is no response, goes in. A heady smell hits him like flowers and bad chicken. Water has spread across the ceiling. Shadows play in her empty room from the swinging dreamcatchers. It is tidier than usual: her duvet, patterned with sea creatures, has been tucked straight and her books have been stacked neatly on her bedside table. Webster, her fluffy toy duck, sits on her pillow. There are no clothes on the floor or any of the little horses she likes to play with. He sees the little wooden animals he carves for her in a straight line along her windowsill: a shoal of fish, a family of cats and a parliament of owls. Her wardrobe is fuller and tidier than it has been all year. He looks out of her window and into the empty garden. He calls her name again. Occasionally the house creaks when he is the only person home, he knows that. A drop of water trickles down the wall. His foot stubs against something hard and he looks down at a trail of rocks, curving around the bed in an oval. They look strange on the blue carpet, the only untidy thing in the room.

He heaps them up in the corner and opens a window to let out the fuggy scent. He picks up one of the colourful Jacqueline Wilson books, turning it over in his calloused hands. He has never read one but will spot them in the quaint Strath Horne Bookshop, to buy for Lauren's birthday or as a Christmas present. She has started taking more of these books out from the library bus. When she isn't looking he will write their titles carefully in a notebook to remember those she doesn't yet have. He'll find her own books lying damp in the bathroom or down the side of the sofa and tell her to take better care of them. His own book collection is limited to what he has picked up here and there in the charity shop or car boot sale, a few music biographies and the works of Tolkien and George R. R. Martin. The small bookshelf in his bedroom is mainly filled with sheaves of sheet music.

He sees an orange bucket next to Lauren's pink rucksack, ridged like a pumpkin with two black triangles for eyes and a jagged mouth. For a moment, he thinks it is new but then remembers the night before. They bought it from the service station. Of course they did. He is almost surprised to picture them out at night, Lauren in her vampire costume. His memory is patchy. An icy cold creeps over his body and he realizes he is still in his pyjamas, his long hair wet from the shower. He stumbles to his room and picks up a crumpled, wet Motörhead T-shirt from the floor, willing himself to try and remember.

The air in his bedroom is unusually damp. To his annoyance, he sees small florets of mould spreading in one corner of the room.

He staggers down to the kitchen with the pumpkin bucket filled with rocks, to throw outside, his knee joints clicking, like Long John Silver.

There is nothing so comforting to him as the smell and crackle of lichened wood in the stove, nothing like the morning when light falls across the table, except where his daughter is curled in a blanket in front of the fire, eating her breakfast. The phone rings like a musical drill and he rises from his chair unsteadily. He looks at the clock on the wall. Just past noon. 'Hello?'

There is a brief silence and then a low, half-whispered voice: '*Hi*, Niall. I hope I haven't caught you in the middle of something.'

'Er . . . not at all.'

'It's Angela.'

'Hi, Angela. What can I do you for?' He tries to sound happy to hear her clipped voice. He stands up and looks at the clock again. 'Hang on. What time is it?'

'Three o'clock.'

Lauren will have been gone for hours. 'Huh.'

'Why?' She sounds genuinely concerned.

'Never mind. So, on you go.'

'Well. I'm not sure if it's even silly of me to call, but . . .'

Niall coughs. 'Oh aye?' He needs to fix the stopped clock. His house is disintegrating.

'Well, I've just been looking out of my window and . . . Oh, I really don't know how to put this, Niall.' Another pause.

He clears his throat again, trying to get rid of the croak in his voice. 'What needs done? Is it that fence that's—'

'Oh no! Oh gosh, no, nothing . . . nothing needs to be *done*.' He hears her take a deep breath. 'I can see someone out of the window, Niall . . .' She lowers her voice further. 'She's been standing there a while now.'

'Where? I mean, who?'

'The orchard. You know, our kitchen looks out on to the orchard? And I had just sat down to read the paper and . . .'

'Wait, is this Lauren you're talking about? She's out with Billy. I mean . . . I thought I heard her back in the house, but she isna . . .'

Angela draws in her breath and it comes out a whisper. 'Lauren? Oh gosh, no. *No*, I haven't seen Lauren. This . . .' Angela's always been one for dramatics. Every month she travels to Inverness for her theatre club.

'Oh,' Niall replies. 'But you're saying someone's in your garden. Right now?'

Another silence. 'It's somebody . . . She's just standing there. I don't know, she *looks* like . . .'

'I'm sorry?'

'She's got her back to me.'

There is silence and Niall thinks something is wrong with the phone. Angela whispers again. 'I just tried tapping on the window and . . . she turned. And it . . . it really looks like her, Niall.'

'Like who? Like Lauren?'

'No! No . . .' Her voice is barely audible. 'She's just standing there. Like she's watching us.'

Niall struggles to form words. 'What you on about? You daft?'

Her voice is louder. 'Hang on. She's turning around now and walking away.'

'If this is a joke, it's not very funny.'

'I'm not *joking*, Niall. Why would I *joke* with you about this? She's just heading to the apple trees at the edge of the copse.' Angela's voice sounds urgently.

'Angela.' It doesn't sound like a joke.

'I'm so sorry, I don't mean to *distress* you, Niall, I just . . . I can barely see her any more, she's walked into the trees.'

There is a long pause. Niall pictures his wife disappearing into the woods and it makes him feel sick. He begins to wonder if Angela is still on the other end of the line when she speaks again. Her voice is different.

'Sorry, Niall?'

'Of course it fucking isn't her.' *You daft cow.*

'Isn't . . . who . . . ? I'm sorry, what – what are we talking about again?' She sounds as if she has just woken up from a deep sleep. She loves to meddle in other people's business but she has crossed a line that astonishes him.

'You *really* want me to believe that? You see some woman, walking her dog or whatever, fuck knows, in your fucking garden and you have the gall to phone me up—'

'Oh! Remind me again, what is it you are phoning about?'

'Angela, *you* phoned *me.*' It is taking everything he has to rein in his anger. Still, he can't help but think he'd like to go over there and talk some sense into her.

'I phoned you?'

'You've lost it. You've actually lost it.'

'I – I'm not sure what you mean. Sorry, I have a headache . . .' He can sense she is trying to straighten herself up. 'What is it you wanted to talk about, Niall?'

4

Outside, the sun has gone down and rain is battering the cloud-coloured sheets on the washing line. Niall watches them but doesn't move; the drip in the utility room increases in speed. He switches the radio off and turns on the TV. A woman is taking small glass bowls from the countertop of a polished studio kitchen and tipping their contents into a larger glass bowl and stirring. She looks at the camera seductively and shows him how to turn flour and butter into breadcrumbs. She explains how to make pastry, leaning gently over the bowl. *Is this for men or women?* he thinks. She is making a chicken pie and smiling with straight white teeth. He pulls the quilt further over him and falls asleep and in his dream Christine is cooking on TV, smiling at him, with her henna-red hair, holding an electric whisk. He wakes up. He fights the quilt off and punches the sofa cushions. His headache punches him back. *How could she be in the apple trees?* he thinks.

On the TV screen now, tiny skiers are crossing a white mountain track between miniature coloured

flags. He catches the same rotten smell again and
wonders if a dead mouse is trapped in the walls.
He turns the TV off and goes outside without a
coat in the dark gale. He slams an axe into logs in
the garden, one by one, on the huge oak trunk he
uses for chopping wood. When he has finished all
the logs he swings the axe into a bush that springs
back at him with thorns. He gathers the firewood
in his arms, takes it inside through the patio door
and throws pieces into the fire so that sparks rise.
He watches the flames creep up. Outside, a buzzard
is sitting on the fence post. He has never seen one
so close before.

He begins to call Jameson but remembers that
Lauren has taken him out. With all the lights on,
there is still a darkness in the house. He sits in the
stillness, angry with the fading day. He sprays
deodorizer around half-heartedly, then pulls on his
woollen hat and ski jacket and takes two paracetamol. He will drive to Cowrie Point and forget
about everything.

Outside, on the doorstep, the rain is spitting. He
takes a breath of damp air through his nose,
thinking of how much Angela winds him up. He
hops into the pickup and slams the door. 'Fuck the
lot o' yous.'

He looks out at Cowrie Point, soft and deserted
in the dusk. The rain hits the windows and it

soothes him. When the rain stops and the sky clears he gets out of the pickup. The tide crackles as it rolls over the smooth pebbles of the beach. The water stretches out in the twilight mist to the large slopes of hills like the resting bodies of giants under a huge sky. There is a tiny house with a red roof on the other side of the firth, evaporating into the falling dark. On a clear day he can usually see white specks of sheep. In the grainy night air he looks carefully for flat stones along the smooth curve of the shore. Once he has found a few he skims them across the black water. The ripples go *one two* for each stone. One day in summer he skimmed a stone and it touched the water six times before sinking. He tries again. *One two*. He is tired. Night is growing; the moon is bright. He skims another stone and a small bald head rises from the low waves. Large dog eyes stare at him. *Sorry, pal, nothing personal.*

He can never look at a seal in the way he looks at cows or sheep or even dogs. He sees another head some way out that sinks back into the dark waves with the first. Seals bring him the words *kingdom* and *folk*. Lauren likes his stories about selkies, seal people, stories his grandmother told him, even though they are often sad. She prefers them to stories of kelpies, folkloric monsters that take the shape of a horse on a beach or river. A few years ago, a girl at school told Lauren that kelpies wait by the water for children to ride on their backs, then gallop into the surf to drown and eat them. For the next two years, Lauren told Niall not to leave her alone near the sea or a loch; it became a kind of game. He feels now that she's getting older he no longer has to reassure her that kelpies are imaginary. Selkies, though, they are *almost* real.

Niall flicks away a fly and smiles a small, dry smile, thinking of how Christine would have brought their daughter up. Naming her was an issue. Christine wanted to choose something 'special', a name like 'Solstice', but Niall refused. He gave in to the name 'Oren', even though it was a name for a boy, meaning *ash* or *pine*. Yet, in the first few years following Christine's disappearance, Oren morphed into Lauren.

He is never usually at the beach without the sound of Jameson's claws on the pebbles and his panting. Niall picks up larger stones, the kind Lauren prefers with long strands of bubbly seaweed attached like hair. Were she here, she would take them home and paint them with faces and sit them to dry out on the breezeblock wall in the garden. Her pebble people. He puts one in his jacket pocket and waves away another fly. They aren't usually so close to the shore. When he, Lauren and Billy walk Jameson down here the two children hunt for the best-looking stones they can find, two each, and line them up anonymously for him to judge. They will often stop for a takeaway on the drive home. He realizes now how hungry he is, and as he turns towards the car his foot sinks into something soft on the grassy bank. It is a mound of shaggy wool, dirty with mud and streaked with red dye across the middle. As he draws his foot back he feels his gorge rise. There is a delicate pink ear tagged with plastic and a head, bone-coloured, already rotting away where the eye should be, black with blood and flies. A sheep that has wandered too far, dead on its side by the shore.

On the short walk down the street from Lindsay's Fish and Chips, Niall spots Catriona, the newly arrived GP whose renovated farmhouse he is working on. She is standing across the lamplit town street in a houndstooth coat and oxblood boots, unlocking her Volkswagen. She smiles at him broadly, her eyes huge and brown. He nods and smiles back, thinking he will see her soon and the oatmeal carpet in her house, waiting to be ripped up.

As he approaches his truck, he bumps into his friend Sandy Ross, wearing a Puffa and the Timberland boots that Niall covets, a Sunday paper under his arm.

'All right?'

'Ni-all. How's it going?'

'No bad, no bad. One too many bevvies last night. Think I lost a few brain cells.' He raises the hot takeaway parcel. 'Soon be right as rain.'

Sandy Ross says, 'Rain, eh. You can say that again.'

'Why do they no wrap it in newspaper any more?'

'Oh aye. You'll have to ask Lindsay!'

'Never tastes as good these days.'

'Well, you can say that again. Hie, listen. I've just thought you might be able to help me with something.'

'Aye? On you go.'

'What it is, right, me and the boys are playing a gig on Tuesday. One of these charity thingmies they have, up at the Castle Hotel. Good money, like, all the same. Onyways, Alec has only gone and broken his wrist.'

'How'd that happen?'

'Well, the thing was, he was painting that new house up on Kirk Street. He was up the ladder, and he says that woman comes in, just opens the door like that' – Sandy does a quick door-opening gesture – 'and of course he's behind the door. Up the ladder. *Boof!*'

'What?'

'Aye, stupid bint. The ladder sort of collapses like that and luckily he's not too far up it, like, it's just a stepladder, but he falls off and tries to put his hand out like that. *Crrrack!* Done for! Very bruised he is too, I believe.'

'He's lucky that's all that's broken.'

'Aye, that's what I said. He's all right; he's fine. The boys obviously won't stop with the jokes about his wrist though.'

Niall gives a laugh that sounds more like a sigh.

'So. We've been looking for someone to take his place on guitar.'

'You need a guitarist for a ceilidh?'

'Aye, that's how we've arranged it. I canna mind, have you seen us? I'm on the fiddle, like.' His smile creases his smooth, tanned skin.

'Aye. I know.'

'And if Alec isna there it's going to throw us off. Course it'd make splitting the cheque easier, eh.'

Niall smiles. 'Aye. True.'

'Well, I've got the set list in the van actually. So are you wanting a look?'

'Sure. Tell me what to play and I'll play it, then.'

Sandy Ross leans on the open door and takes Niall through each song on the set list. He fetches his new guitar from the boot, which Niall admires. He takes it under his arm, going through some of the chord progressions.

'That's a nice instrument you've got here. Beautiful.'

'Thanks very much. One of these Ovations. You wanting a shot of it on Tuesday?'

'Seriously?'

'Aye. Just to say thanks, like.'

Niall thinks about this. 'No, you're all right actually. I'd be best just using my old Bessie, you know? Just in case I . . . fuck it up.' He laughs.

'Ach, come off it now, how will you?'

'I don't know, but I just know what suits me.'

Large, grey drops of rain begin to fall again.

5

When Lauren finally comes home from Billy's in the dark, her dad is gone. She takes the wet sheets from the dark line and puts them back in the washing machine. They smell awful, or maybe it's the utility room. She pushes back the unsettling feeling that brushes the hairs on her arms and the back of her neck and stays still, listening. The house feels untrustworthy. She wonders what her dad might be doing and if the woman is hiding somewhere still. They don't have an attic or a basement. She has searched all the rooms, or all the rooms she can open.

Whenever Lauren feels scared in the dark, she lets it wrap around her, opening up her other senses until she becomes part of it, moving as silently as she can. She creeps to the stone hearth and sweeps out the grey ash into a dustpan. Then she piles the fire with kindling, as she often does when her father is out in the evening, laying down a piece of firelighter with half a peat block and striking a match. A burnt match is one of Lauren's favourite things and she breathes it in, wafting the stick around with its thin trail of smoke. She wants to feel protected.

As the fire takes hold, she grabs the apple she took earlier from Billy's house and forest birch twigs from her pocket and scatters the pieces of wood out in front of her, with a few dry leaves. She lays the apple on the stone hearth and cuts across its circumference, splitting through the core, pressing down hard on her pocketknife with the heel of her hand. She opens the two halves, revealing a five-pointed star shape in the middle of each. She flicks the seeds on to the floor with the tip of the knife and takes a stubby pencil from the table. She draws a question mark on to the curled strip of birch skin, then throws these birch pieces into the fire, whispering:

'Birch in the fire goes.
Tell me what the Lady knows.'

She watches them crackle and dance, then throws the apple seeds into the fire. They pop in the flames and she loses her thoughts to the heat.

When the flames die to embers she feels warm and safe in the dark house. The numbness in the walls has gone. She chops up the browning apple in the kitchen and puts the pieces on a plate with a blob of peanut butter.

She begins moving between rooms, switching on the lights, another ritual she saves for when she is alone. The only door she cannot open is the one to the locked room, by the front door.

She goes into the back room again. She wishes her dad would buy them a big TV like Billy's. Maybe if he took on more jobs. She could make posters to advertise. He is sporadic with the work he does take on, but likes it that way. She wishes she could read his palm, too, to find out what kind of person he really is. She wonders if bad people's hands are different to everyone else's.

But there are other questions too that his hands cannot answer.

She wants to play her CD, the soundtrack to *Frozen*, her guilty pleasure, but she cannot find it. Has her father really tidied it away? She rummages through the cupboard on one side of the fire in the back room, running her finger along her father's albums, a strange mixture of heavy metal and folk. She remembers that the last time she looked in this cupboard it was a mess, with CDs lying out of their cases and odds and ends of guitar paraphernalia: string packets, picks, the black snakes of electric leads. When she opens the cupboard an overpowering smell, like rotting meat and honeysuckle, hits her in the back of the throat. The cupboard is very neat and, after reading the names of several CD spines, she realizes they have been arranged in alphabetical order.

With her hand over her mouth and nose to mask the putrid smell, she finds the *Frozen* soundtrack in between a group of albums by Faith No More and Na h-Òganaich. The shelf has also been decorated with a line of small polished stones, pale yellow and a glassy purple. Lauren holds one of each up to the light and puts them in her pocket.

She plays the CD in the stereo of the alcove. At first the music makes a strange, mournful noise and she thinks she must have taken the wrong CD. A woman's voice wailing. She takes it out and rubs it with the sleeve of her sweatshirt. The second time around the music plays clearly.

She goes upstairs to get another jumper and is taken aback by her tidy room, filled with a similar heady scent, sweeter than before. Her books are ordered by her bedside table and the bed itself is made, with her stuffed duck, Webster, sitting happily on a pillow patterned with octopuses and jellyfish. There are no clothes on the floor or any of the little horses she likes to play with. All her clothes are in her cupboard and her wooden menagerie marches along her windowsill as though they are heading to Noah's Ark. *Thanks, Dad*, she thinks, feeling sure he must be a good person, who doesn't hurt anyone. She is pleased she made him a cup of tea before she left that morning.

She sits and thumbs the pages of the spaewife's leatherbound book on her bed, to find what she must do. She realizes it has become very late, as she goes out into the black garden, scooping up four jam jars on her way.

For a brief moment, a bat flutters in the trees. At the back of the overgrown shrubbery is a patch of lavender and herbs. Imagining her mother planted these, she tries to tend to the plants while keeping them hidden. She wants to make sure it's neat in case her mother returns, but she tells herself off for thinking this.

She picks three stems of lavender, three of sage and three of double-flowered camomile for each jar. Back in the house, she throws rice and salt into the jars and places them at the four points of the compass, touching each with a wish for the safety of the house. As she walks through the hall, she tries to look for clues: drops of blood or strands of hair. But the house is clean.

She takes three stones and places them on the hearth. She listens carefully, but there is still no sound of her father's truck in the drive.

She goes up to his messy room and watches the dark stretch of road below. Sometimes there are absences she can't explain. She has tried to stop feeling worried if he doesn't come home right away. There's a game she plays. From his window she can make out the shape and colour of the cars as they pass a lamp post on the single-track road. Their headlights between the fir trees and endless fields beyond. She speaks one word of a sentence with the passing of each car. Sometimes ten or twenty minutes might elapse between vehicles. It depends which day it is. Sometimes the traffic vanishes mid-sentence.

A small car. 'Where . . .'

Empty road. She sees a large bird, a buzzard, swoop down and sit on a fence post.

A white van from the bakery. 'Is . . .'

Empty road. Her dad is a good person.

Alan Mackie's jeep is coming back from the town. 'My . . .'

Empty road. She hopes he's safe.

Empty road.

The pickup. The pickup. The pickup. Jameson starts barking and runs down the staircase with her.

Niall comes through the door: a cold, wet coat and beard and hat. He lifts Lauren in his arms and swings her round.

'DAD.'

'You're home early!'

She observes his face closely, its lines and pores. 'No. *You* came home late.'

'Sorry, toots. Ran into Sandy Ross. He wants me to play with his band on Tuesday. How about that?'

'Can I come?'

'I think it's too late for wee lassies like you.'

'I'm not a wee lassie.'

'No. You are a very grown-up lady who likes . . . wait, is this that *Frozen* again?' He laughs and swings her once more, teasing her that she's too old for the likes of Disney; then he goes to the kitchen to stoke the boiler and put the kettle on.

'Dad,' she shouts through to him.

'Aye?'

'Thank you for tidying my room.'

'What?'

'Thanks. For tidying my room.'

'I didn't tidy your room – you did. Nearly tripped over those stones. They're in the garden.'

'What? No, I was out—'

He has disappeared back into the kitchen, clattering pots and pans as he serves up their dinner. She notes that he didn't look sad, angry or secretive when she spoke to him. He didn't look any way at all.

Over a plate full of sausage and mash Lauren asks carefully, 'So when are you playing the ceilidh?'

'Tuesday.'

'And I'm not allowed to come?'

'Afraid not. I'll play you a private gig and you can dance to that. You and Billy. And Jameson.'

'No way.'

'No way, José.' Her father smiles into his plate. 'So. You won't mind staying at Billy's that night then?'

'When?'

'Tuesday.'

'No—' She picks at her mashed potato. 'Dad. Billy's not even going to be there. They're away.'

'Where?'

'Disneyland Paris.' She forks a small cloud of potato into her mouth. 'So can I come with you?'

'Ach, no, Lauren. We'll have to find someone else. How about Vairi, eh? Know how much you love her.'

'Dad, stop joking me.' They eat the rest of the potato in silence. As Lauren picks up the plates, she says, 'Can I go to Angela's house?'

'No, you cannot.'

'But why? They're not on holiday. Ann-Marie is home.'

'Aye. Maybe Ann-Marie can come around here. I don't know. You're just not going to Angela's.'

'Why not?'

He sighs. 'Just . . . Now's not the time, Lauren.'

She knows better than to say any more and dries the dishes as he hands them to her one by one. 'Do You Want To Build A Snowman?' plays for the fourth time.

6

Lauren waits with Billy in the rain for the school bus, dirty white with peeling letters: *Lighthouse Coaches*. Everyone calls them *Shitehouse*.

She takes her place in one of the middle seats next to Jenny Gunn, from the year above. Lauren steals a glance at her fake leather jacket with its black studs.

'It's from New Look,' Jenny says.

Lauren has never been to New Look. Jenny always dresses more like the older kids at the back of the bus. She looks up to Diane and her friends who wear a lot of dark eyeshadow with bright nails. Lauren wonders if Jenny has only made friends with her because she knows Diane. She knows next year when Jenny starts the secondary school, she will be smoking with those girls at the bus stop in Strath Horne.

'See that old lady who lives across from me,' says Jenny. 'I think she's a witch.'

'How?'

'She scares me. Vairi Grant was over at hers the other Sunday and we heard these noises coming from her house. Cackling.'

'Maybe they were just chatting?'

Jenny tips her dark curls back. She leans closer to Lauren, her baby-blue nails catching the fluorescent light as she cups her hand to her mouth conspiratorially. 'We knocked on her door once and all these cats came out? She is like' – Jenny changes her voice to a reedy old lady's – 'He-l-l-lo . . . Ca-n I hel-p y-ous?'

Lauren giggles, but really she feels nervous. She can't imagine what Jenny would say if she ever found her granny's book. People think she and her father are weird enough already.

'I think that Vairi Grant is in on it too. Think they hexed me. You're to watch out for them. Hu-bble bu-bble . . .'

'Och, quit it.' Lauren says this good-naturedly, as though she isn't really bothered. She turns and wipes a patch of the misted window. In the pane along someone has written GRANT MACBRIDE IS GAY I.D.S.T. which stands for If destroyed, still true. Lauren draws a stick man that begins to trickle lines of water from his body.

The bus passes black goats on the steep hillside. A buzzard hovers high over an empty field. An abandoned croft with a rusty roof sprouts tufts of grass. In the distance the hills rise into mountains and the rocks grow bigger and more jagged. They stop at the Murrays' farm and Eilidh Murray climbs on to the bus. One girl is telling someone, over three rows of seats, that she has 205 pets: 'Two dogs, two cats, a rabbit . . . and two hundred sheep.' Lauren starts inking stars on her pink rucksack until she feels sick. She always wears a grey skirt and green sweatshirt for school, with any T-shirt she likes underneath. The T-shirt she is wearing today is midnight blue with a wolf standing on a crag in the moonlight. Another wolf, made of mist and stars, looms large in the sky behind it.

A hand yanks her plait from behind. She turns towards the seats behind her and sees Maisie MacAllister and another girl from her class looking carefully out of the window.

'Em, what are you looking at?' Maisie says. 'Mind your own beeswax.'

Her classmate, Katie, laughs beside her. Lauren turns around and sinks back into her seat.

In front, Maisie's brother Stuart is telling Billy about oil rigs. It is all he will talk about, given the chance. 'It's semi-submersible, see. You've to watch it doesn't sink.'

'When I go to Disneyland Paris tomorrow I think there's gonna be a ride that's semi-submersible.'

Lauren wonders whether the MacAllister kids were in the forest the previous day after all. She is about to ask Stuart when the hand yanks her plait again, to more laughter. Jenny, a blur of black hair beside her, whips round in her seat, pointing a pastel fingernail. 'I saw that. Yous two quit it.'

'What are you talking about?' comes the reply.
'Leave her alone.'
Lauren pulls her knees up towards her. 'It's OK.'

The day passes quietly. Lauren's Primary 6 class draws pictures of ancient Egyptians on coloured paper and sticks them to the walls. Lauren draws Tutankhamun with a blue and yellow headdress. She learns how to spell 'sphinx' and writes it six times in her best handwriting.

In Maths she helps their textbook's series characters, Olivia and Rajesh, to solve puzzles as they trek through the rainforest. She has to separate blue spiders from red spiders and see how many stones they need to build a temple. How high it will be. At what angle it slopes.

At morning interval, she buys Highlander crisps from the tuck shop and eats them sitting against the radiator in the girls' cloakroom, licking salty crumbs from her fingers. Most of the children are playing outside, but she prefers to go unnoticed here, in the warm. The space is empty today, apart from her classmate Rachel Munroe, who is practising the fiddle over by their row of coat pegs. Rachel comes to school every day with a sleek, high ponytail that swishes back and forth when they play sports. She writes everything in scented gel pens.

If people play a musical instrument at school, it's usually the fiddle or the chanter. Each student learns the same tunes in the same order, by ear. The chanter players like to huddle together in the playground to practise together. Mr Muir, with his puffy red cheeks, is their teacher, priming them for the high-school pipe band.

Marching around the village on a Saturday night, playing the bagpipes while everyone watches, is Lauren's idea of hell. She loves the fiddle though. The school fiddle players prefer to play alone at lunchtimes. If two are in the cloakrooms at the same time, they'll compete with each other. Rachel is now running the gamut of the primary-level repertoire, each song a little faster and more complex than the last.

Lauren doesn't have official lessons like the others but their teacher, Sandy Ross, comes to her father's now and again to play guitar with other men. He usually teaches her something on those nights and she is allowed to stay up later and listen. The songs they play most are about travelling round the world and missing Scotland and learning things the hard way. Songs that bring most men to the brink of tears, before they belt out a chorus to stop themselves. Lauren will sing along too and let her feelings ride high. Just as certain songs are only played at certain midnights in Scotland, particular emotions

are only permitted in particular circumstances such
as these. Whenever the men grow rowdy with drink,
she takes herself to bed.

Lauren has stopped recognizing the songs
Rachel is playing, so when she pauses, Lauren
asks, 'What was that? After "Merry Boys O'
Greenland"?'

'"Da Full Rigged Ship". Are you still playing.'
This sounds like a challenge rather than a question.

'Now and then.' Lauren is determined not to feel
small.

'Can you play "Mairi's Wedding"?' Rachel replies.
'I just learned it.'

'No. I can play "Bonnie Tammie Scolla".' This is
the second song you learn on the fiddle after 'Baa
Baa Black Sheep'. It's respectable, Lauren thinks,
it means you're not a baby. She thought it was
called 'Bonnie Tammy, Scholar' at first and imagined
a girl who was pretty and cool walking around
with a pile of books.

> Where have you been all the day,
> Bonnie Tammie, Bonnie Tammie?
> Where have you been all the day,
> Bonnie Tammie Scolla?

Her father had soon put her straight, explaining
that Tammie was a boy's name, the same as Tam
or Thomas, and Scolla was a Shetland surname. It

was disappointing. Boys are not bonnie, in Lauren's view, not bonnie enough to sing about.

Rachel does not think 'Bonnie Tammie Scolla' is respectable. 'Oh, that's easy,' she says, cocking her head to one side.

Lauren wants to tell Rachel her gel pens smell like hot puke, but instead she says, 'And "Donald Blue".' This is a lie. 'Donald Blue' is a complicated tune, like lots of bright boats bobbing at different times. She always imagines Donald Blue at the helm of one of them, wearing a navy Guernsey.

'Are you serious? You want to play it?' Rachel holds her fiddle out, calling her bluff.

'Nah. Play "Mairi's Wedding" then.' This song is one of Lauren's favourites, one of the most advanced for kids their age, and Rachel plays it faultlessly. Her fingers dance over the neck of the fiddle, so fast Lauren can hardly follow. While she plays, Rachel's eyes stare ahead vacantly.

You learn fiddle tunes by watching what your teacher does, again and again, until your body knows the music without thinking. If you do stop to think, you usually make a mistake. The lyrics run through Lauren's head:

> Plenty herring, plenty meal,
> Plenty peat to fill her creel,
> Plenty bonnie bairns as weel,
> That's the toast for Mairi.

When she is older Lauren wants to be a woman like the one who comes alive in this song, someone with a generous smile, someone everyone loves.

> Red her cheeks as rowans are,
> Bright her eye as any star,
> Fairest of them all by far
> Is our darling Mairi.

Lauren wonders if a song about her mother would sound the same. Maybe it would be very different.

Rachel finishes on a flourishing chord and gives her foot a little stamp.

'Is Sandy teaching you?' Lauren asks.

'Yeah.'

'He's my dad's friend.' She hopes the tone of her voice says *I know him better than you*. Next time he's round, Lauren will ask to learn 'Mrs McLeod', the third tune in sequence. Lauren imagines Mrs McLeod like her Primary 3 teacher, with big skirts, round glasses and black hair in a bun.

When she comes back to class after interval, she finds each of her coloured pencils have been snapped in half. Her father bought them as a treat from the supermarket.

She looks around. Maisie is watching her from another table and swivels her head back to face the teacher.

* * *

At lunchtime Lauren stays in the cloakrooms, their walls an oak tongue and groove. She watches the girls from the year above kneel on the coarse grey carpet in a huddle and pull their coats over their heads to tell ghost stories.

'What are you doing?' asks Lauren, knowing fine well. She stands close to them, then kneels gingerly.

Jenny sticks her head out and a giggle rises from under the bed of winter coats. 'It's just for P7s. You can't join us, sorry. I'll get a row.'

'Who says?'

'My mum.'

'How?'

'Because.'

'But—'

'*Because of your mum, Lauren,*' a voice says from under the coats.

That evening Lauren sits eating cheese and beans on toast on the sagging sofa, her legs curled to one side. She watches her father tuning his guitar.

'Dad.'

'Yes?'

'Do you ever hear people say things about us in town?'

'Say things about us?'

'Yeah.'

'Why would they be saying things about us?'

'*Dad.*' She waits for him to speak and he doesn't. 'Stop being like that.' When he still doesn't respond, she carries on, feeling tears prick the corners of her eyes. 'You *know* they speak about us. You're pretending everything's OK. Well, I've been pretending to you. People at school give me so much shit.'

'Hey. Lauren. Watch it.' She's got his attention now.

'How can you tell me not to swear? You don't care. Have you even got me a babysitter for tomorrow?'

He shakes his head with a plectrum between his teeth. 'Oh *God*, Lauren. Have you not asked Ann-Marie?'

This was never something he told her to do, as far as she can remember. She tries to stop herself from crying, tracing a piece of toast on her fork around the geometric pattern on her plate. 'No.' She sniffs. 'You never said anything. Can I go round there?' She hates the way her voice whines like this; she sounds so young.

He gets up, gives her a hug and then goes back to his plate. 'Jameson. Stop begging. Lauren, come on now. No. Give them a phone. She can come here.' He begins to play 'The Mountains Of Mourne'. *So I'll wait for the wild rose that's waiting for me.*

'When will you be back?' She had thought she was going to confront him, but he has managed to slip away, again.

He stretches. 'Need to get my capo.' He stands up to retrieve the guitar clip. 'Early enough. Maybe eleven.'

She knows he will be closer to four in the morning.

7

Lauren is opening a packet of Monster Munch when she sees Jenny standing in the playground. The neat primary school sits on the top of a hill built in Victorian sandstone, with high square classrooms, separate entrances for boys and girls, and a large brass bell in an arch on top of the slate roof. There are only a few houses to each side and bare playing fields stretching to the woods. The wind is rattling the flagpole. Skinny boys play football. A haar is coming in from the coast.

'Jenny?'

'Yes?'

'Do you want a crisp?'

'Cheers.' Jenny takes one and crunches it. Her lip gloss catches some of the crumbs.

Lauren tightens her ponytail. 'Will you tell me a ghost story?'

Jenny shakes her head.

'Why not?'

'I told you yesterday.' Jenny cocks her head to one side.

'What did you mean, though?'

'I don't want to make you upset.'

Lauren looks down at the black tarmac. A chocolate wrapper blows past them. 'I'm not upset about . . . *that*.' She tries to sound as though she knows exactly what Jenny is referring to.

'It made your dad really sad. My mum said he wasn't seen in town for weeks after.'

'Just tell me? I'll read your palm.'

Children race around them shrieking in the playground, echoing in and out of the square concrete shelters in the centre.

Jenny stares at her gloomily and helps herself to another crispy claw from the packet. 'I'll tell you this one story, OK?' she says mid-chew, 'but don't tell anyone I did. People say there must be this guy, who lives up in the woods. OK?' She looks over her shoulder. 'So, my uncle was telling us, his friend, he saw something strange when he was walking his dog up in those woods one night. The ones near where you and Billy stay. He's walking up there, deep, deep in the trees as it's getting dark and the dog goes off for ages.

'So. He shouts her and nothing. Starts to think she must have gotten lost. It's getting really dark and he can hardly see his own hand in front of his face. Then he hears the dog come out of the trees at last, panting. He can make out she is dragging this huge big stick she's got from somewhere, poking out both sides of her mouth, you know. Trailing along the ground.'

'Uh-huh.' Lauren doesn't like this story.

'When he gets to his car, he opens the boot for the dog and the light comes on. He notices that the stick is wrapped in some kind of material or some sort of thing. Some rags. The dog is staring up at him, really pleased. Her tongue hanging out, you know. Then the man looks down and notices a shoe, a trainer, on the end of the stick. He realizes it's not a stick at all, but his dog has dragged out a human leg.'

Lauren squashes the crisp packet into her pocket and feels the same as when the tide is sucking away from her feet, drawing her into the sand. 'I've got to go to the bathroom,' she says.

'I thought you were going to read my palm,' Jenny says, but Lauren is already walking back to the overheated girls' cloakroom, angry at herself for being such a baby. The place is empty and feels cavernous compared to the sharp winter light outside. She takes off her coat, sits on the floor and presses her back hard into the white-ridged radiator. She lets the heat seep into her skin until it scalds.

It is lunchtime at Catriona's farmhouse, but Niall still has to get rid of some built-in cupboards from the living room. His stomach is cramping with hunger, but he pushes on against the blaring radio.

His conversation with Lauren has stuck in his craw. He did his best to make light of things, keep things moving. The truth is, he hadn't known she was getting stick at school. She had never said much about the place. He had an inkling but he couldn't bring himself to ask her more. *Not much of a dad*, he thinks to himself. His mind skips over to the drinks cabinet in Catriona's kitchen. *Not much of a man. Not much of anything.* She has Jura single malt and Harris sugar kelp gin; he's looked. *No wonder she left you.* He tries to focus on unscrewing a cabinet from the corner of the living room, reaching into the dark corner, feeling for the bracket. *Lauren will too. One day.* The screws have been drilled in too tight. He tries over and over to take the little bracket apart, but his fingers feel thick and dirty against the rounded edges of the plastic block. *Not much of anything.* He puts pressure on the screwdriver until he is almost shaking, his teeth clenched.

The screwdriver slips and stabs him in the hand.

'Fuck's *sake*.' He wheels back, his jumper catching on a nail that is jutting out from the back of the handle. He throws the screwdriver against the wall and twists round to free himself.

He tries to wrench the cabinet door off its hinges with his bare hands. It doesn't come off, but just scrapes against his skin until it bleeds. 'Piece of *shit*.' He thumps the cabinet hard and tries again, with no luck. He grabs the hammer from his tool kit and launches himself against the wood, hacking it with the claw. '*Fucking piece of shit!*' His voice is loud over the radio.

He hacks until his back is slick with sweat. The cabinet starts to come off the wall through sheer force, ripping patches of the plaster. It's come apart now but he keeps hacking, because it feels too good. '*Absolute fucking bastard.*' He is stamping on wood and tearing plaster, his arms and hands catching against splinters. He can't let go of the hammer. His hair is sticking to his skull and his shirt is clinging to his back.

He kicks the remains of the cabinet with another groan and peels back, teeth bared, to see Catriona standing in the doorway.

For a second, he sees terror has exploded across her face. She dips her head and shuffles off to the kitchen, gently closing the door. Niall is left panting, surrounded by shards of wood and snowy flakes of plaster. '*Fuck*,' he breathes. The clouds are moving fast outside. He switches the radio off. Shadows leech through the filmy window. He can feel the blood pumping in his ears. '*Fuck.*'

He begins to tidy up his tools carefully. Catriona is the kind of no-nonsense woman who wears corduroy trousers and pays him cash in hand. When he first started the job, he had to arrive at 7.30 a.m. as she was leaving for work. She always looks so fresh-faced in the morning, with smartly ironed shirts that give him a clean, warm feeling as he lays down his tool bag on the terracotta hallway tiles.

He had no idea she would be home this early. They have fallen into a pattern on the days that Niall works on the house. When Catriona is home from the surgery and he is finishing up, Niall will switch off his radio and look up towards the hallway. Usually the milk-white kitchen door is closed, but sometimes it is a little ajar. He doesn't usually hear her arrive, only the fuzz of the radio and the rumble of the kettle. He always waits for a few moments behind the door with its cold brass handle before entering the pristine kitchen. The smell of fresh paint will be hanging in the air and he will tell Catriona he is popping out to grab more adhesive or pipe surrounds, or simply that he is heading home. She never seems to take much interest, or minds how sporadic he can be. A few times he has gone into the kitchen to say he needs things when he does not. She will barely look up, her laptop open like a clam on the wooden table, its flat screen illuminating her clear-skinned face.

This has fucked up everything.

'Catriona,' he says quietly against the closed kitchen door.

He hears a murmur in return and lets himself in. She looks up in her round tortoiseshell glasses.

Her caramel foot is high on the table's newspapered edge and she is stretching forward to paint her toenails peach. He notices her hand is shaking. A glob of polish is stuck to the newsprint over a story about a car crash. He can't think of what to say. Every time he opens his mouth he remembers how loud his voice was and how the plaster was hanging off the walls. She has untied her black curly hair, bringing out the smooth curve of her eyebrows.

'That's me off,' he says.

'Excuse me?' The eyebrows raise.

Niall clears his throat. 'That's me off.'

She stares at him hard. 'Right. That's it, is it? You're off. Charming.'

He wants to evaporate. 'I'm sorry. I didn't know you were . . . I'll make sure there's no damage done.'

She is shaking her head. 'Have a bit more . . .' Her arms gesture around her helplessly. 'I mean, I shouldn't have to . . . you know?' She is being brave, but the fear is seeping through.

He coughs. 'I'm sorry. It's been a bit of a tough job, aye.'

She looks at him as if he's the last line on an optician's wall chart. He drops his gaze to the ground and reaches for the door.

'People talk, you know,' she says.

'What?'

She shakes her head and says, 'See you Wednesday,' then goes back to painting her nails, as if he has already left the room.

The afternoon passes slowly at school. The teacher chalks words on the rolling blackboard. They take turns to read from a children's novel about the Highland Clearances and the Countess of Sutherland. She used to live up the road in a white turreted castle full of deer heads and lion skins. The story is about the villainous Patrick Sellar and his flaming crofts. There are scared mothers, hungry children, sheep, dirty tenements, girls at harsh looms, lost fingers, seasickness, the windy deck of a ship, Hudson's Bay, trading posts, fur and pine. Lauren thinks of the empty fields that stretch around them like patchwork and imagines twin landscapes in Canada. In under two hours, you can reach the most northerly part of the Scottish mainland and stand three hundred miles west of Norway. Lauren wonders why the crofters didn't go there instead.

Before art class, the children spread newspapers over their tables and put on their fathers' old paint-stained shirts. The teacher tells them to paint their favourite fairy tale. Lauren carefully paints a cow leaping over a crescent moon while the dog plays a fiddle under jagged stars.

'Did you know', says Lauren to Gary, the boy who sits next to her in an Aberdeen shirt every day, 'that you can see shapes and animals in the stars? Star signs. They tell you what will happen to you in the future.'

Gary is busy painting a black horse and doesn't answer.

The light starts fading before three o'clock. Lauren watches it from the vertiginous sash window. The bell rings. Girls and boys separate and mill out to their cloakrooms at opposite ends of the building. The lights flicker and the narrow corridor is extinguished into black.

The sudden dark makes the girls bleat and shift close together. The teacher's raised voice can be heard, telling them to keep calm, she is getting a torch. 'Everyone this way to the main door. Everyone this way. Turn around.' Children jostle Lauren on both sides, shrieking and chattering. She finds it hard to breathe. An instinct to run floods her, but she's hemmed in.

Someone to her left pushes Lauren and laughs. The torch beam passes over the crowd and she sees Maisie MacAllister at her shoulder. 'Lauren! Are you afraid of the dark, Lauren? Are you?' Maisie disappears again as the torch moves on.

'Scaredy cat!' another girl whispers behind. 'Scaredy cat!'

'She'll be bawlin' her eyes out.' Maisie, back beside her, gives Lauren a harder shove and she stumbles. She feels another leg hit her shin and falls hard.

'Uh-oh!' Snorting laughter. Her face is hot and she starts to cry without a sound, her burning cheek pressed against the ridged, itchy carpet. She tries to reach for something against the moving forest of legs around her. Her hands brush against one and another kicks her. Someone takes her outstretched palm and pulls her up. The hand is adult, but delicate. It lets her go and she feels a light pat on her back as she is carried along by the stream of noisy children, following the torch beam which has now moved in front of them. She tries to look for the figure who helped her up as she moves away but sees only the shapes of little girls behind her pushing out of their cloakroom. Another taller girl blocks her view and she realizes she has reached the light of an external door.

Lauren spots Billy and hurries to walk beside him. 'How's it going?' he says. He never seems surprised to see her. She starts to say something, but then shrugs as they walk towards their school bus in the twilight.

When he's finished work, Niall meets Sandy for a pint at the Tavern. It is smaller and dingier compared to their usual haunt, the Black Horse Inn, but the pints are slightly cheaper. The bar is on a hill – a main road – and a window stretches across two walls, overlooking the rolling peatland, its heather no longer in flower. The moon has appeared, shining over the rugged afternoon.

Niall remembers coming here as a teenager with his group of friends on the never-ending summer nights, when the hills were purple from June to August and they felt unmoored from the rest of the world. He remembers learning to fish on the long midsummer days of June and July, when the bright sun begins to set just after 10 p.m. He would go out with his friends to remote lakes in the woods catching rainbow trout, drinking from yellow tins in rowing boats, whether they were allowed to or not.

Niall sits in one of the beech chairs and recognizes a man across from him as someone from school.

'Kenny! You all right there? We're getting some pints in,' he says to the balding man seated alone with the crossword. 'You want something?'

'Hi there, no, you're OK actually, thank you.' Kenny gives Niall a funny look. 'I hardly ever see you about these days.'

'I'm about,' Niall says, trying to read his expression.

'Still got your wee girl and that?'

'Aye . . . of course.' Some people in the town still ask him these strange, cold questions. Niall looks up and sees the barman is now looking over at him. As Niall catches his eye, he looks away.

'Sandy!' Kenny brightens.

'Hello hello,' says Sandy.

'Still at it with the ladies?'

'Well, you know.' He winks.

'Still doing those house calls?'

'What can I say? Gotta give the customers what they want.' They burst out laughing as Niall shakes his head and orders three beers.

8

Lauren's father looks unusually smart in a kilt, shirt and waistcoat as he stands by the back room's sliding glass door. His ponytail is neat, and he has trimmed his beard.

'Why are you wearing that, Dad?'

'Have to, don't I?' He begins to pace the room, frowning. 'These guys I'm playing with? This band. You know what it's called? The "No Troosers" Ceilidh Band. What that means is – before you start giggling – you have to wear a kilt. Naff, really. But money's money.' He takes his old semi-acoustic guitar out of its case, flipping up the latches, checking it over. He starts to play the opening to 'Paranoid'. 'I'm not sure that's what they'll be wanting, is it?' He stops. 'Sing this one to me, Lauren, why don't you?' He starts playing 'Bonnie Tammie Scolla' loudly, as he knows she's trying to learn it. He points the guitar towards her, with a nod. She begins to sing:

'*Where have you been aw the day, bonnie mammy, bonnie mammy . . .*' Her father hasn't noticed, so she carries on. '*Where have you been aw the day bonnie mammy Chris . . .*'

He stops the music and stares.

A shadow passes the hall window and there is a loud rap at the door.

'Right.' He shoves the guitar in its case. 'That'll be Ann-Marie.'

She enters the hallway in an ice-blue anorak, her short hair in tufts from where she has pulled off her knitted hat.

'Hullo, how are you?' Ann-Marie says. 'Hi, Lauren!'

Niall says, 'Aye, no bad, yourself?'

'Yeah, I'm OK. Exams and stuff.' She sounds out of breath and her nose and eyes are watery from the cold.

'I see. You were missing home, then?'

'Yeah. It's been ages since I've been here properly, you know? Nice to see people again. Vairi. Alan popped by the other day. Dad's giving me some more driving lessons. I'm almost there.'

'Uh-huh.' He looks down at his guitar case and sighs. 'Right. That's me off then. Lauren – don't be giving Ann-Marie any cheek, you hear?' He pulls Lauren's head to his chest and kisses it, then takes off and slams the door.

Ann-Marie turns towards the locked living room.

'No,' says Lauren. 'C'mon this way, through here. Just put your jacket on the staircase.' She leads

Ann-Marie to the back room, with its worn sofas and table, while they hear the pickup's engine start its low growl, then fade away.

'Oh, it's lovely and warm in here.' Ann-Marie smooths down a blanket on the armchair.

'Do you babysit other people?'

Ann-Marie shakes her head, smiling. 'I'm at boarding school. Hang on. Did that lamp just switch on?'

'Which . . .?' As she speaks, Lauren can see it is the salt lamp, glowing pink again. 'I'm not sure . . .'

'Maybe it was on when I came in.'

Lauren looks around and sits on the carpet by the dying fire. 'Our TV isn't very good at the moment.' She would rather be at Ann-Marie's.

'It's OK. I don't think there is much on tonight anyway.' She looks around the room. 'Do you have Wi-Fi?'

'I don't think so. We've got a computer over there. It has internet.'

Ann-Marie looks at the PC on its beaten-up Formica desk, in the corner. 'It's OK. I can still get some 4G.' She pauses. 'A bit. I forget what it's like here.'

'I have my own mobile, but it doesn't have the internet.'

'Really?'

Lauren takes out an old Nokia.

'That's a nice-looking phone.'

'Thanks.'

'People text you?'

'Just my dad, really.'

'None of those girls, those girls at school you mentioned? Because—'

But Lauren is already shaking her head. She can tell Ann-Marie wants to ask her more, but instead Lauren motions to look at her touch-screen phone. The cover is shaped like a bucket of popcorn and the screen bubbles with coloured squares. Behind these, there is a picture of Ann-Marie with a blond-haired boy. Their heads are close together, on a beach. Lauren can see parts of the boy's scarf. They are both smiling.

'Who's that?'

'That's my boyfriend.'

Lauren squeals. 'You have a boyfriend!'

'Yes, I do.'

'What's his name?'

'Rory.'

'*Rory and Ann-Marie sitting in a tree. K. I. S. S. I. N. G.*'

Ann-Marie rolls her eyes and tries to find a video with a cat on a treadmill, but the internet doesn't work.

'Can I use your bathroom?'

'Sure.'

Ann-Marie is gone for quite a while, even though she knows where it is; Lauren can hear creaking in a different part of the house. She wonders if Ann-Marie is nosy, like her mother Angela, but decides it isn't important. She likes her too much.

When Ann-Marie returns, Lauren asks, 'Can I meet your *boy*friend?'

She shakes her head. 'Shhh. He doesn't live here, does he?'

'Ask him to visit!'

Ann-Marie laughs. 'Oh! Your dad forgot to say – when's your bedtime?' She raises her eyebrows, like a threat.

Lauren looks at the clock. 'It's six thirty now. Not for a while. He's going to be home late. I know it. Ann-Marie, you don't want to stay here late, do you?'

'He's up at the Castle Hotel, right? My parents are too. It's for charity. To help people who aren't very well.'

Lauren scrunches up her mouth, thinking.

'How was your day at school?'

'OK.' She catches the smell of something rotten, like meat left in the sun, but different, more floral.

Ann-Marie looks over at the lamp again. 'Do you mind if I switch that off? It's bugging me.'

Lauren nods. They are next to the kitchen, but she is sure her father hasn't left anything out to rot.

'So,' Ann-Marie continues, 'school is just OK? What did you learn?'

'About pyramids.'

'Pyramids?'

'When a pharaoh died, they buried all his things with him in the tomb. We had to write what our favourite belongings are.' She remembers once a mouse died in the wall, but this doesn't smell the same way.

'That . . . you would have buried with you? Hmmm. I'm not sure about that.'

'Why?' She feels embarrassed by the smell. The dripping from the utility room seems to be getting louder, somehow.

'Have you told your dad about that?'

'No. I said I wanted my Jacqueline Wilson books buried with me.'

'I see.'

'And Jameson might be buried with me. But he would have to die too.'

'Oh, Lauren. Are you still playing the fiddle?'

'Yes.' Surely Ann-Marie can smell it too and she is just being polite.

'Do you want to play something for me? What have you been learning these days? Can you play "Mairi's Wedding"?'

'Can you read me a story at your house?'

'Why not here?'

'I don't like it here.'

The house is called the Elms. It is made of dark brick and black slate. The panes are painted white. There is a well-kept walled garden with topiary hedges and rose briars. A red hen house and a white duck house stand adjacent in one corner of the garden. The edges of the sloping grounds are dotted with birch trees. Lauren's feet slip unsteadily in the gravel as she crunches up the dark incline to the house. Ann-Marie is wheeling her bike after giving Lauren a backie down the forlorn hill to her house. She looks over at her. 'I forget how dark it gets here. In Edinburgh there are always people around, and so much light. It's so quiet here. So quiet.'

Lauren can see that she is spooked and trying not to show it. 'The quiet feels calm, though.' She stops in her tracks and gestures for Ann-Marie to stop too. 'Just stand here.' It is so quiet she can hear Ann-Marie breathing in the cold. 'Your eyes can see better than you think, if you let them. The dark is a good thing. My dad says *the dark is useful*. It's useful for rabbits and the little animals, as well as the big ones. The worst you can do is try and run away from it. Then you'll really feel scared.'

Her father often walks the dog in the dark, when the moon and stars are so bright they can shine the way. Even when they don't, she knows he lets his eyes open up and he never ever runs. Now she lets her body melt into the dark and lets the other senses – hearing, smell – work harder. It feels somehow relaxing to be hidden away in the night. The air is dry and clear as glass. It cuts through her gloves to the bones of her fingers. Her nose begins to run. 'Come on,' Ann-Marie says and they walk up the drive.

The wide hall grows thick with heat from the open fire Ann-Marie has made. The only other light comes from a Tiffany lamp. There is a thin bench with red leather padding in front of the hearth. Years of smoke from moss-covered logs and peat has sunk into the oak panels and velvet. The particular smell is as comforting to Lauren as her father's stew.

'I know what we can do!' says Ann-Marie. They go down into the huge kitchen and Ann-Marie takes out a clear package from a cupboard in the island. 'Have you ever toasted marshmallows before?'

'No! Can we?'

'Of course we can!'

Ann-Marie finds sharp iron skewers. Lauren enjoys driving them through the pink flesh of the marshmallows. She lines up the white ones, thinking about the white of the young woman's dressing gown, the girls talking behind her back at school. She pushes the thoughts away, not wanting to break the spell of this happy moment.

Back upstairs, the two girls draw the bench close to the hallway fire and Ann-Marie shows Lauren how to hold the skewer just above the flames, to toast it without burning. Lauren copies her move-ments carefully and the marshmallows begin to soften and bubble brown.

'We'll text your dad, won't we? Will you text him? Don't want him wondering where you are when he comes home.'

'Yes. OK. He's going to be annoyed.'

'Why?'

Lauren notices the oil painting of a gun dog with a pheasant in its jaws, half in shadow on the wall. She has never really paid attention to it before. There is blood soaking its mouth. Below, on the mantelpiece, are silver-framed photographs and a candelabra holding unlit used candles that have sunk into themselves.

'When do you use that?' she asks.

'Oh. We can now.' Ann-Marie takes a large box of matches from behind a photo frame and strikes a flame. Lauren collects empty matchboxes. She has decorated a couple at home with silver glitter and pictures cut from newspapers. Inside she keeps things that are small and precious to her – a tiny shell, a palette of eyeshadow from her mother's vanity case, a foreign coin. Sometimes she will use them for spells, too, and bury them in the ground. Lauren watches the match glow blue, orange and yellow. She watches the flame catch the burnt, sunken wick of the first candle. Ann-Marie uses the same match to light the next candle and the next, her back straight, concentrating.

'Did you know that candles have magic powers?' says Lauren.

'Er . . . no, I didn't.'

'Well, they do. Blue means protection. Yellow means happy. Red means love.'

'How do you know that?'

'We have a book at home.' Lauren doesn't ever mention *the* secret book, but she talks about others. She picks at a corner of the bench where the red leather has cracked and yellow padding spills through. 'It's one of my favourite books. *Candle Power: The Inspiring* – something – *Ritual and Magic.*'

'What do white candles mean?' Ann-Marie says.

'I can't remember.'

'Let's look it up.' Ann-Marie begins tapping on her phone. 'White is . . . "Psychic development. Purity. Truth." That sounds good, doesn't it?'

'Yeah. What does the first one mean?'

'I don't know. Look. There's a poem you're meant to say when you light the candle.

"Flickering candle,
Enchanted fire,
Grant me what
I so desire."

They watch the three small flames move. '*One two three* . . .' Lauren holds her breath. Ann-Marie points to her phone screen and they say the last part together: '. . . *So shall it be.*'

The lamps and candles flicker and the room turns black. Lauren grabs Ann-Marie's hand and they try to see each other in the dying flames.

'That can happen,' says Ann-Marie, her voice a little shaky. The bulb has blown. The room feels very cold and damper now, Lauren notices, as though they are underground.

Back downstairs in the bright kitchen, the Irish wolfhounds rise from their ancient baskets and sniff around the girls' feet. Lauren does not want to pet them with her clean hands. The dogs look up at her, and one tries to rise up on its hind legs, its nose almost touching hers.

'Down, Rowland!' says Ann-Marie.

They eat quietly for a while, leaning against the untidy island. A bowl of ageing fruit, wine stains, bills, a corkscrew and a gardening fork litter its marble surface. 'Ann-Marie.'

'Yep?' Ann-Marie has her mouth full of marshmallow.

'You know how you said I should tell you if those girls gave me any more bother?'

'What have they been doing now?'

'It's just . . . They don't like me. I feel like they're going to play a trick on me.'

'How could anyone not like you? They'll be jealous of you.'

Lauren shakes her head. 'No, they're not. How would they be?'

'Because you're different.' Ann-Marie puts her arm around Lauren in a half-hug. 'You're cool, Lauren! Come on. Tell them to go and . . . kiss your bahookie.'

Lauren giggles.

'Shall we put on some music?' says Ann-Marie. 'What do you like?'

'Um. I like *Frozen*.'

'OK. I don't have that.' She picks up the greasy kitchen stereo by its handle and they go back to the hall by the fire.

Ann-Marie plays synth music and Lauren begins to dance, sitting on the wood floor, swaying her arms above her head.

'My parents really like them. They're from the eighties,' says Ann-Marie. 'They're called Duran Duran.' She skewers another marshmallow.

They bring candles back to the fire, to light the room, now the bulb has blown. The fire crackles. Part of a thick branch breaks and falls into the flames with a rush and snap.

'Ann-Marie? Some girls were talking and it made me wonder. Where do you think my mum went?' Lauren's words rush out like water. She sees Ann-Marie go still as she continues. 'I once asked Kirsty about it, but she said I have to ask my dad and my dad doesna want to talk about it.'

Ann-Marie looks Lauren straight in the eye. 'Yeah?' She nods encouragingly. Her mouth closes.

Lauren can see the shape of her tongue moving, as if dislodging food or finding the right words. When she speaks, it is in a more formal tone. 'It's difficult. And the truth of it is, Lauren, I don't know what exactly happened.' She gives a puffy-cheeked sigh. 'I wish I did. Diane and I have always said that.'

'What do you mean?'

She gives a searching look and closes her eyes. 'Sorry. I'm sorry, pal.' She puts her arm around Lauren once again. 'It's hard to talk about.' She pulls away, leaving her hand on Lauren's shoulder. 'We don't know where your mum went to. Nobody does. She left, one day. When you were little. She didn't say where she was going.'

'But *why*?' Lauren's eyes and nose have begun to grow moist in frustration. She has never wished so fervently to be an adult.

'*Why?* Exactly. It's something that really bugs me. It doesn't make sense. Diane's been saying the same. We're so sorry and we just don't know.' She twists a section of her fringe. 'I remember Christine from when you were a baby. I was very wee. She was lovely. I really liked her a lot. She sometimes looked after me.' She sighs and squeezes Lauren's shoulder. 'She loved you very much, Lauren, don't you forget it.'

'What was she like?'

'Well, she was quite un*u*sual. She had this long hair that was' – she laughs softly – 'all over the place. She wore cool clothes. She liked things like this,' she says, nodding towards the candles. 'Like candles. And I remember once I had a headache. She put her hands on my head, like this.' Ann-Marie puts her hands over the crown of Lauren's head, her fingers joining at the hair parting, the heels of her hands pressing Lauren's temples. 'Then she lit a candle and got rid of bad energy with her hands.'

Lauren feels a slow burn of anger that she tries not to show. 'How?'

'By moving them around and throwing away the bad energy, getting it away from me. It made me feel calmer – relaxed and not so anxious and in pain. She made me laugh doing it; it was like a game. I remember her being a very warm person, your mum.'

Lauren's eyes are huge in her face.

'Maybe you should talk to Vairi about her. Vairi was good friends with her.'

'Vairi?' Lauren asks.

'Yeah, I know. She doesn't seem like the friendliest person at times, does she? But she believes in some of the same superstitions that your mum believed in. My mum says they used to cook together.'

'What did they cook?' She feels detached and as if she wants to be back at home.

'I don't know – you should ask Vairi. I'm sure she'll tell you. She was nice though. I remember this one time, at the beach. It was really cool.'

Lauren feels a dark wave pass through her.

'We were walking the dog, drawing in the sand and stuff. Then Christine told me to stay still and close my eyes. When I opened them, she had drawn a circle around me, and covered it with rocks, pebbles, seaweed and shells. She said it was a special circle, called a cairn. No, wait, a "cai*m*". It was giving me power to, like, protect me.'

'Protect you from what?'

'I don't know. It was just, like, magic stuff. Superstition. Protect me from bad spells. Bad witches. Bad people.'

Lauren picks some dirt out of one of her finger-nails and doesn't look up. She wants Ann-Marie to stop bothering her.

Ann-Marie puts her arm around Lauren. 'I'm sorry, I said too much. I don't know. Believe me, I'm trying to find out more. Christine was so lovely. She wasn't like anyone else here. That's why I remember her so well, even though it was a long time ago. I always remember her.' Ann-Marie pauses. 'She gave me birthday presents.'

'Why did I never get birthday presents?' She feels her nose sting.

'No . . . no. So . . . listen a minute. I was about seven – or eight – when she gave me the last one, the summer before she went away, a bit younger than you are now . . .'

Ann-Marie pulls herself up and takes the curv-ing red stairs two at a time. Lauren follows her reluctantly. As she climbs she is sure she can hear dripping from the basement down below. The staircase is cavernous and dingy, and she drags her hand along fleur-de-lis wallpaper. At the top, Lauren sees a splinter of light from Ann-Marie's bedroom.

The walls are dark purple and stuck with glossy posters of actors Lauren doesn't recognize and a blurry Magic Eye picture. An art nouveau fireplace blossoms with flower-shaped fairy lights. A lava lamp bubbles above. In the corner of the room is an orange labyrinth of plastic tubing for rats. Ann-Marie is pulling a candy-striped shoe box from underneath her big iron bed. She brushes off a layer of beige dust from the lid. 'Guess it's been here a while.'

She thumbs through a pile of papers and cards. 'Ah, look,' she says, 'here's a card from Alan Mackie. I thought I had chucked them all out. And here it is – a birthday card from your mum and dad.'

'Doesn't Alan creep you out?' Lauren asks.

'He did send me a lot of birthday cards,' she replies. 'Well, one every year, from when I was about ten. And some presents. Two years ago he sent me a swimming costume and my mum asked him to stop.' She shrugs and holds out the other card. It is light green, with a Celtic knot hand-stamped on the front. 'So sweet, eh? *Happy birthday with love from Christine, Niall and baby O.*'

'Baby O?'

'That means you.'

A strange feeling rises up as though Lauren is being made to wear something she hates. Ann-Marie continues: 'She gave me a ring with that kind of design on it one year. I loved it, but I don't know where it's gone. Maybe in my jewellery box. Here.' She takes out a circular quartz pendant on a silver chain. 'How cool is this? I remember she gave it to me for another birthday – I think it was that summer – and she said it had special powers. It was gonna be good luck, to protect me – the circle, you know? I believed in it. I used to, like, run around the garden casting spells and stuff. Sorry, Lauren.' She holds it out. 'Here. You should have it. I want you to.'

Lauren feels nothing as Ann-Marie fastens it around her neck. She may as well have picked it up off the pavement. 'Talk to it. Talk to it and maybe you will be talking to her.'

'I don't *want* it,' Lauren says, then louder, trying to tear off the necklace, 'I DON'T WANT IT.'

The clasp snaps and the pendant springs across the room.

'Lauren.' Ann-Marie kneels down.

'*No.*' She flinches and ducks away.

Ann-Marie takes a deep breath. 'I am going to try and help you – I've decided. It will just take some planning. I—'

'No, I don't need . . . *help*! She doesn't care, she never, *never* cared.' She spits out the words and wrenches open the bedroom door. She looks for somewhere to hide and be alone, scratching her nails along the bannister as she stalks the tartan carpet of the corridor. She hates the house, hates every old inch of it.

She slams herself inside the bathroom on the landing and leans her hot back against the cracked white paint of the door frame. It is a cold room, with thick towels draped on a rickety railing and green potted plants, lined up next to cloudy glass bottles that skirt the room. She moves to a faded yellow bathmat in a sea of delicately painted blue tiles that flow into tangled floral wallpaper. Still clothed, she climbs into the empty claw-foot bath. Her jeans brush against the ceramic. A copper-coloured shower head looms like a poisonous flower. Sitting with her knees tucked under her chin, she pulls out the pocketknife and snaps it open then shut, over and over, listening to the swish and click. Water drips from a corner of the ceiling. The black mildew around the edges of the tiles melts away, as does the rest of the bathroom, its wallpaper peeling in the corners. She feels her chest gently pumping air in and out as if she is observing another body. She wills herself to be like a creature in a shell at the bottom of the ocean. As she levers open the knife again she begins to whisper the words:

'Strength of dark,
Strength of light,
Give me power beyond my sight.'

The words become a loop of sound against the slap of the knife that echoes in the bath. After some time, she becomes aware of a gentle knocking against the door.

'Out in a minute,' she says. Lauren runs the cold tap slowly, so the water creeps to meet her toes. She holds the knife under and watches the water cascade off the metal. As icy water slides under the soles of her feet and up to the edge of her jeans, she hears Ann-Marie creak away outside. She closes the knife and lays it ceremoniously on the side of the bath. Taking a few more breaths she splashes the tap water over her swollen eyes and mouth, pressing her fingers against her eye sockets and lips. Her clothes get splashed, but she doesn't care. She gets up and looks at herself, expressionless in the mirror, measuring how still she can make herself, how unblinking, how cold.

The dripping is getting faster; the pipes rumble within the walls. There is a clear full moon shining into the room, a reminder that things will change. On the dresser is a bottle labelled *crème de corps*. She wants to try some on her forearm, but has to hit the end of the bottle, like ketchup.

On one wall in the bathroom is a photo collage behind glass. She didn't notice it earlier when she was angry. There are pictures of Malcolm, Ann-Marie's father, when he had more hair, holding Ann-Marie and her brother Fraser's hands on a skiing holiday. He is a surgeon and Lauren hardly ever sees him. Angela looks very similar in the pictures to the way she looks now, but thinner and with bigger glasses. Lauren's eyes move between pictures: puffball dresses, white birthday cakes, Siamese cats, Christmas lights, banana-boat rides. Ann-Marie and Fraser grinning in a rubber dinghy with four of their cousins, all with short dark hair and orange lifejackets. In one photo, Ann-Marie is a little girl standing next to a grown-up girl, who is smiling broadly with sunglasses. A bit more grown up perhaps than Ann-Marie now, and with glowing, henna-red hair. She is smiling, in an indigo tie-dye dress. Lauren looks at it again. The faces are tiny, and the film is over-exposed, but Lauren is drawn to it, squinting.

Downstairs one of the dogs starts to howl. Ann-Marie starts to shout at them and sounds more childlike. Lauren tries to find her phone and then remembers she left it in her bag downstairs. In the half-light on the landing, she sees a glass dome encasing a stuffed bird. It is sitting on a gnarled branch with peeling lichen. The bird is large and pheasant-like but obsidian black, with red, leathery eyebrows and a tail that looks just like a Spanish fan. Its long neck is stretched upwards, as if it is reaching for something with its blunt white beak. It looks too dusty to come alive. She can see its eyes are fake.

When she finally goes to find Ann-Marie, she is sitting by the fire, acting as though Lauren has only been away for a couple of minutes.

'Those pictures in the bathroom. Ann-Marie, is one of them my mum?'

Ann-Marie thinks for a second. 'Yes, sorry, I didn't realize.'

'Do you have any more? We only have one in the house and . . .' The photograph sits on a table on the landing, her mother's young face looking hopefully off camera, her hair decorated with tiny plastic butterflies.

'What? You only have one photo of your mum?'

'Yeah. I think my dad has more. I've tried to get him to show me but it makes him upset. He—' She was about to say, *He drinks too much*, but stops herself.

'If I find any more, I'll give them to you, but I'm not totally sure we do, sorry. Hey,' the older girl says, looking into the flames, 'do you want to know a secret? You can keep a secret, can't you?'

'Yes.'

Ann-Marie looks at her.

'Cross my heart, hope to die, stick a nee—'

'OK, yeah. Look.' She pulls up the side of her T-shirt to show a large black tattoo on her hip.

There are tendrils, tentacles of some creature, similar to an octopus but a stranger shape, with a pointy head. There are dark-blue ink splotches over her stomach.

'Oh my God! When did you get that?'

'In Edinburgh.'

'When?' Lauren can't take her eyes off the twisting limbs.

'A month ago.'

'What is it?'

'A squid. It captures its prey with its two front tentacles, like this.' She wraps her arms around Lauren, who tries to twist away, tries not to laugh. 'Then it tickles them. Like this.'

Lauren pushes her off, not able to keep a straight face.

They sit in silence for a while, then Lauren says, 'Was it sore?'

'A little. Actually, yeah, really sore.'

'My dad says it's sore. He has some. But he says I'm not allowed. Do your mum and dad know?'

'They found out. The school told them. No one's very happy with me right now. My mum's trying to pretend everything's fine, but she went mental. Yeah.' She looks out of the window. 'They sent me home. Coming home's weird. It feels so empty. My dad—' She catches herself mid-speech.

Lauren realizes she must be too young to talk to about these things, but she tries. 'You got in trouble?'

'Um. My dad doesn't want me to tell anyone, but I'm suspended. Like, banned from school for a while.'

Lauren reflects on this. 'Why did you do it?'

'Sounds stupid now, but I thought it was beautiful.' She pauses. 'Don't say anything to my mum and dad. Or my brother. They don't want anyone to know. They made me promise.'

'When you take a shower, will it hurt?' Lauren points to Ann-Marie's side.

Ann-Marie laughs. 'No, it'll be fine.'

One of the dogs runs into the hall, agitated, howling softly at her. 'What's wrong? Hey. Do you want to go outside?'

The dog runs into the games room and paws the corner of the door that leads outside to the garden. Eighties pop bounces out of a room somewhere.

The dog, either Rowland or Fergus, turns to look at Ann-Marie and barks. Lauren sees its brother hiding under the billiard table. It crawls towards the door and starts to howl too.

Ann-Marie sighs, 'OK then.' As she reaches for the door key, the porch light comes on outside.

Ann-Marie stops. 'Hello?' There is no sound. She rolls up the blind and looks through the square panes of glass. The outside light stretches over the gravel into the dark trees.

'No, you're not going outside.'

The dogs start a cacophony. One goes back under the table, whimpering, and the other dog begins to scratch at the door again as it barks.

'*Quiet.*' She turns to Lauren. 'Oh! Look at these guys. It's nothing. Probably just a bird. Or a bat. They're such numpties. OK, so do you still want to stay over? I'll text my parents. They'll be fine with you sleeping in the nursery upstairs.' She goes over to the kitchen window. 'There's an extra blanket in the wardrobe. I'd better stay and sort those dogs. I don't know what's gotten into them.' Lauren doesn't ask why she's not letting them outside.

The nursery is full of lace. Lace over the brass bed, lace curtains. Lace on the dresses of the dolls that sit on a rocking chair with teddy bears. The walls are cream and there is a white enamel sink in one corner. A grey dolls' house sits under the window. The floors, like most of the floors in the house, are polished wood, covered here and there with old rugs. In this room, by the bed, is a large sheepskin. Lauren kneels down to touch it. It is softer than any sheep she has met.

She reaches around in the cavernous wardrobe and finds the blanket. Then she wraps it around her, sitting cross-legged on the edge of the white bed. Under the counterpane is a grey quilt. It's so quiet. She looks at the rocking chair of toys and they look back at her. A bald baby in a long christening gown, its skin the colour of a peeled apple. There is a little girl with black ringlets under a straw bonnet and a teddy bear with glinting buttons for eyes. A light, the porch light, comes on outside. She gets up to look. Below, a dog shoots into the dark. Lauren tries to see out. Through the single-glazed glass, she hears Ann-Marie calling 'Rowland!' Then, more quietly, 'Oh. *Oh my God.*' A bush obscures the porch light, but she can see the edge of a female figure and, when she looks more closely, the bunched white towelling of a dressing gown.

'Are you . . . ?' Ann-Marie's voice rises.

The back of the woman's head is nodding. She spreads out her arms to each side, the palms facing away, and shakes her head.

'What? I'm sorry . . . You look so cold.'

The woman turns, her arms still half stretched, and begins to walk away. Lauren notices the porch light shines in a different way upon her. She is solid but not quite opaque.

'*Where are you going? Hello?*' Ann-Marie sounds frightened. As the woman turns, she raises her head to look straight up at Lauren in the window. She smiles and Lauren ducks down out of sight. The photograph from the bathroom glimmers in her memory.

Frightened, she slides under the cold counterpane and switches off the lumpy bedside lamp.

The outside door clicks shut. There are footsteps on the stairs and snatches of a familiar song. '*Where have you been all the day . . .*' Lauren shrinks down into the bed covers. '*Where have you been all the day, bonnie . . .*' The bedroom door creaks open.

'Hello, Lauren? Are you asleep?' Ann-Marie whispers.

'No,' Lauren breathes back.

'Are you all right?' Before Lauren has a chance to answer, Ann-Marie begins to sing in a low, lullaby voice.

'Up a hill and doon a brae,
Bonnie Lauren, Bonnie Lauren,
Up a hill and doon a brae,
Bonnie daughter Lauren.'

Lauren sits bolt upright. 'What?' She switches on the bedside lamp. She realizes the base is covered in seashells.

'Hey. Sorry. It just popped into my head.' Ann-Marie looks puzzled.

'*Daughter Lauren?*'

'I said *Bonnie* darlin *Lauren*. What's wrong? Where is that song from again? I'm sure I know it.' She sings again. '*Bonnie Lauren Mackay.* Happy?'

'Please, don't. Who were you talking to?'

'What?' Ann-Marie comes up to Lauren's bed, her silver jewellery catching the lamplight.

'Who was it?'

'Huh?' Ann-Marie's face is blank.

'The woman you were talking to. Outside.'

Ann-Marie stares at her. 'Lauren,' she says in a half-whisper, 'I wasn't speaking to anyone.'

'Yes, you were.'

Ann-Marie sits on the edge of the counterpane, pulling the ends of her jumper over her hands. 'No, I wasn't.'

'Why won't you tell me? I'm not lying. I saw you.'

Ann-Marie sighs. 'What did you see?'

'A girl. You were talking to someone.'

'I was?'

Lauren nods.

'And you know who she is?'

Lauren hesitates. 'I think so.'

'Who, then?'

'No. I don't. Really. It's hard to explain.'

'Right. I was calling the dogs. They were running off too far. That's who I was talking to.'

'There was a girl, a woman.'

Ann-Marie looks out of the window. 'Whatever happened, I think you should get some sleep. I'm texting Diane up the road, to see if she's on her way. Rowland's still outside. God, he's never normally like this.' Her phone begins to buzz.

'Ann-Marie?'

'It's Diane calling, sorry.'

Lauren talks quickly. 'I saw this lady the other night and—'

'Sorry, I think I should answer. We can talk about this tomorrow? Try and get some rest. I'll tell my mum and she can tell your dad.'

It looks a bit like her, Lauren doesn't manage to say. Ann-Marie snaps the light off and closes the door with a hush of air. In the pitch black Lauren falls into a hazy sleep. The last thing she thinks of is white candles.

What could be some minutes or hours later, Lauren hears two voices downstairs against music that sounds like an angry factory. She climbs out into the cold room and puts her ear to a ridge between the floorboards. There is a third voice, male and scratchy.

Out on the landing and hiding behind the heavy bannister she squints into the yellowy hall below. Diane, who lives up the road, is swaying her black ironed hair, a green bottle in her hand. 'Let me talk to him!' she is saying in her croaky voice.

Ann-Marie appears by the fire, licking her thumb. They have been toasting marshmallows again. She is talking on FaceTime to someone Lauren thinks must be Rory, her boyfriend. She catches him saying, 'What you up to? Couple of dafties.' The music rasps and drones.

'We're having a party,' says Diane. Each of her eyelids has a perfect black flick of liner and her mouth is the shade of blackberries. 'We found her parents' booze.'

'But we haven't found my dog yet,' says Ann-Marie. She tosses the phone on to a ratty velvet cushion. 'He keeps cutting out.' She looks at Diane. 'You're pissed.'

'I amne,' says Diane, too loud. Her tone of voice makes Lauren want to laugh, as if she's inviting an audience. She takes off her tartan shirt, so she is just wearing a black cropped vest. The fire is making the room too hot. Lauren creeps down a few more stairs. Ann-Marie is facing away from her.

Diane says, 'So you got sent home for a tattoo, is that it?' Her voice is drawn out with wine. 'See, when I got that one on my arm, nobody gave it a second glance, man. I wouldna last two seconds, like.'

Lauren can tell she's pretending to be amazed and dumb, but her voice is hiding something meaner. She carries on. 'Sounds like you get a punny eccy for as much as fartin'.'

Lauren shoves her hand over her mouth in silent, almost painful laughter. A punny eccy is what secondary pupils are given when they're in trouble.

Ann-Marie flushes. 'There were other reasons.'

'Yeah, like what?' Diane is chewing on something.

'They caught me smoking on the roof.'

Diane rolls her eyes.

'And they said I was being too "aggressive".'

'Huh?'

'With a teacher. That Mr Hutchinson I told you about.'

'Old Hutchy.'

'Yeah. I drank too much one night and I "made a scene". He said he had reason to be worried about me. More like scared.'

Diane laughs and Ann-Marie relaxes. 'But hey. About that thing, anyway,' she says, putting a hand on Diane's shoulder. 'That thing you told me about, in the pub?'

'What?' Diane is already distracted by her phone.

'Shhh.' Ann-Marie touches her friend on the shoulder and points to the ceiling.

'She can join us! *And her dad.*' Diane raises her eyebrows.

'*Diane.* Look at me. I'm talking about . . .' Ann-Marie still has her back to Lauren and half mouths or whispers something to Diane – it's hard to tell. 'You know? I just couldn't stop thinking about what you'd said.' She points to the ceiling again. 'She doesn't seem to know anything about it either. So I just wanted to tell you. I'm gonna find out. See if it's him or not. We owe it to Christine.'

'You're mental.' Diane looks towards where Lauren is hiding.

Lauren's heart starts thudding and she scrambles back up the stairs, the carpet burning her palms.

'Hiya!' shouts Diane and Lauren freezes like a lizard. 'It's past your bedtime, isn't it? Hey, come down here for a selfie, c'mon.' Diane's voice sounds like it is flowing out of a jar. Lauren clambers down shyly, her bare feet slipping on the hardwood floor.

'Come here, yous two, it's for my Instagram, eh.'

Lauren feels a small bubble of joy as the two older girls huddle around her. She smells nylon, hair products and something else, a mulchy-sour smoke.

'Amazing, guys,' says Diane in a way that is making fun of them or the situation, Lauren can't quite tell. She always sounds like she is about to lose her voice. 'Hey, Ann-Marie says you were doing spells, candles and that?' When she speaks Lauren sees silver flashing out of her mouth, through her tongue.

'Kind of,' says Lauren.

'Can you do one on me?'

'OK,' says Lauren, secretly pleased. 'Sit down. On that chair, there.'

Diane looks at her as though she is wondering how tall she is.

'Here.' She grabs Diane's palm and stretches it out flat. The underside feels dry and chunky silver rings graze Lauren's own smaller hand. One is coiled like a snake around Diane's finger. 'Why are you laughing?' Lauren asks.

'Because I'm hungry. Hey, come on. Can you really do this?' Her breath smells like burnt lemons.

'Yeah,' says Lauren. She peers at Diane's palm. 'Your heart line has a lot of disruption. You have had a lot of hardships in your life. You fall in love easily.'

Diane looks at Ann-Marie, then back at Lauren, her pupils as big as beetles. 'Is that it? I already kinda know that stuff.' She smirks.

'Hey now,' says Ann-Marie.

Lauren drops the pale hand. 'No, I can. I can do it. I can tell you your future.'

Diane frowns with her marker-pen eyebrows.

'Give me a card deck. I know how to read cards,' says Lauren.

'Like a – what? Like a magic trick?'

Ann-Marie cuts in. 'She means like tarot or something.'

Diane's face changes. 'You've got tarot cards?'

'At home, yeah.' Lauren's voice is rising like water. 'But I can do it with playing cards. Have you got some?'

'Hang on.' Ann-Marie jumps up and skids in her socks to the games room. She slides back with a battered pack of cards.

Lauren feels their anticipation like energy that wakes her up. She closes her eyes and feels something else, another sense waiting. She picks up the card pack in her left hand, turns it on its side and begins to shuffle with her right, looking from one hesitant teenager to the other. 'OK,' she says. 'Let's start with something simple.' She always remembers a phrase from the spaewife's book: *You don't read it, you re-form it.* Lauren has memorized the meanings in each number, the emotions and the power of each symbol.

Out of the corner of her eye, she sees a woman standing in a grey-white robe by the flickering fireplace, but when she turns her head it's just the shadows dancing.

'The clubs are the clubs as in Tarot,' she says, cutting the deck in three and shuffling. 'You know, the sticks, the wands. The hearts are the cups. Think of your heart like a cup of, er, feelings.' The girls are drinking in her words. 'The diamonds, they're shiny like stars, like coins, like pentangles.'

'Mind that shop Pentangle,' says Diane. 'In Inverness.'

'Hey,' says Lauren, feeling a flow of something commanding, snapping Diane back to focus. 'So that's three of them, right. Clubs, hearts, diamonds. Then, last, we have spades, right? You cut with a spade; you cut with a sword.'

'OK,' says Ann-Marie, trying to understand.

'Right,' says Lauren. 'Think of three questions.' She has so many questions, bubbling up inside of her, as she tries to focus. Why can't Ann-Marie or her father remember what she remembers? The young woman's eyes were so piercing, so unforgettable.

'But wait. Don't tarot cards need to be, like, magic ones?' says Diane.

'No, this is fine, honestly. Tarot is a card pack. An old card pack, from Egypt. But then those other pictures got added.'

'Yeah, so what about the death card and that?' asks Diane.

'I can't do those now, but it's fine anyway. Think of three questions.' She feels the same power as when she rides Kirsty's horse, bringing it to focus, moving it forward as she lays out three cards face down in front of her. 'Ask a question. The answer has to be yes or no. Or maybe.'

Diane gazes at the ceiling. Her lipstick has nearly all been washed off with beer. 'Um. OK. Am I going to pass my exams?'

'That's your question?' Ann-Marie says.

'Yeah. What else am I gonna ask?'

Lauren turns the first card over. 'Ten of spades.'

'Is that good?'

'You don't really need exams to go far.' She smiles hopefully, and Ann-Marie starts to laugh.

'What the hell? OK. Does anyone bloody fancy me then? Will I have a rich husband if I fail all my exams? Am I going to marry a rock star?'

'That's three questions.'

'Will I marry a rock star? Man or woman, I just want them to be rich.'

Lauren lifts the next card. 'Four of diamonds.'

'Is that good? Diamonds should be good. Like, with four diamonds, I'd be well on my way.'

'Yeah, it is good. But don't get too greedy. That's what it means.'

'I'll be fine.' She laughs and sucks on her roll-up. She's enjoying this now. There are embers in her eyes.

'You'll be rich, but you might not share it.'

'OK, fine by me. Next one. I've got a question. Am I ever going to get out of this shit hole?'

Lauren feels taller, older. She turns the final card. 'The joker.'

'You're fucking kidding me.'

Ann-Marie splutters, balled up in the armchair.

'It's all right for you, you live in Edinburgh, *Auld Reekie.*' Her voice is veiled in insincerity, as though she is making fun of the world, always.

'It isn't that bad,' says Lauren. 'You'll travel. Either in a real way or in your dreams. It's a "maybe" card.'

Diane blinks. 'Oh my God, that's amazing. I fucking loved that, Lauren. And you're only, like, eleven years old. Jesus.'

'I'm ten and a half, actually.'

'How good is that, Ann-Marie? Do you want yours done?'

'No, I'm tired. I'm going to shout the dog again. Lauren, you should really be in your bed.'

Ann-Marie leaves and the flames in the fireplace flicker and drop and a cold draught passes through the room. The air feels sharper, as if it has metal edges. Lauren has a feeling there are still three people in the room.

'Hey,' says Diane. 'Do you want to try?' She holds out her smoking roll-up in the pinch of her thumb and finger. It doesn't smell like the bus stop.

Lauren knows her father would hate her doing this. It seems dangerous, yet for a brief moment, she inhales the coarse smoke that burns a trail down her throat. The scent is good, like a dry, burning garden. It follows her up the stairs to bed.

That night her dreams are close and cold and she can hear someone walking over gravel. The capercaillie is stretching its throat out in its glass dome. There is a rising and falling of syllables, stretching in long waves of sound. The names of the dogs being called. The floor of the bedroom is covered in pebbles and someone in white is walking towards the bed. She sits up and the lace curtains fall from the window. The room is the same temperature as the woods before snowfall.

9

There are six men in the band, two Niall has not met before: one old and portly with a full grey beard and the other young and gangly with ginger hair cut into a mullet. Another man he recognizes from a Burns supper a few years ago, lean and rangy with a Rob Roy shirt. And Don from the ironmonger's, a short, neat man. Niall watches them as they climb the small set of stairs to the stage and shake hands. The ginger-haired boy is wearing tartan trousers.

'And what are those?' asks the old man.

'These? Thought they're pretty good, like.'

'This is the Nae Troosers Ceilidh Band, son! Did y'not think tae wear a kilt?'

The old man laughs and begins to play his accordion, which protrudes like an extension of his belly. The rangy man and Sandy Ross set up their electric fiddles. Don takes out a few yellow cans of Tennent's from his backpack and offers them around. He drinks one sitting behind the drum kit as the ginger boy takes a swig and picks up his bass guitar.

'Is it legal for you to drink that?' the old man says.

'Hey, Sandy.' The rangy man is ignoring the ginger boy and nearly everyone else. 'You're in a good mood the day. New bird on the scene?' A couple of jeers rise from the band.

'I couldn't possibly comment,' says Sandy, raising his hands in mock innocence, before smirking into his beer can. His eyebrows are so neat, Niall wonders if he waxes them.

Niall shakes his head and takes out his guitar, a few paces from the rest of the group. They are the kind of men he might spot in the pub or the post office but would not say hello to, except for Sandy Ross, who seems to be on good terms with everyone. A moth-eaten deer's head hangs above the stage, its glassy eyes frozen forward. The hall is dim, the thick castle walls decked in red tartan banners that match the tablecloths in the dining room next door, where the guests are eating cranachan.

A woman enters the hall with a tray of wine. 'I'm Aileen. Welcome.' She looks around at the cans of beer. 'I see you've already made a start!'

The guests enter from the dining room to the ceilidh hall. The women wear dresses in shades of autumn leaves and holly. The men wear Bonnie Prince Charlie jackets and kilts, their long socks the colour of moss.

'Ladies and gentlemen, good evening!' Sandy's voice reverberates into a microphone. The audience cheers, tipsy. A few people shout back amid a current of chatter.

Niall catches sight of Angela and Malcolm whispering to another middle-aged couple, weary and grey-haired. He hopes he won't have to talk to them. Angela always acts friendly, but he knows she looks down on him. Sandy Ross strikes his foot against the stage, a sign to play the opening song. Niall comes in on the guitar at the right beat and steadies himself. He grins at the men around him as if they are old friends. They finish the song. Niall picks up his can from the floor and takes a long gulp.

'And we are . . .' Sandy calls out, 'the *No. Troosers. Ceilidh. Band!*'

Applause ripples. Someone whoops.

'To start off the night, we'll play one everyone knows . . . Gaaay Gorrrrdons!' His voice rises and falls in an arch. 'Go on, ladies and gentlemen, find your first partners for this evening. Anyone here need told how to dance this? Nope, good . . . C'mon! Don't be shy now!'

The crowd begins to assemble itself into pairs, making a border of couples around the edge of the room, the men with their arms over the women's shoulders, the women holding the men's hands, ready to be turned around the rectangular hall. The chords sound and they are off, their footsteps smothered with the music. Niall's eyes follow Angela and Malcolm as they parade stiffly through the dance, turning one way and then the other. He stops watching them and becomes lost in his own movement of fingers and arms and keeping rhythm with the rest of the band.

It isn't long before everyone is up on the dance floor. The music, as 'heuchter-teuchter' as it is, soon takes him over and his body starts to work with the group. Sandy Ross and the other fiddle player thread in and out with the accordion player while the drummer keeps him right. They are men who know what they must do: keep time, keep together and get drunk people up on their feet and out of breath. That is it.

Women soon dance without shoes, their hair falling loose from chignons and clasps, their make-up smudging. Men's faces turn ruddy as they clap or clump along sets of six and flex their arms, turning women. Niall smiles at men, often older, who proudly curve their free arm above their heads, fingers pressed together. He sees teenagers not taking the dances as seriously as their elder relatives. Instead of setting to their partners during the Dashing White Sergeant, one group mimes 'Night Fever' moves before carrying on in the traditional way. Niall's brain sinks in and out of the music. For a few moments he feels strangely elsewhere.

When the band takes a breather, setting down their instruments and spreading out across the stage,

Niall says to Sandy, 'I could do this every day of the week.'

Sandy shakes his head, laughing. 'Aye, crowd's not bad the night, eh.'

'You know,' says Niall, animated, 'Lauren hates this.'

'This?'

'Well. No this, she's no been old enough to go to these. She hates it in PE, you know, the social dancing. It's starting again soon, for Christmas.'

'Oh aye. I remember that. Remember it well.'

'It is all right for you, the girls had to form a queue back then.'

Sandy laughs. There's something steely about it.

They stand for a while and watch the other people drink and talk. The hall is large but has heated up too quickly, the narrow castle windows coated with steam. The old man in the band comes to join them. Niall says, 'I was just telling Sandy, my daughter, she hates, you know, dancing with the boys. I can't say I blame her.'

The old man coughs thickly. 'Well, that'll soon change! But aye, I remember. It's terrible, all that carry-on. If you're the last one to be picked, it's *terrible*. I used to stretch out my sleeve for girls to hold, instead of my hand.' He laughs with Sandy. Another man, the one in the Rob Roy shirt, comes up to the stage carrying pints from the bar. Niall takes one. A hip flask of whisky is in his back pocket, for later.

'Yeah,' Niall says, 'they take the mick about who is dancing with who and that. She gets hung up on it.' If only that was all of it.

'Well,' Sandy says, 'look at this lot. We've been up and down Caithness and across Sutherland and had a smashing time. Some of the stories I could tell you. After this night, we're taking a wee break. But surely she'll be glad of knowing the dances some day, eh?'

The old man interrupts as he turns to Niall: 'That reminds me. I met' – Niall can tell he is stopping himself from saying *Christine's mum* – 'Lillith, a few times she was over, way back. I was sorry to hear when she, you know. Last year. I was sorry. I hope you're keeping well.'

Niall shrugs. The funeral had reminded him what an old bitch she had been. 'Aye. I'm no bad. Thank you.' He picks up his guitar as the band begins to reassemble and guests drift back to the dance floor. One man passes close to the stage with a toothbrush in his sock instead of the traditional *sgian-dubh*, a hunting knife, looking for a good time. The crowd are in high spirits, especially for the most well-known dances.

He catches a glimpse of someone, a woman sitting at the back of the hall, with the same hair colour as Christine. He can't quite see her face. When he is drunk, thoughts have a habit of intruding like this. As he plays, he pictures Christine, the first time she arrived in town from Edinburgh. He saw her buying a box of oats at the local grocer's with a west coast accent. The summer was cool and bright, and she was hardy enough to wear a green spaghetti-strap vest. His attention was caught by a Celtic band tattooed at the top of her pale arm. He was freshly tattooed himself: an intricate cross on his left shoulder blade. Her dark-blonde hair was dyed with henna and in a complicated braid. Later, she liked to wear it in two plaits. He used to call her Minnie the Minx because it annoyed her.

Niall keeps drinking for most of the night and before the final dance, Orcadian Strip the Willow, he staggers up to the back of the hall, but can't find the woman among the seats. Feeling sheepish, he makes his way along a winding corridor to the posh guest toilets to piss and swig the last of the whisky from his hip flask.

Leaning against an empty cubicle, he remembers that when he met Christine in the grocer's in Strath Horne, she was wearing a long black skirt and her necklace with the purple stone, but these details could easily be inventions of his imagination. He said hello quietly to her as she was leaving. When she turned towards him he saw how truly beautiful she was and how she was some years younger. Eighteen. She looked at him suspiciously, her head only reaching his shoulder. He noticed he was standing too close to her and stepped away. In the castle bathroom he shakes his head and washes his hands.

When he finds his way back, he cranes his neck again, towards the seats, but they are empty. The one hundred or so guests have formed a single line of men and women facing each other. He still feels a dizzying strangeness but jumps back on stage to play with the rest of the band. As the crowd begins to turn and weave, a headache makes its way up his skull like a web. He looks around the room. Some people have become sloppy in their dancing, nearly spinning over and falling into each other, leaning too close, their heads back, misjudging their steps. His stomach lurches. He sees the younger group standing at the beginning of the line, whooping exaggeratedly as if the whole night is a joke. A young man with curly hair is keeping his partner close, trying to hold her gaze. She looks over her shoulder and slips out of his arms, as the dance demands, to spin with another man before returning to him. Niall's arms feel heavy. He notices a figure again, at the back of the room. Someone is sitting in a chair by the door, watching, but he can't make her out properly in the crowd. Sweat grows cold at the nape of Niall's neck and he concentrates on playing as best he can, but still his stomach roils as his arms and hands work without thinking.

Another memory drifts back to him. A strange one, this time. A bath awash with blood. Bloodstains in the sink. Teeth. He tries to recall if he was in a fight at some point. Concussion. His nausea grows. He remembers washing someone's hair in the bath. A woman's long hair, dark with the water, flipped forward over her face. Blood in the bath. Teeth in the sink.

He has stopped playing the guitar. Sandy is looking at him, most of the men are. He tries to carry on and keep his balance. As the last song nears an end, he makes his way off stage again. He snakes around the edge of the dancers to the nearby staff toilet. He looks back, squinting, and sees it is Catriona sitting at the back of the hall. He has not noticed her dancing all night. He pushes himself into the stinking cubicle and hurls up vomit. He takes a mouthful of water from the grubby sink and spits, then wipes his face with his sleeve. He pushes his way out again, taking one last look around the main hall. The final chord has just rung out and the dancers are breathless. He makes for the back door and sharp air. The stars are clean, hard chunks of light and he starts to feel better. A heavy hand smacks his shoulder. Malcolm.

'You all right there, our man of the hour?'

'Aye, I'm fine.'

'Fantastic music this evening. Angela and I had a *whale* of a time, really fan*tas*tic.'

Niall nods. 'Glad to hear it!'

'Did Lauren let you know? She's over at ours. Best place for her, really.'

'Oh, right, no. She didn't tell me.' His mouth is tight. His head has cleared. It's the last time he's asking Ann-Marie to babysit. He takes out his phone for the first time that evening and tries to hide his embarrassment with a laugh. 'I tell a lie. She's just starting to use this mobile I gave her.' Malcolm is not getting the better of him.

'Well, makes sense for us to get you home then. We can pick up your car in the morning.' They walk back into the hall.

'No, I'm fine actually.'

'We'd really rather . . .'

'I'm all *right*.'

Malcolm moves his hand back from Niall's shoulder as if he has touched a stove. The guests are dispersing and the castle staff are clearing glasses and stacking the velvet-backed chairs around them. Aileen snuffs out the white candles in the alcoves.

'Well. Niall. It's nearly two o'clock; I have to insist. Angela's taking one for the team, as they say, staying away from the strong stuff, being the chauffeur tonight. Now, there's a man who looks like he owes you something.'

Sandy is gesturing to him by the stage and Niall goes over. He has almost forgotten he needs to be paid. It comes in a white envelope, a tiny £60 scribbled in the corner.

'Now,' says Sandy, 'I can't thank you enough.'

'Cheers,' says Niall, 'appreciate it.' It is less than he was expecting.

'You all right there?' asks Sandy.

'Aye.'

'You had to make a quick exit?'

'Yeah, I dunno, I wasn't feeling too great.'

'No bother. Make sure you do something nice with Lauren, eh?'

'How do you mean?' Niall swings his guitar on his back.

'Lauren deserves something nice—'

'She's only ten.'

'Aye, sure. I took my niece to Waltzing Waters the other month. She loved it.'

'Oh right. *Waltzing Waters*. Uh-huh. I have bills to pay for her, you know.'

'Just a thought, pal. Do whatever you want.' He looks at the hip flask sticking out of Niall's shirt pocket.

Niall puts his hand on Sandy's shoulder and looks unblinkingly into his grey eyes. 'No, you're right. I'm no the best father.'

Sandy grins up to the ceiling. 'I wasn't saying that, Niall.'

Niall turns, shaking him off. A woman winds out of his way. Too late, he realizes it was Catriona. 'Well. I'm not. Don't—'

Sandy pulls him back, yanking his arm hard, to speak in his ear. 'Dinna gie us that. I know you've bills, Niall.'

The sound of his own name is irritating. 'Get *aff* me, man.' He is relieved that Catriona and any other young women in the room have disappeared.

Sandy's voice is heavy with self-importance. 'Thanks for doing me a favour. Now, you going to be OK getting back? I'm putting you in the car with Malcolm Walker.'

In the nursery, Lauren hears a low sound that crawls into her sleep: heavy tyres on gravel. Then there's Angela's soft voice downstairs and her father, louder and less controlled. Malcolm's voice rises in a question. Her father answers against the groan of the stairs. The nursery door opens and he lifts her in his arms. 'Stay sleeping,' he says, his voice heavy with alcohol. 'Stay sleeping.' He carries her downstairs on unsteady feet, through the back door, the air changing from old furniture to the burnt wood, to night air. He whispers to another person, 'Don't worry about it. No, no.' But they get into a car that smells of carpet cleaner. It moves smoothly. She half opens her eyes and sees lights. The car stops and they are outside again, with a thud of the door. Her father whispers something harshly. Angela's voice is too low to make out. Lauren feels Niall's waterproof coat as he carries her into the house and up the stairs. The smell of her old blankets. A sense of disappointment. She hears her father slam the door to go back outside. The air is faintly fetid. She goes to the window to open it and sees him sitting on the low wall in the bitter cold, a bright ember from his cigarette falling into ash.

In the small hours, Lauren is restless in the dark. She hears the beating of wings close to her bedroom window. She winds the corner of her woollen blanket tightly around her fist. The worry dolls are asleep now, under the pillow. Each one knows a secret question. She thinks of the girls in the cloakroom and the way they know something too. The dog with the leg. Whose leg? A man up in the woods. She imagines the girls' mothers knowing her mother in a way she does not. She is trying to grasp at something she doesn't even know the shape of. Did her mother fall out with her father? Did she run away because she didn't like him and his music and his drinking? Sometimes, when she is lonely, part of her wishes her mother had taken her with her, to somewhere exciting. She imagines her in a vintage sports car or drinking cocktails at a party held in her honour, somewhere in a city.

She hears the loud fluttering again, by the window, but when she looks out there is nothing but the night sky. The moon is as big and white as an empty dinner plate. Outside in the garden she sees large birds perched on the fence posts. The silhouettes of buzzards, a white barn owl, rooks. There are shapes moving on the lawn, little animals, pine martens and stoats chasing each other in circles by the herb garden. She looks over to her left and sees a fox, its ears facing forward. Another appears and Lauren is rooted by the window, watching.

Sometimes another feeling creeps up her spine like fingers. She has seen the looks children give her at school, the way some keep a wide berth. She hears about birthday parties the day after they happen. She can feel the rumours invisible around her in the playground, like text messages travelling from one kid to another. Once someone asked if it was true that her house was haunted. Another asked her if her dad had spent time in prison.

When Niall wakes he spends a few moments trying to remember where he is. The room feels damp. It is November dark. He can see a white beam shine over the patterned fabric of the curtains. The sound of a giant vehicle. A snow plough perhaps, or a long-distance lorry. It's colder than usual this year. There is a softer glow coming from the streetlamp in the road and the luminous green of his alarm clock. He turns and sees the outline of a body next to him. A hump in the duvet like a small range of mountains. Above, on the pillow next to his, he makes out the curve of an arm, lying still in the deep grey. He squints at a river of hair on the pillow. A faint, calm smell, a familiar smell. Honeysuckle. Long, long hair he wants to touch. He reaches out but his hand feels the cotton of the pillowslip. He sits up and pats around in the dark, touching nothing but bedding. He stretches his leg out to the empty mattress.

He feels a kiss on his neck. Two cool hands of another person over his eyes, arms reaching from behind. Slim, soft fingers. The chill of a ring next to his eyelid. Another kiss, warm breath, hair brushing his neck. The back of his T-shirt creeps up and a cold draught touches his bare skin. He stays very still. More kisses on his rigid back, now slick with sweat. She is kissing his tattoos. A hand on the hollowed middle of his spine.

He tries to turn around but hands push him down lightly on to the bed. The faint shape of long hair is hanging over him. He can smell her. He knows.

Her breath tickles the crook of his neck and shoulder as he turns on to his side. There is the sensation of her unclothed body against his. Then the body shifts away. He turns violently and kicks the duvet to the floor. He smooths his hands over the sheet. He kneels. He presses his head against the mattress. He begins to weep. Another light in the road passes.

10

When Niall arrives at Catriona's that morning, he lifts a corner of the old flagstone along the side of the garden wall and cannot find the spare key. He flips over the whole stone, which has now rounded at the edges with time. The wet soil underneath is bare, except for two pink earthworms and a cluster of ants. He walks back over the grass, noticing it has been left to grow untended. He rings the doorbell.

After a few minutes he decides to text Catriona, but she opens the door as he is tapping out a message.

'Hi, Niall,' Catriona says, her voice thick. She is wearing a grey waffle robe and her hair is swept back under a wide band of cloth. 'I'm not feeling well today.' She hugs herself in the draught of the doorway and turns back towards the stairs.

'Heavy night at the ceilidh?' he mutters.

'What's that? I'm all stuffed up.'

'I was just wondering,' he says, 'are you wanting a cup of tea or something?'

'No, no, thanks, I'm fine.'

'If you don't mind me saying, you're awful peely-wally,' he says gently. He hopes this will sound charming, caring. She looks in need of something hot, the peppermint she likes. 'Are you sure?'

She pinches the bridge of her nose and nods. Her eyes are swollen and her lips cracked, but she's still beautiful. He remembers the way she was watching the band and that maybe she doesn't think so badly of him after all. He hopes he didn't look too strange, stumbling off stage.

As she creaks up the stairs, Niall is left on his own in the kitchen. He stands for a moment among the clean white walls and polished chrome. The guilt from his last visit is making his stomach ache. He needs to explain somehow. He's been thinking it over. He carefully fills the enamel kettle with water and finds the right cupboard for the mugs, which he sets down as quietly as he can on the shining counter.

Carrying one mug, he calls her name from the hallway. The walls are still bare and new. He wonders what she might hang on them, old photographs or maps he thinks, rather than paintings. Spending time decorating people's houses has given him some idea of these things. Sunlight shines through a stained-glass door panel. It is an unusual piece of glasswork that apparently dates back to 1905, when the farmhouse was built.

The second time he calls Catriona's name, he hears nothing, so he takes the stairs, slowly, listening. The landing is sunnier than the hallway. He stops at the five doors in front of him and listens again. There is a low murmur behind one and he knocks and opens a bedroom door gently. The sun is dimly shining through a yellow curtain.

Catriona is fast asleep, her mouth slightly open. Niall looks down at his heavy work boots, grey with dust and paint, on the oatmeal carpet. He moves quietly over to one side of the copper-framed bed and places the peppermint tea in its new white mug on the bedside table, next to yellow tulips. A slim phone lies on the double bed's empty pillow like a surrogate partner. There is a MacBook at the end of the puffy bedspread, playing an American drama. Catriona's frame looks small and childlike as she lies in a foetal position under the bedclothes. He stands watching her chest rise up and down. She isn't wearing a bra under her pyjama T-shirt. An acoustic guitar is propped in the corner, surprising him, and a pair of shiny heels have been kicked off by the large mirrored wardrobe. He can't remember if she was wearing them last night.

He hears a rustle as Catriona turns her head towards him and her face changes into fear and panic. 'Niall . . .'

'No, no, don't worry at all,' he whispers, starting to walk out of the door. 'I just wanted to say sorry. The thing is . . .'

She takes a deep breath.

'The thing is . . .'

'Please. Please leave me alone.' Her voice is distant and rough. They stare at each other for a moment.

'Hope you like the tea,' he mutters under his breath as he leaves.

11

The next day, when Niall is driving home from Catriona's, he remembers his conversation with Sandy. Of course he knows that Lauren deserves something good. Especially now he knows things aren't right at school. 'Slick bastard,' he says to himself. He didn't even know Sandy had a niece, but he imagines them now, on their happy family trip out. His thoughts are interrupted by the drama of the landscape that surrounds him at this particular part of the road. He can't help but marvel at the tawny expanse of forest and hill, rising on either side for miles. He reaches the top of the hill near their village and slows the pickup, looking out at the mossy green patchwork of the land, the silver loop of the burn, the red herd of grazing deer and the burnt-orange bracken. In these rare moments he feels godly.

As he makes his way down the hill, the feeling channels out of him and he becomes an ordinary man, who has a daughter. He doesn't often appreciate how lucky he really is to have a daughter. He doesn't like to think it, but one day she'll leave him. He wants to make her something special. A home-made pie. The kind of pie Desperate Dan might eat, with two horns sticking out of the pastry.

Back at the house Niall leans on the counter by the oven and thinks of Christine using it for her bakes. They inherited the house from his childless uncle when he died of a heart attack. Her relatives from the west coast were always sending her things for the house. He decided it was why she seemed to get away with so much, the way she was comfortable with being indulged. It gave her an unshakable confidence but there were times he loved her for it.

He remembers how mesmerized he had been that first day they spent together after meeting at the grocer's. How she took his calloused hand in hers and traced his dry palm with her little fingers. The way, without blinking, she looked into his eyes and told him he had experienced trauma but that he had a good handle on his emotions. It was the first time they touched. He laughed and clasped his hand over hers and looked into her ice-blue eyes. 'That's not true,' he said and kissed her.

He doesn't speak to her family, only exchanging a few emails when Christine's mother Lillith passed away last June. Every December a Christmas card used to arrive for Lauren, but there would be nothing for him. He always meant to take Lauren to visit her grandmother but he never managed to. He told himself that work was getting in the way and then it was too late. Deep down, he was scared there was too much suspicion hanging in the air, which kept him awake at night.

Standing on a Shaker chair he has made himself, he unsticks a thick recipe book called *Cooking Up a Storm!* from the top of a kitchen cupboard.

He fishes out his well-thumbed graph-paper notebook, filled with precise, pencilled measurements of flooring and cabinets. Biting his lip, he copies down a list of ingredients.

The supermarket, a Co-op, is twenty-three miles away, in the town of Duthac. Lauren loves their trips to buy food and he feels a strange guilt going there without her. There is something about the abundance, the neat arrangement of perfect vegetables, the brightly lit aisles of magazines, cleaning products, toiletries, and the choices offered. The synthetic smell of baking. She loves the supermarket café, or rather canteen: its chairs attached to tables with iron tubing; the yellow glow from the metal serving hatch; the steam of overheated meat and swirls of Danish pastries; the comforting smell of the coffee machine. On Saturday mornings in midwinter father and daughter will sit with steaming drinks looking out at the snow.

Niall does not like the overhead lighting today, however. It is too bright and makes him aware that he hasn't showered. He tries to glimpse himself in the thin side mirror of the dairy aisle, but only sees part of his unkempt beard. He goes to the magazine rack, his heavy, chapped hands fumbling on the bottom shelf to pick up a copy of *Pony* magazine with a pink cellophane package stuck to the front. The handles of the basket feel too thin and the wire digs into his palms as he walks past a huge display of boxed fireworks. He finds onions, flour and cider, but misses out some herbs: 'one bay leaf' doesn't sound like it will make much difference. Perhaps he can find something in the garden. He hasn't considered the pastry itself until now. He asks a teenage shop assistant, Kayleigh, where he can find its ingredients. She gives him a doubtful, blue-eyeshadowed look and suggests he buy a roll of something pre-made from the chilled aisle.

He buys some extra things: instant coffee, more budget cornflakes, blue milk, own-brand beans, apples for Lauren who loves them, like her mother. He stands in the queue behind a family scanning Catherine wheels.

Driving back through Duthac he stops by the ironmonger's, a dark shop cluttered with floor-to-ceiling tools and materials, with its own familiar smell of chalk and rust. Squeezing between tins of paint, plant pots and power drills, he buys caulk, nails and sandpaper to fix the leaking roof.

At home, he dumps the ingredients on the kitchen counter and sits frozen on the sofa in his coat, summoning up the energy for the meat of the dish.

He claps his hands together, then heaves the sliding patio door open to the chilly garden. He hoists himself up on to the first concrete ledge, bedded with shrubs, and walks up the path to the bushes at the back that lead to a sloping field. Here he keeps a small vegetable patch that mostly animals benefit from.

At the edge of the bushes by the fence, he crawls on his hands and knees and feels around for a wooden box. It is cuboid and weathered, about two feet long and eight inches wide. His knee bones ache when he crouches and his tightly laced boots cut into his ankles and feet. His hands are almost as rough as the box, which has darkened with algae. The door board of the box, which he built himself, is closed. He drags it out, feeling the weight at the end twitching. He stands and up-ends it, then opens the sliding door and peers into the black.

He plunges his hand two feet down into the narrow space until he feels fur jolt against wood and grabs velvet ears, dragging the rabbit out as it kicks its thick hocks. Quickly Niall grips its soft neck with his other hand and, before it can bite him, he jerks the rabbit's head right back. He feels the neck snap and the body fall slack. He checks its liquid eyes for any signs of myxomatosis, then takes hold of its feet and stretches its dangling body downwards before lying it out on the garden path. He has to admit it looks cute.

When he has squeezed out its urine, he takes a knife from his pocket and makes a shallow incision in the animal's chest, careful not to break the slick white skin underneath that houses the guts. He sticks his rough fingers under the brown fur and tears a straight line down the animal's stomach, splitting the pelt. Alive only a few moments ago, its body is still supple and skinning it is easy, like stripping thick wallpaper, until the body is naked and red.

Niall opens up the animal's insides and cuts out slippery black intestines, then kidneys. These he will give to Jameson later. He cuts off the head and the feet, tossing them over into the field for the foxes and buzzards to get to.

He takes the small red body to the kitchen, where he rinses and butchers it, leaving him with meat for the pie to braise and bake in the oven.

He sinks back into the sofa for a break. The clock ticks; the ceiling drips, reminding him of sand slipping through a timer. Feeling tired, he listens to a curt answering-machine message about tiling from Catriona on the hallway phone. He left before she came home today. Her voice is cold, but still syrupy. He doesn't know how long it will take him to fix this leak in the utility room. He thinks he'll probably have to climb up on the roof and check the vents and flashing. It can wait. To mask the dripping, he plays an Iron Maiden album on the paint-flecked stereo. He lays out the cans and packages on the worktop and begins to slice carrots, cutting in time to the music. There isn't much to it; cooking isn't so different to joinery.

The clouds shift and a bright day comes through the kitchen window, catching dust motes and things that need to be replaced or fixed. After an hour's work, the light fades and the house feels emptier. He watches the dark oven and the bulb that has been dead for years behind the murky glass door.

When Lauren gets off the bus the light is dim and there is a sharp bite in the air. Billy has been away for three days. It is Bonfire Night and as she walks alongside the mossy drystone wall on the road to her house, she smells dry branches and leaves burning somewhere. Vairi passes her on the road, walking her two tiny dogs. Lauren greets them, nervous of their yaps.

'That's you from school then?' says Vairi.

'Yes,' says Lauren. The wind rises and she begins to feel her eyes sting in the cold.

When Vairi coughs, Lauren remembers she might die soon.

'Back in my day, of course, there was no school bus,' says Vairi, pointing down the road, a gnarled finger sticking out of her long twill coat sleeve.

'I had to cycle in, past that forest, down the big hill, rain or shine. Aye. You kids are lucky now.'

Lauren says, 'Is that right?'

'That's right. That bus started 'bout thirty year back, aye. This is too cold for November. I think we'll have snow soon. Mind how you go.' She begins to totter off down the road in her lace-up brogues.

'Vairi?'

She turns. The dogs stand stock-still.

'I just wanted to ask. Ann-Marie's back now.'

'Yes, I've seen her come and go.' She frowns as though the wind is too strong and starts to turn away.

'She says you knew my mum. You were her friend.' She has to raise her voice against the rustling of the trees and bushes.

Vairi looks at her and smiles like a pumpkin. 'I knew your mammy, aye. I still know her.'

'What?'

'Someone like her. She was a special lassie.' She licks her wrinkled lips. 'I don't know what your daddy's told you, but someone like that never really leaves, ken. I thought you'd realize that.' The wind sets the leaves in an orange papery swirl around their feet.

The back of Lauren's neck feels itchy against her scarf.

'Look, look at that bird over there – that buzzard.' Vairi points over the road. The bird perches like a lost glove on a fence post, its sharp yellow talons almost invisible. 'She is watching you.' Vairi's voice croaks. 'And your mammy will be watching you too. Just like that birdie. They're very territorial. And your mammy is wise, like these ones. They may not look it, but they are. And that one over there knows how to help folk too.'

'Buzzards help people? How is she your friend?'

'They appear as a warning sign, of sorts. To watch out for what's ahead. And the truth is' – now that there is a story to tell, Vairi has resigned herself to the pavement in the silver November light – 'your mother and I didn't get on at first. I thought she was wild. And she was. Wild. She didn't have any family near by, they were from somewhere else, further north, on the west coast.'

'I know,' says Lauren.

'But I could see that she understood some things. Eventually, I saw that.'

'What sort of things?'

'Oh, traditions and the like.' Vairi stops, and looks ahead down the road, then back behind her. 'Things my granny used to do for good luck. Y'know, superstitions, perhaps.' She looks down at her two dogs as they pull on the leads. Then Vairi whispers: 'She still does. I still talk to her.'

Lauren recoils and looks at the long road towards home. 'How?' She is daring herself. The curiosity is feeding a skinny part of her. She finds the antler handle, deep in her jacket pocket, and clenches it in her fist.

'How? She's . . . present. In my dreams, and in the evenings recently I've seen her. I know you see her too.' Seeing Lauren's disbelief, she goes on, 'I know Christine. She's visiting to say there's trouble afoot. Most don't remember seeing her though, do they? Most don't want to, that's the thing. It's a kind of shock that passes over and they push her away out of their heads. I can see from your face that you do see her though. I'm right. After all this time, she'll be back for a reason. Protecting you, like her over there.' She gestures to the buzzard. 'You see your mammy. And you remember her, of course.'

This is too much. Lauren turns and starts running towards home, her school shoes slapping on the broken pavement as the wind draws tears from her frozen face. *That auld wifey.* She hears her father's voice in her head. *That maddie.* The day has almost faded. A timber lorry passes, piled with rocking logs that look set to roll away. She starts walking, out of breath. Her creased black Clarks pinch from the running and she wonders whether to ask her dad for a new pair. She is nearly home now and can see the kitchen light through the shrubs. *She's visiting to say there's trouble afoot.*

As soon as she twists the back-door handle, Jameson starts barking. 'Jame-son,' she says, then louder, 'Jame-*son*.' A guitar album is playing quietly.

She runs upstairs and hears her father call her as she goes. The temperature drops when she reaches the landing. She prises off her tight shoes and wiggles her toes in the chill. Her socks are odd, one striped yellow and the other pink camouflage. All her socks seem to be separated from their partners and have to make do together. That's how she thinks of herself and her dad: a pair of odd socks. Sometimes Niall won't notice she has run out of clean clothes until it is too late. Maisie, with her perfect Chelsea boots, has whispered to other children that Lauren doesn't wash. She can't bear to tell her father that they call her a scaff. Lauren dumps her bag and coat in her dark bedroom. The dark makes her less-than-real. She feels around for the softness of her dressing gown to slip over her school uniform and take the day away. Downstairs is quiet.

She creeps over to her father's room and slides on her belly under his bed. The floor is thick with dust. She pretends she is a car mechanic fixing up a lorry. In the dark, her dressing gown is a deep-blue boiler suit, with her name embroidered over a top pocket. She reaches around for the bumpy plastic shell of her mother's vanity case. It isn't in the usual spot. She has the urge to put on her mother's lipstick. It makes her feel safe, almost protected.

The festering, flowery smell has crept up on her and she slides out again, sneezing with the dust, and looks at the bed from this different angle. The room is too gloomy, so she fetches a rubbery black torch from the hall cupboard, kept for power cuts.

Peering under the bed again, she sees the make-up case pressed against the back wall. As she tries to slide back under, the torch wobbles and falls, rolling into a couple of bin bags. She heaves them out, and finds they are full of her father's muddy boots and trainers. Back under the bed, she also prises open a battered shoebox full of electricity bills and bank statements. Her father would go nuts if he knew she was here, but that's partly why she likes doing it.

As she tries to turn around, her torch beam shines up towards the bedframe. The wooden slats above the vanity case have been marked with tiny drawings. When she looks closer, she sees there are perfectly printed stars, lines and circular symbols. Lauren traces her finger along the grainy surface of one illuminated slat. She can't work out if the symbols have been inked on in the same way she inks stars on to her school bag, or if they are somehow burnt into the wood.

She gives the vanity case a push so that it slides out the other side of the bed. She clambers over the untidy mattress and unsnaps the locks on the case, catching sight of her own fingers in its internal mirror. She wants the red lipstick that sits in a top tray, the one she wore at Halloween, but there is only a small black obelisk in its place. She rummages deeper inside the box and finds it is filled with stones: fluorite and rose quartz and pebbles of labradorite, among her mother's make-up. She finds a lipstick eventually, but it is a different colour, pale pink in a rose-gold case, rather than the deep red of Halloween. She picks out a small palette of silver eyeshadow and brushes it around her eyes until she looks like a girl from the future. She pretends she can read people's minds.

In the back room downstairs, seventies rock thumps and the table is laid for two. She draws the hall doorway's velvet curtain behind her but Jameson snuffles through and sits under a forbidden dining chair.

Her father calls from the kitchen, 'Nearly done now.'

She leans through the steam of the food hatch. 'What is it?'

'Making a pie.'

'Is . . . today special?' She wonders whether he is drunk, like the summer he made pancakes at four in the morning.

A clump of hair is hanging between his salt and pepper eyebrows. 'Nope!'

She hurls herself backwards into the main room like a rock star. Further away from the kitchen, she begins to smell something sour that isn't his cooking. It is the same smell as under the bed, and when

Ann-Marie came to babysit her. She keeps dancing. The same smell that is not rotting meat or dead flowers or a mouse trapped in the walls, but something like it. After a couple of minutes, she realizes her father is watching her dance from the kitchen hatch, his face pink like ham. 'You know,' he says, moving in time, 'I should show you how to play this. I think you could pick it up, if I showed you.'

'No I couldn't!'

He disappears, and she hears the clanking of plates and metal. She stops dancing. A current of frosty air brushes her skin, even though the fire is steadily building. Shadows start to grow from under the doorway curtain, like a tide edging in. For a second she is sure she sees the shadow of a person behind the curtain, and then it is gone.

Lauren shivers and lights a stubby candle in a piece of carved antler. She can hear the utility room dripping under the clatter of cooking.

Niall carries in the gigantic pie ceremonially, the brown edges of the pastry bubbling with gravy. 'Here we go. Like Desperate Dan, eh? But it's rabbit, not cow.' He raises his eyebrows at the burning candle. 'You wanted to add a touch of class, did you, kiddo?' In the candlelight each move Lauren and her father make is projected on to the wall as something larger and more theatrical. The sour smell is growing and Lauren wonders if he can smell it too.

She wrinkles her nose and makes shadow animals – a rabbit, a dog and a bird. Its wings end in huge feathery fingers, like a buzzard.

'Ach, I forgot to cook vegetables and that,' Niall says.

''S OK. What's that smell?'

'What smell? Your fingers look like feathers there,' he says, pointing to the shadow. 'Now. How much of this are you wanting?'

'Don't mind. However much.

'Dad,' Lauren says, chewing a chunk of meat.

'Yes?'

She swallows it down and it sticks in her throat. 'This is really good.' It would be, without the smell.

'Thanks, love.' He tucks a napkin into his collar and takes a bite thoughtfully. 'It is actually, isn't it?'

'Jameson'll be wanting some.'

'They'll all be wanting some.' He spreads out his arms happily.

'Who's they?' Her teacherly voice is a way of showing him affection.

The patio doors opposite the table are now a deep-black rectangle. The room has a strange humidity.

He smiles and shakes his head. 'So, do you have homework today?'

She is about to eat another forkful of pie, but stops. 'Dad . . . you sound really serious.'

'I can be serious.' He is looking down at the plate of his own cooking.

There is a soft knocking noise. Lauren's shoulders lock and her voice comes out as a whisper. '*Dad.*'

The smell is overpowering now. Their heads turn sideways to the sliding doors. A gaunt face comes forward out of the dark, peering in.

Lauren shrieks, bolting back in her chair.

When the figure moves closer out of the dark, they can see it is the woman in the dressing gown.

Nausea roils in Lauren's stomach. Niall puts a finger to his lips as he slowly gets up from the table. The woman takes a step back, her face expressionless. Lauren grips the seat of her chair. 'Dad?' she whispers. 'Don't open it!'

Before she can stop him, Niall carefully turns the key and slides the door open, making a slow *shhh*. The young woman reaches up and takes hold of his hairy face in her slim hands. He looks down at her with curiosity as he did on the road.

She looks past him, with her huge eyes, at Lauren. She is beautiful, if gravely ill. Her jaw is slack and her skin clings tightly to her skull. An icy draught blows in from the back garden. The woman takes a seat at the candlelit table and Lauren looks over at her dad, who is sliding the door shut. As she opens her mouth to speak, Jameson starts a howl that turns into a chain of barks as he runs into the room, then out and up the stairs.

Niall walks slowly to the kitchen. The woman follows him and Lauren stays seated, too scared to look over, hears them murmuring. He brings out a large white plate, a glinting knife and fork. The woman takes a seat again and he puts the plate down in front of her, at the head of the table. Lauren gets up from her chair, the blood rushing in her ears. The room has grown darker.

The young woman reaches out for her hand, but Lauren backs towards the door. 'Dad? What's going on?'

Niall strokes the woman's hair. The temperature has dropped, despite the burning fire. 'I'm sorry. I'm so sorry.' He is talking to the woman, not Lauren, and then kisses her hard on the dry mouth, his hand in her scraggly hair. Lauren feels as though she is sinking into the carpet, but then she realizes it is the tables and chairs that are rising, floating off the ground.

Lauren runs out of the room to the top of the stairs and sits there panting, remembering everything Vairi told her. When she finally opens the bedroom door the woman is sitting on her neatly made bed.

She turns her head to one side and smiles at Lauren. She is missing several teeth. She looks kind.

At once, the room feels warmer and Lauren doesn't feel so afraid. The woman pats the duvet beside her and Lauren sits. The edges of the room feel fuzzy. She feels the warmth of tears against her eyelids as she pushes her face into the woman's dressing gown. When she is up so close, she can see there is a translucent quality. Light shines through.

The woman strokes Lauren's hair and Lauren curls into her body. She doesn't smell unpleasant, but familiar, of how she imagines the moon might smell, or a flower that only bloomed in winter. The woman shows her a silver ring on her finger, two hands holding a crowned heart, and then holds it out in her palm. They hear distant explosions.

Lauren pushes the ring over her finger but it slides off again. She props herself up against her pillow, relaxing. The woman puts the ring on Lauren's thumb, gently closing her fist. Lauren's body feels heavy and tired. The woman, with her gaunt mouth, sings a gentle, familiar song. Lauren lies back on the bed and rests her head on the pillow. The woman stops singing and pulls the duvet over Lauren. As she begins to fall asleep, Lauren sees the young woman looking down at her in the low light and realizes then that they share the same colour eyes.

12

After Lauren has left for school, Niall goes out to the work shed, taking a cheese sandwich with him and a small jug of milk. Clear flakes of sleet are falling softly, sticking to the cobwebbed window. He turns the heater on high and sands and varnishes cabinets for a few hours. They are for another local woman, older and widowed, who lives in a croft up the coast. Alternating jobs means he never gets bored. He's not avoiding Catriona. At around three o'clock the sleet stops, and he hears a bird call outside. He stands tall, blinking at the sudden interruption, breathing out the sawdusty air, dry from the plug-in heater. He carries on varnishing, listening again for the bird call, but it doesn't come. The shed door creaks open with a 'Hello?' It is Kirsty, Billy's mum. She sounds out of breath. Her face looks washed-out without her usual make-up and her red-squirrel hair is wild.

'You OK? How was your holiday? Sorry, been in here all morning. Take a seat. Mind that axe.' He points to a new oak chair he has made.

'Wow, this looks beautiful.' Kirsty gazes at him for a brief moment, relieved. 'Oh, the holiday was fine,' she says. 'Lovely. Really lovely. Craig and I haven't been getting on so well recently, so I know the holiday was for Billy and Lewis really, but, you know, it gave us some time together and I think we needed that. The food was awful though. Never mind. I brought Lauren a little something.' Niall notices now she is holding a bright plastic bag. 'We . . . we got back late last night. There were delays from Manchester to Inverness. We didn't get in until around three a.m., would you believe? And Billy had school this morning, you know. It's an early night for him tonight.'

He feels sorry for her, looking so washed-out and a little haggard. 'Are you wanting some tea as well?'

'Oh. Yes, please. Thank you,' says Kirsty.

'I've got the full works here.' He points to a scratched kettle in the corner and a box of Scottish Blend, next to the jug of milk.

'No sugar for me, thanks. How've you been, then?' Kirsty asks above the hot bubbling of the kettle.

'Fine, aye.'

'Are you sure?'

'Sure, sure.' He leans back on the work bench.

'It seems some odd things have been happening while we've been away, don't you think?'

Niall adjusts his position a little. 'How?'

'I ran into Angela. Well, she was on her way to see me actually, when I was taking the horse out.'

'Uh-huh.' He starts to make the tea.

'And . . . she was a wee bit shaken up. She says that there was a strange sort of . . . something strange has happened to their house.'

'What do you mean?'

'She showed me. It's . . . it's like there has been a storm, I suppose. Can you remember? Was there a storm last night? We were straight to our beds and dead to the world. There was a circle – and I mean a perfect circle – of *debris*. And quite large rocks actually. Around the outside of their house.'

'Debris? I didn't hear a storm.'

'Yes. You know when it's low tide and there's a line of seaweed and that on the shore? The debris? The same thing has happened in a circle around their house—'

'Seaweed?'

'With leaves and sticks and rocks. Around the house. No seaweed.'

Niall sips from the hot mug, frowning.

'I don't know,' says Kirsty, to herself more than Niall.

He crosses one free arm over his chest, tucking his left hand under his right armpit thoughtfully. 'Is this someone having a laugh?'

'No – well, I don't know, it looks too kind of *natural* for that. I was wondering if there was something in the ground. The way the rocks were in a circle like that. And the ground was burnt.'

'The ground?'

'Just the way it had formed. And burnt like, you know, when you've had a bonfire, but in a circle. Big. I went and saw it myself earlier. It was weird.'

'Maybe there was a storm, or a wind of some sort, aye. I don't remember last night.'

'I . . . I don't know. I didn't hear anything, to be honest.'

'So, what are they doing about it?' He scratches behind his ear and runs a hand over his long hair.

'Well, I think . . . I think she mentioned calling the police.'

'The police.'

She folds her hands on the table. 'I think maybe someone broke into their house.'

'Huh?'

'Well. She doesn't remember a thing, but apparently Ann-Marie heard things breaking in the house, she said. This was before she saw the circle.'

'Things were breaking?'

'Plates and dishes,' she says. 'Downstairs. When they were up in bed. Well. Ann-Marie told her this, this morning. And loud noises. Screaming, apparently.'

'Screaming.' He looks up at her. 'And the plates were broken?'

'Yes, but only Ann-Marie heard them breaking. Maybe those two had had a big nightcap.' She laughs hopefully, before becoming serious. 'Ann-Marie thought someone was in her room. It was dark, but she says she heard her desk being dragged around, towards her door.'

'What?'

'Yes, she was terrified. When she woke up, her desk was up against her door. And her room was a mess, or that's what they're saying.'

'A mess how?'

'Angela didn't go into too much detail.'

'Ann-Marie. Sleepwalking. Or drunk. She's how old now?' He leans back again.

'Niall. I don't think she's like that. But then, what do I know?'

Niall gulps half his tea down.

She pauses. 'Teenagers do like to get drunk.'

'Maybe that's it.'

'I've seen them, down at that bus stop in town. And the other strange thing that happened was that apparently Sandy's house was set on fire. Did you hear about this?'

'Kirsty. You're having me—' He stops himself as he remembers the stones in Lauren's room. Hesitantly, he pulls a chair next to her, over snaking wires.

'No, I'm not. That's what I'm saying: it sounds as though they've had a time of it. Someone was saying they saw smoke coming from his house, or his garden. A lot.'

'Not his bonfire,' he says flatly.

'It started off as a bonfire, I think, yes, but then something happened, and the fire caught the downstairs. One of the windows is black, apparently. Or maybe it was his door.' Kirsty stares down into her mug and traces her finger over a chip in the ceramic, chewing the dry skin on her bottom lip. 'I don't know if that's related to the break-in or whatever it is at Angela's. But we need to be a bit more careful round here. The Walkers are thinking of getting a new security system.'

'Is that right?' He hesitates. 'The fire, at Sandy's, that just sounds like he isn't keeping an eye on things. Bonfires can be dangerous. I had one the other month, burning scrap, and, you know, you've got to be careful. The circle around Angela's house, that could have been teenagers, playing pranks again. Or a storm, as you say. The winds.'

'What?' She looks up at him.

'Have you seen any teenagers up here?' he says.

'No, well, there's Diane. I mean, who knows about her friends. But she wouldn't do that to Ann-Marie now, would she? They've been such friends since they were wee.'

'Thick as thieves.'

'But then the house is so big, who knows who she – Ann-Marie – was inviting over, eh?'

They sit with their own thoughts for a while, in the golden gloom.

'She's always been a nice girl,' Kirsty says. He notices how she looks at him sometimes. A shy sideways look, like a sparrow.

'True. I suppose I'm saying there could be a simple explanation.' Niall tries to recall a shred of anything that she says happened which he could have noticed, but his memory has emptied out like a bucket.

'It sounded strange to me. I think Angela was right to call the police.'

'Hmm,' says Niall, knocking back the tepid dregs of his mug. 'She's a one, that one. Angela.'

'How?'

'Oh, nothing. As long as she's not wanting me to go and fix something, that's fine.'

Kirsty rubs her eye and shifts in her seat. 'Well. I do feel calmer now. I mean, we're just literally in the door from Paris and – I usually feel so safe here, you know. Paris is a different matter. Police, guns, everywhere this time.' She crosses her legs and props up her chin with one hand. 'And now I'm coming round yours for a blether like a mothers' meeting.' She sighs and his face softens for a moment. 'Craig left early for work,' she continues. 'Anyway, you haven't seen anything strange, then?'

'That Angela,' he says, shaking his head, remembering her odd voice on the end of the telephone. 'That Angela is full of stories.'

*　　*　　*

On the school bus home, Lauren can't find a free seat at first. The rain pelts the roof while the fan heater hums at full tilt. She is carrying a cumbersome collage of a bonfire, made from red cellophane and brown felt stuck to thick cardboard. She hopes her dad likes it.

She spots two empty seats together, which is strange when the rest of the bus is so busy. As she shifts over towards the window, a drip falls from the ceiling and trickles down her neck. She hoists the artwork away from the water, propping it against the steamed glass.

The bus doors gasp open and a boy, Callum McColl, climbs into the aisle.

'Here, Callum,' yells Maisie from a few seats behind, 'you take my seat, I want to sit beside Lauren.'

Lauren freezes and jerks her head at the boy to come and sit beside her and ignore Maisie.

'Don't do it,' Maisie carries on to Callum. 'And she fancies you anyway.' Maisie swings her body round into the seat next to Lauren's and thumps down with her heavy Disney rucksack. 'Hey, Lauren! How ya doin'?' The mock sincerity in Maisie's tone is light, but present. 'How's it going there, pal?'

'What do you want?' says Lauren.

'Excuse me, Lauren, that sounds a bit rude!' Maisie scoff-chuckles and looks sideways at an imagined audience.

Lauren folds her arms tighter and focuses on the window and the trees blurring by like smeared paint. Maisie's braying is difficult to tune out.

'Oh my God, Lauren?' She makes a choking sound. 'Did you have . . . an accident?'

Lauren looks round slowly and sees Maisie pointing to a large damp patch at the edge of her seat, below the ancient Shitehouse roof that is patched with gaffer tape.

'Oh my God,' Maisie says again. Then louder, standing up to address the rest of the bus: 'Oh my God, Lauren's wet herself.'

A cruel sneer rises from some unseen children in nearby seats. A few begin to crane their necks, as if Lauren is a strange animal. She sees Jenny, near the front, gawking at the commotion. Lauren feels her cheeks grow hot and pulls her knees up to her chin. She is angry and starts to explain, but her words are drowned out by chatter. Lauren looks for Billy, in his familiar red woolly hat. He is turned away, on purpose she thinks. Maisie prods her shoulder. 'You're disgusting . . . Here—' She grabs hold of the hair on the back of Lauren's head and tries to force her face down into the damp, scratchy seat edge. Lauren headbutts Maisie's shoulder, hard. A gloating cheer rises again, from a couple of boys in front. Lauren feels like a cow locked in a feeding fence and thinks of her pocketknife, hidden in her bedroom. She jerks back and her foot stamps against the bonfire collage, crumpling the card and cellophane. Maisie jams Lauren's head low, her hands scratching either side of Lauren's ears, pulling her towards the puddle of leaking water. Grey drops trickle down her neck, smelling of stale rain mixed with rotting food.

The bus jolts over a pothole and Lauren feels a surge of nausea. Then Maisie tugs out a little clump of her hair as someone else drags her away.

'Hey. Hey.' A throaty voice. Lauren peers up at the lanky figure of Diane, her black hair falling over one side of her face. Her clothes always look like they have been worn for two days running. Diane slams Maisie back in her seat, with a hand firm against her shoulder. 'Here, Maisie' – she speaks low and close and smoky – 'stop being such a lesbian.'

'Get off me,' Maisie says, snatching her shoulder back and squirming in her seat. Diane turns around to the back of the bus, without looking at Lauren. Maisie is silent for the rest of the bumpy journey, staring across the aisle at the fields rushing by.

13

On Saturday afternoon, Sandy passes by Niall's house to pick up a cement mixer. Niall hasn't been over to Sandy's for weeks, even months. He lives in a detached cottage closer to the town and has told Niall he is building an extension.

Lauren seems mesmerized by Sandy, the way someone might watch flames dance or snowflakes fall.

'Hiya,' he says. 'Look. You've got something—' He reaches behind Lauren's ear and a five-pound note materializes between his fingers.

Niall shakes his head, stammering, 'Look – Sandy . . .' He remembers their conversation at the ceilidh and wants to ram the fiver down his throat. Lauren is giving her best polite smile. He can't take it away from her. 'What d'you say, Lauren?'

'Thank you, Sandy.'

'No bother, champ. How's that fiddle coming along?'

Niall wonders what it is about the man. He always looks tanned, so much so that Niall thinks he must use a sun bed. He has hair to match his name and a bench press in his front room.

'Did you have a fire up at your house the other night?'

'Fire?'

'Yeah. Someone mentioned you had a fire the other night and it set the downstairs alight.'

Sandy's laugh is generous. 'You're having me on. God, no. Just shows you, doesn't it? How the rumour mill works, eh? You can come and have a look. Not a sausage.'

Lauren giggles.

He continues. 'I am going to a fire*work* display later, but . . . Hang on, I remember this. I heard it was here in the village where this fire happened, now you mention it. A couple of guys down the pub were talking about some kind of bonfire, but that was back last week. They were saying it was down at Alan Mackie's house, as a matter of fact. And then this week it's me.' He shakes his head, raising his eyebrows. 'Anyway, thanks again for your help the other night, pal.' He lifts a clinking bag. 'I got us some beers.'

'Oh, cheers.' Niall tries to sound genuine. Lauren is opening her fiddle case, flipping up the silver latches.

'Yeah, the band's coming on pretty well actually. Looks like we might be headed for the big time. Imagine me, famous!'

'Oh yeah?' Niall opens a bottle of Joker IPA.

'BBC Scotland are doing a piece on folk music in the Highlands, you know, and rumour has it they could be interviewing me.'

'Well, that'd suit you down to the ground.'

Sandy smiles broadly, his teeth unnaturally white. 'Ha! Well. Fingers crossed. We've got this bothy kitted out to practise in. Here, speaking of the devil, do you ever see that Alan Mackie about?'

'Well, yes, you know he stays just down the road.' Niall sinks into the sofa and gulps from the bottle, while Lauren practises her finger movements on the neck of the violin.

'Just keep an eye on him, won't you? I get a bit of a funny feeling.' He lowers his voice. 'Seen him pestering Diane in the Black Horse the other night. He needs to watch himself, that one.'

'I can't not think of him as Mr Mackie, you know. Since school.'

'Aye, I know, always one for girls, that man. I remember it, when he was teaching us PE.'

'No. You're serious?'

'Aye, I'm telling you, just keep' – he looks at Lauren – 'keep an eye out.'

14

Sunday morning stays dark for a long time. Lauren hangs over the side of the bed and reaches for her pocketknife. She can still feel the sensation of the young woman's fingers in her hair, her palm cupping her skull. Recently, Lauren's thoughts about what this means have been swirling to the surface like silvery sediment, loose and difficult to contain. Maybe if the woman is who Lauren thinks she is, she will appear again. Maybe this means her mother is never coming back. Lauren opens the knife up in her hands: bright metal glinting from antler. She stares at her eyes reflected in the blade, then snaps it shut.

When it finally arrives, the dawn is buttery. A robin sings in the hazel outside. The crystals spin in the window and one produces a rainbow against the cream wall. When she opens the curtains, the world is white and a silence has fallen.

The jet obelisk from the make-up box has been placed carefully on her bedside table, next to the worry dolls. Her father is using the buzz saw in the garden. She can recognize the different electrical devices he uses: the buzz saw, the hedge strimmer, the lawn mower, the sander.

As she gets dressed, she takes a blue biro from her pencil case and, in front of her wardrobe mirror, she draws on her right side. A creature with many tentacles, difficult to capture. She tries to finish it but can't draw the same way as her reflection.

Lauren trudges up to the white woods before lunchtime, her old blue joggers ballooning over her wellies. She knows Billy will be back from church before too long. Snow doesn't make any difference. She identifies bird calls and spots robins among the branches heavy with snow. She hears a crow and hums the Welly Boot Song under her breath as she clears a path around the hut in a circle. The stones have vanished; just the indented soil is left. She wonders if Maisie has been here again, but it feels too weird a trick for her to play. Lauren chews the chapped skin on her lip and thinks her father might be hiding something. He wouldn't come up here, though, and do this. Lauren's coat is thick but the air still sifts through the zip and stings her cheeks. She looks up at the blue, clear sky and believes it will snow again. She feels safer with Jameson, who stays close, his nose to the ground, padding through the paths she clears through the bracken.

* * *

When Billy arrives, the light is already slipping away. He wants to play armies again. Lauren, feeling less disturbed, says they can if they use the walkie-talkies.

'I want a dog like Jameson,' Billy says. His nose is red, and he sounds out of breath in the cold. 'I think he likes me better than you. Do you not, Jameson? He likes me.'

'He does not,' Lauren says. Disagreeing is almost fun.

'Does.'

'Not as much as me. Jameson, do tricks.'

Jameson looks at her, then sniffs busily along the forest ground again.

'No, he can do it. Jameson. Give me your paw.' She holds her palm up. 'I want Jameson to be a show dog. We can compete together. Maybe go on *Britain's Got Talent*.'

'Army dogs aren't show dogs.'

'He's not an army dog.' She shakes her head to herself, as if she's older than Billy, not younger.

The snow deadens sound between the trees. Billy is now a general, ordering Lauren on a special reconnaissance mission and teaching her how to fire a gun.

'I know how to fire a gun. My dad has one, a real one,' Lauren says. 'He showed me how to use it.'

'No, he didn't.' He rolls his eyes.

'Did.'

'Go and bring it out next time and give me a shot.'

'Maybe,' Lauren says, more to the trees than to Billy. The bones of her toes feel like shards of ice. She notices another buzzard sitting on a branch further away in the oncoming twilight. 'I like the snow,' she says. 'Everything so still.' Snow is hopeful to her.

Billy is breaking a large branch apart and doesn't hear. 'It wasn't this cold in Paris. It was nice.'

'Do you ever stop wearing that hat?' she asks, pointing at his Aberdeen FC beanie. She remembers two years ago when his uncle gave it to him for Christmas.

'Not in church,' he says.

'No, I bet you love it so much you sleep in it.'

She tries to grab it off his head and he pushes her away, gently but defensively. 'You're not an Aberdeen supporter,' he says, half smiling. 'You don't get to touch it.'

'Whatever, pal,' she says, knowing it will irritate him, and walks away to collect more stray twigs to twist around the den. They hardly ever sit in the hut, but Billy has suggested that maybe one night they'll camp there, in the summer.

She finds Jameson digging in the ground with deep concentration, as though he has found a rabbit. As she gets closer, something small and hard chips into the air, catching the snowy light. She watches it fall into a pile of leaves that are dusted with snow like iced biscuits. She upturns the mulch with a crooked stick, poking around for it. In this part of the forest there are no birds. The snow here is untouched, like mounds of sugar, except for the occasional line of a deer's track. She can feel the chill through her wellies, seeping into her socks. She prods around some more until she finds a dull piece of metal: a silver ring. When she picks it up she sees that it is shaped like hands holding a heart. She tries to catch her breath in the cold, and the forest and Billy and the rest of the world fade away. She holds the ring tightly in her fist, as though this is the only thing she has in the world.

'Mum. *Mum.*' Her tears are hot and she finds herself on her knees, her legs being too weak to hold her. She does not know what is real any more. And yet, she feels the slippery, metallic coldness against her fingers and opens her hand again. The ring is still there. She wipes her eyes and cheek with a snowy glove, pulls her hand out into the freezing air and slides the ring over her thumb.

She walks the short way back, calling Jameson to heel.

The sun is sinking and the walkie-talkie twitches with static in her other hand, before Billy's voice comes through: 'Lauren. *Lauren.* Where've you gone?' She can see Billy's outline growing larger as he walks towards her. The clouds hang heavy, like wet wool, and stars start to appear through the trees like large, shining stones at the bottom of a river.

The temperature has fallen with the sun and Lauren hugs her padded arms to her padded body.

'It's already dark. Come on,' he says. 'I've got homework to do.'

The thought of school tomorrow sits in her stomach. They gather various belongings and treasures scattered around the camp – some plastic binoculars, a handmade catapult, a rusty teapot, a length of rope – and put them inside the hut. They argue about whether to take home the packet of bourbons that have been stolen from Billy's larder, before deciding to leave it in the supply tin, half buried in the frozen ground.

They walk back down the looping path, banked by snow-laden ferns, towards Clavanmore. She likes Billy walking beside her like this, in his Aberdeen beanie. He's like a big brother, but with a better face and hair. Lauren rolls the silver ring between her index finger and thumb, in her pocket. Darkness seeps into the forest and the white snow fades to a dark grey, then darker still, until the world is black.

15

Niall wipes away the grouting and stands back. 'That's me done for today,' he calls. Catriona hasn't heard him, but everything has seemed back to normal since she was ill. She must have forgiven him. He reaches into his coat and takes a sip from a rectangular flask.

He walks out through the darkened corridor, over tiles he has laid himself, to the kitchen, where he can smell cooking. It is a nice house and he likes being part of it. He pads through the open door and sees Catriona standing at the countertop in black leggings and an oversized shirt. Her feet are bare on the terracotta tiles.

'Watch you don't catch a chill,' he says.

Uncertainty flickers across her face; then she gives a tight smile. 'Oh, I'm feeling loads better now.' Her nose still sounds blocked.

A couple of trout lie on the glass chopping board. She picks up one and slides a long, thin knife under its left fin, cutting deep towards the head. Her bouncy hair is tied back with a polka-dot ribbon and her short nails are painted a cherry-juice red. A high, winding guitar plays a riff he doesn't recognize from a silver stereo. She turns the fish over and begins to cut the other side. He clears his throat and she springs up.

'Niall. Sorry, I'm a bit flustered today.' She shouldn't have to apologize; he knows he was the one who overstepped the mark.

'You're all right,' he says.

'How's the floor looking?'

'Pretty good.' He smiles hesitantly.

She looks back at him matter-of-factly. 'OK, thanks.' She proceeds to snap the head off the fish, gently, throwing it into a poly bag hanging from a drawer handle.

'Those local?' He tries to sound good-natured, friendly, but wonders why it seems so hard.

'Huh?' She turns back towards him, headless fish in hand. 'Yeah. I caught them at the lochans.' She shrugs, and he watches the way her plump mouth moves.

'You're into your fishing, are you?' he says.

She laughs again, as if she's embarrassed, and turns back to run her knife down the fish's back, rippling the silver scales. Her hands are smooth and young. The kitchen smells of butter and lemon.

He walks over to her and stands just close enough to hear her breath as she begins to fillet the fish.

'So that's me done for the day,' he says. He wonders what she likes to drink. He wishes he could ask.

She takes a couple of seconds to register what he has said and how close he is standing. Her body stiffens. 'Thanks very much, Niall, I appreciate it.' The knife scrapes against the spine of the fish as she separates it into two halves.

He steps back and props his hand on the edge of the marble-effect countertop that he fitted a few months ago.

'Mind those fish guts,' she says.

He looks at the golden hoop through her ear, then at his boots on the tiled floor and the good grouting he has done. Her brown feet look so delicate next to his. 'Any plans this evening then?' He can't quite leave this beautiful room.

'Yeah, actually.' She looks down and makes another cut into the side of the second fish. 'Yeah.' She glances at the black window. 'I think you know him maybe,' she says, turning over the second fish and positioning her knife just under its fin. 'Sandy Ross?'

'Oh aye,' Niall says. *Oh aye.* 'How d'you know him?'

'Well, we got chatting at a folk music night when I first moved here. He asked me to come to the ceilidh the other night. I didn't even want to try and dance, I didn't really know many people, apart from those who visit the surgery. So I just watched him and . . . and you, of course.' This last part is only a politeness. 'That was after he took me to the lochans the other weekend and showed me, you know, how to catch these. Pretty nice of him. I just stuck them in the freezer.' She cuts deep behind the brain of the fish. 'Maybe that's how I caught the cold.'

'Maybe,' Niall says. The bastard.

'So, you know, he's actually going to pop round and try one of these, he said.' Her voice trails off.

'Right, uh-huh,' Niall says. 'I'll see you tomorrow, then.' He can feel his heart beating in his chest. He needs to get out.

'See you, Niall,' she says absently.

'Go easy on the bevvy,' he mutters as he leaves, but she doesn't hear him.

He plans to go home, but finds himself taking the turning for Strath Horne instead. Leaving his tool kit in the pickup, he walks, dazed, into the Black Horse Inn.

The back door is locked. Lauren rattles the handle several times, but she can't get back into her house. Her dad never mentioned he would be out this evening. He never usually is on a Sunday, even though he still often works, keeping odd hours. She takes out her single spare key on its puffin keyring and jams it into the lock.

Inside, it's dark and cold with a shaft of moon-light falling upon the stairs from the window. The clouds have drifted, and the night is clearer than the day. She does not know how to stoke the boiler. She pulls her father's heavy dressing gown from the hook on the back of his bedroom door and wraps it around her, rolling up the sleeves in wide folds. The end trails behind her like a cape as she walks.

Up in her bedroom she lays her tarot cards out on the bed. A draught creeps across her shoulder blades and, for a moment, she gets a strange feeling of a hand, reaching out of the darkness. She shakes her head and shoulders and shuffles the dog-eared cards. She flicks three across her bed, face down, then puts her hand over the first card and asks it to tell her what is going on. The next one she asks what is getting in the way. The third she asks what will fix the problem.

Lauren takes a moment to clear her mind and push thoughts about time and school away, as best she can. She turns the first card over on the bedspread. The High Priestess stares back at her with blank eyes, her face placid under a strange horned crown. She sits between two pillars, one black and one white. These, Lauren knows, stand for the bad and the good, the dead and the living, the end and the beginning. Meanings refract through symbols like sunlight. The woman's necklace is shaped like a 'plus' sign, showing she is like both of the pillars she sits between, two opposites in one person. There is a wall of red split fruit and dense leaves behind her. A sliver of yellow moon lies at the woman's robed feet, like the joined horns of a Highland cow. Lauren props this woman up on the windowsill.

She turns over the second card. It's the Hermit: the obstacle. He is a thin, white-bearded man with stooping shoulders under a long, hooded cloak. In one hand he holds a tall yellow staff, and in the other a lantern. Inside the lantern is a pointed, shining star. It's as if he has taken it from the sky and imprisoned it there. He walks over craggy grey ground.

This is a card Lauren doesn't know very well. She flicks through the spaewife's book and finds an old, shaky note written in the section on tarot:

The Hermit: his right haund holds the Lamp o' Truith, its star guidin those who dinna ken the way. His left haund holds the patriarch's staff to bide by dern, saicret paiths, using his lanesome nature and knawledge to find his way. His cloak signifies he is unseen, discreet, cannie. His saicrets are no for awbody.

She places the Hermit, the obstacle, next to the High Priestess on the window ledge and turns the final card. A hand reaching out of cloud, clutching an upright, shining sword, from which golden leaves or flames fall. The tip of the sword meets with a small gold crown and drooping wreaths.

Lauren flicks again through the pages of the note-book. Written in another sloping hand are the words *The Ace of Swords signifies clarity, raw power, triumph.*

Thick flakes of snow float down diagonally outside her bedroom window, increasing in speed.

She places the card next to the others before reaching down and tucking her knife inside her rucksack.

There is the dripping sound again. When she goes to take a look downstairs, the dripping speeds up, faster and louder. She looks around the kitchen and at the ceiling to make sure nothing is wrong. There is a rank smell coming from the utility room that gets stronger when she opens its dark door. She switches on the top light and it sparks. She jumps, and backs towards the door. In a dark, far corner she can make out what looks like blood, spattering down from a crack in the utility-room ceiling. Water doesn't fall that way.

Lauren's chest feels like a deflated balloon. She tries to breathe. The blood is falling into the bucket her dad has put out to catch the drips. She notices the smell of iron. The blood pools on the top of the chest freezer, the colour so dark it is almost black. She runs without turning to see if it was really there. When she closes her eyes she can see the woman, protecting her. Her face placid, like the tarot card.

Lauren sits in the sagging armchair and watches an Italian cookery show blankly for an hour on the TV. At the closing credits she realizes the windows have turned black. She texts her father: 'Where are you? @ home.'

Next up is a game show, but Lauren can't answer any of the questions.

'In which city would you find the Bridge of Sighs?'

'Glasgow,' says Lauren in a spaced-out monotone.

'Let me repeat that. In which city would you find the Bridge. Of. Sighs.'

'Glasgow,' says the contestant.

'The answer is, in fact, Venice. Sorry about that – you're going to go home this evening.'

Lauren leaves the game show on and makes toast. She tries to imagine what her father might be doing, but everything she thinks of seems ridiculous.

She picks up the heavy Bakelite phone and calls Kirsty, who tells her to come over for dinner, she has made spaghetti.

'I was watching a show about spaghetti,' says Lauren.

'I saw that,' says Kirsty. 'It's what made me think. So you don't know where your dad is?'

'No.'

The garish tartan carpet is stained and gives the Black Horse a certain smell. All year round the windows stay shut. A light-up Santa stands on a

shelf behind the bar. It is always there. Scots prov-
erbs hang in teak frames against the bare drystone
wall. Phrases like *Lang May Yer Lum Reek* and
Haste Ye Back, by the entrance, written in swishing
calligraphy.

'Hi, Hamish,' says Niall to the landlord as he
takes a seat at the bar.

'Niall,' says Hamish. 'What're you havin'?'

'Niall!' Diane pulls herself up from the bar fridge
and leans across. She is only paid to collect glasses
but has been known to pull a pint. Hamish sometimes jokes that she is trying to grow up too fast.
Diane says it's because she needs money fast.

'How's yourself?' she asks him.

'Usual! How's tricks?' He looks over at Hamish.
'Just a Tennent's.'

Niall takes himself to a cushioned corner of
the platformed seating area and sips his lager. He
wipes the foam from his mouth with a frayed
sleeve. The skin over his knuckles is cracked
and the backs of his hands are veiny. He is an old
thirty-five, with prematurely grey hair. He wonders
how much older he is than Diane and if she is
still in school.

'How's your mother keeping?' he asks her as he
plods back up to Hamish for another pint.

'You finished that off quickly,' says Diane and he
grins, in a way he hopes is charming. Can he be
charming? Does Catriona ever think he's charming?

Diane notices him looking at her and cocks her head. 'I saw your daughter the other day, when I was at Ann-Marie's. She's such a wee character.'

Niall is caught off guard. 'Ho, well, you can say that again, aye.' He coughs. 'More of the same, please,' he says, hoisting himself up on a leatherette stool. Hamish pours the drink in silence. The fruit machine flashes electric treasure in the corner.

'Quiet in here, eh?' he says and drains half his pint. Hamish looks up from a newspaper that is spread out on the countertop and nods.

'Good day?' It is another man at the bar, whom Niall now realizes is Alan Mackie, wearing a forest-green jumper and tweedy trousers. He stays staring at his drink as he speaks.

'I've had better. How's yourself? I didn't see you there,' Niall says. He squints at the 'Dear Deirdre' column Hamish is reading.

'Had better days, have you? Have a whisky with me,' says Alan. 'On me.' He lifts up his little water jug. 'Two more, aye. The man needs it. Doubles.'

'No, I couldn't . . .'

Alan replies with a wheezy chuckle. 'Aye, you can. Here' – he directs his voice to Hamish – 'who's playing this Friday?'

'Sandy Ross and his pals.'

'I could do without hearing his name for a while,' Niall mutters.

'What? I thought you were one o' them,' says Diane from the corner, spraying Pledge on to a glass tabletop and wiping it.

'Aye. Well.' He balls his fist and stretches it out absent-mindedly.

'Right then. Here you go, gentlemen.' Hamish slides two tumblers across to Niall and Alan.

'Cheers.'

'Thanks very much.' Niall feels queasy at the sight of the whisky, but he has to drink it, to keep going. As he takes a sip he imagines himself here, sitting like Alan, talking to younger men in twenty years' time. Lauren will nearly be the age he is now. Maybe she will have a family of her own. This seems as real as Niall one day becoming President of the United States.

'I know I ask you this every time,' Alan says, 'but how are things going, with Lauren and everything?' He hesitates. Alan is always trying to get him to talk about his feelings.

'Aye, it's not about that,' says Niall. 'No, it's fine. Just work.'

'I remember when I lost Moira,' says Alan. He shakes his head. 'I hope you don't mind me saying, but you never really . . . "get over it", as they say.'

Niall looks straight at Alan, noticing his gym teacher is old now, with deep-grey hair. He thinks about what Sandy said and the girls he went to school with. 'I haven't lost her in that sense,' Niall says. 'She might, you know – we might hear something.'

Alan nods, raising his hand to signal he has crossed a line. 'Well,' he says, 'just thought I'd check, you know.'

Hamish turns on the music, folk rock, signifying that the evening has started. Niall finishes his pint in silence and remembers when Christine would sing, her voice crystalline over his guitar. The song makes him remember her feathered earrings and the way her hands hovered over bodies, to cleanse them. She was always cleaning and cleansing souls. Purifying. He once asked her to cleanse the kitchen and she made as though to slap him. It was always a joke.

The music changes to 'Letter From America' by The Proclaimers.

'D'you think there'll ever be another indie ref?' Alan asks, his whiskered face crumpling at the question.

'Who can say, Alan?' says Hamish, absent-mindedly turning a page of the newspaper, seemingly unfazed by Scottish politics. 'Who can say? Anything happens these days.'

Niall feels a leathery hand grab his as Alan leans over with some effort, reeking of BO and baccy. He has the urge to pull it away.

'I know it sounds awful,' Alan says, 'but you have to be happy. There are a lot of ladies out there, you know? I know – it sounds awful and you can tell me to fuck off for saying it.' He grins.

Niall smiles uneasily while he checks his wallet for the next round. Nevertheless, his thoughts wind their way back to Catriona and the pattern of her work trousers stretching taut over her backside. He coughs. Diane looks over at him. It's the end of her shift and she's pulling on her coat. He tries to give her a cheery smile, while the next girl takes her place at the bar.

After spaghetti at Billy's, Lauren watches Sunday-night television with his family. Kirsty and Billy's father Craig have a glass of white wine. As usual, Craig keeps himself to himself; his pinched mouth has little to say. A couple of times Kirsty and Craig exchange a look. The second time Billy's father gets up in his seat and says, 'I'll go over the way. See where he is.'

'Give Sandy Ross a call first,' says Kirsty.

After some time, Craig comes back.

'The drive's empty,' he says, 'and I gave the door a good chap. No answer.'

'You know what those two are like – they'll probably be out together.'

16

Alan Mackie sits on his own now at a corner table, watching a game of darts played by three tourists from out of town. He laughs with one of them about something. The accordion player from Sandy's band is telling a story to a couple of older men, their heavy bodies wedged on to rickety, Draylon-cushioned bar stools. Niall is never able to make friends in that way.

People in nearby villages used to probe him about Christine's vanishing in less sensitive ways than Alan Mackie. He knows people want to ask him about what happened.

He's sure there must be rumours too. Because she was always a maddie, always a strange one. Her disappearance was the last strange thing she did. These thoughts hurt more than remembering her as she was, or how he saw her. There is a word that he knows must float behind his back and it creeps to his mind, shamefully. *Witch*. He once found a book about familiars lying by her bed. He insisted they didn't have any pets. The dog came after she disappeared.

He takes a while to warm up to anyone new in the bar and is used to regulars giving him sad or wary nods, and asking after Lauren, which makes him talk even less. He likes the quiet company of the old boys who never ask questions that are too intrusive, like Alan. He finishes his pint and steadies himself to get out, saying goodbye to no one.

He carries on down the dark village road to the Spar, with its glowing fir-tree sign. The wind picks up, pushing against his face, wakening him. The shop is too dear, but he uses it when he has to. They are building another supermarket, an Aldi, on the outskirts of the small town on a patch of empty land by the forest. People in the town have been talking about this for months.

He walks through an aisle of 'Scottish produce': oatcakes, shortbread and the chilled cheese counter with its faintly sour smell. The light is too dim for a shop and there is a low hum of white noise that he barely perceives. His reflection wobbles over the glass of the deli counter.

The primary colours of the cereal aisle stand bright against the grey-tiled ceiling and floor. The cartoon characters – Snap, Crackle and Pop and Tony the Tiger – have changed since he last bought a packet years ago, but he doesn't notice this either.

His sense of time has floated away. He passes Highland Spring and Schweppes, his footsteps heavy, and picks up two glass bottles with red labels. He snaps out of his empty daydream and notices someone else in the aisle.

'Hi, Niall.'

Christine's voice.

He turns, cradling the vodka in his arms. Someone is standing with her back to him in the drinks aisle. He is not sure now that she has spoken. She is slight, short, with a black beanie pulled down to the collar of her ice-blue anorak. Her head is lowered, examining a row of Lambrini.

He looks down at the waspy yellow sign for a special offer, running his hand over his chin, feeling the greying stubble scrape his palm. He managed to shave this morning but didn't shower. He puts the bottles back on the shelf and takes two other, discounted brands, with a clink.

The small person turns around, startled.

'Ann-Marie.' His voice is croaky with booze.

'Hi, Niall.' Her eyes dart about, never quite meeting his.

'You old enough to be buying here?'

She takes her hand away from the shelf, but then reaches out for a bottle of Gordon's gin.

'My dad's outside. He asked me to nip in and pick up a few things.'

The arm furthest from his is down by her side, holding a large white bottle. He remembers she is on a school holiday.

'Your dad's on the Bacardi these days?'

She puts the rum back on the shelf and looks down at the vodka in his arms.

'Be careful,' Niall says as she disappears around the corner.

When Niall takes the vodka and a pack of Tennent's to the counter, he sees her again, standing in the cereal aisle, staring at the Special K, her beanie tugged down low. He can see she's nervous about something.

Jill is at the counter, as usual, unsmiling and distant. Her hair is short and yellow-blonde. She scans the bottles, then the beer. He gives her his credit card and opens his mouth to say something about Ann-Marie, but thinks better of it. Jill asks if he wants to spend five p on a poly bag. She is not from the area. Niall only knows her name is Jill because it is pinned on her geometric blouse. No one in this town ever comes close to being as beautiful as his wife, not even Catriona. Guilt seeps through him.

It has been ten years. No one in the town ever looked like her back then either. The other girls from school brushed their hair back into perfect ponytails, the tops of their heads hard with hairspray. Other women cropped their hair, sometimes leaving it long at the back and short at the sides. In lots of small ways, the town has never truly left the nineties.

Sportswear is popular for men and women: joggers, T-shirts printed with holiday destinations. Other women wear tight jeans and sequinned, off-the-shoulder tops for cigarettes and pints at the pub. He found these girls pretty and exciting at one time – they were the only girls he knew. But they treated Christine like a foreigner.

The bottles clink in the bag as Niall carries them out of the shop. As he leaves, he passes Alan Mackie in the doorway, still smiling from the pub.

'Whup!' Alan says. 'We've got to stop meeting like this! I'm getting a few for Duncan's place.'

Niall nods, not knowing which Duncan he means. Alan eyes him with mild curiosity.

Making sure no one can see him, Niall sits in the pickup and takes a yellowing plastic cup, part of an old thermos, from the glove compartment. He unscrews the red cap from the vodka bottle and pours himself a drink, neat. He never learned what Christine really thought of him, even to this day. She was mad but calm. Daydreamy at times, at others anxious. In a good mood, she would act as though she was humouring him and that nothing passed her by, because she had seen more of the world than he had.

Soon after they met, they went to the big beach near Strath Horne for a walk. There was little wind and families were out on the sands. Dogs were running with driftwood and children were jumping off the rocks Niall had jumped off as a child. He told her a story and used the word 'jamp'. She corrected him, and he tried to carry her into the water. He picked her up in a fireman's lift and she kicked her legs and screamed, and he noticed a family he knew staring at them, so he put her down among the sand dunes. She kissed him, and they lay there for a long time.

The road is dark, and he is not near a streetlamp. He waits, sipping the vodka at first, then taking deep gulps. He sees Ann-Marie walk out with a heavy bag, its contents unclear.

He turns on the engine and leans out of the open window. 'Hie!'

She ignores him.

'Hie! Ann-Marie!'

She stops and walks over to him.

'Are you wanting a lift home?' he says.

'No, no,' she says. 'I'm fine.' She looks at the thermos cup in his hand. 'Thank you.'

'Where are you off to?' he says.

She starts to walk away, pointing ahead to somewhere vague. 'I am meeting . . . Just meeting my dad. Don't worry.'

She leaves, her light jacket fading into the ill-lit street.

He sits in his own thoughts for a while, but these kinds of memories are like rocks rubbing against raw skin. He prefers to believe they happened to another man. Often this seems true. He likes to use his work shed and take trips to the timber yard when the memory of this man feels too much like himself. These days he has been making a cabinet that needs sanding. New chairs he has finished are stacked in the corner of his work shed, waiting for varnish. He will never get tired of the smell of varnish. Much of the furniture in the house he has made himself.

The previous month, an English shopkeeper at a furniture place in town had asked whether he wanted to supply his work as a 'local artisan' and have his photograph taken, to put in the window. But he said no, he wasn't 'arty', not like Christine.

Niall drinks another cup of warm vodka and begins the drive home, passing some teenagers who are walking to the bus shelter, where Ann-Marie is sitting on its sloping red bench. He stops the truck some feet ahead, and notices the teenagers do not seem to know her. He drinks another cup of vodka and gets out of the pickup.

'Hey.'

Ann-Marie looks up.

'Hey, hop in. I'll give you a lift. You don't want to get the bus.'

Ann-Marie smiles reluctantly. Her bag clinks as she rises and walks over to the pickup. It is fully dark now.

'Here, take a seat,' says Niall. He steadies his hand on the passenger window and frost stings his palm.

'Thanks, Niall.' Ann-Marie opens the passenger side and snowy air blows in. 'Are you OK driving?' She is still standing, holding the door.

Niall takes a minute for her words to sink in. Then he says, 'Y'all right? I'm all right. We're fine now. I don't want you going home on your own.'

'Thanks, Niall.' She gets into the pickup, clutching the bag on her knees with one hand, the other gripping the handle in the truck's door as he starts the drive back to their village.

'So,' he says. His breath comes out in steam.

Ann-Marie shifts in her seat. 'So.'

Niall turns the radio dial and a chat show fills the pickup, along with the smell of anti-freeze blowing out from the dashboard. The wipers start squeaking. There is a comedian who sounds serious, talking about how Christmas is getting earlier each year. Niall starts off into the empty road, swerving a little and then righting himself.

'You sure you're OK?' asks Ann-Marie.

'Aye-I'm-fine-why.' One word melts into the other.

'You . . . don't seem your usual self.'

'I'm fine! Never better. Never. Better. Women, y'know.'

Ann-Marie smirks. 'OK.' The black road merges into the black landscape either side of them, with tiny dots of light in the distance and catseyes glowing up from the tarmac, one after the other.

'It gets so dark now. It feels so much later than it actually is,' she says.

Niall stays silent. A lorry charges in the other direction, almost clipping the wing mirror.

'Niall.'

'Aye.'

They drive on in silence. Niall changes the radio station to the one he prefers at this time of day. They are playing a run-down of the best folk of the seventies. He can feel Ann-Marie relax a little beside him.

They pass a snowy field outside the village. Christine once took him up to the standing stones there, for a solstice picnic in the sun, by the ancient burial ground. She was always doing these things.

Before she moved to Strath Horne, Christine had found paganism in the city, becoming one of the performers at the Beltane fire festival. He had never been to the spring event itself, but he knew it was about body paint and nudity and sex. He had heard that there were orgies. She had danced naked with fire. He would ask her for her stories before he went to sleep some nights. He nicknamed her friends from that time, the New Age students, 'the hobbits'. Fucking Beltane. It had meant nothing to him, before he met her, except running up a hill like a madman and shoving your face in the April dew. And bonfires. He must admit he has a soft spot for them now. She used to call them 'need-fires' and make bannocks. She celebrated the sun. She was a child of seventeen when she moved to Edinburgh, but lied about her age. No one could tell her anything. She painted her nails vermilion and made posies from rowan branches. He would tease her later, hearing these stories, and tell her she needed to keep away from the rowans, that the branches would burn her, that someone would dunk her in a river.

Once a farmer complained that he had found ivy garlands around his cattle in the field some way from their house. No one ever admitted to this. Christine looked as though she had no idea about the incident, yet Niall remains convinced to this day it was her doing.

Ann-Marie clears her throat in the dingy pickup. 'I wanted to say . . . Lauren was asking the other day. About . . . I thought I should tell you. She seems quite disturbed.'

'What?'

'She . . . she seems troubled. She wanted to know about . . . her mum.'

The truck drifts out to the middle of the road and Ann-Marie clutches the handle.

'Y'all right, Niall?'

Niall suppresses a hiccup and mutters, 'Fine.'

'I just thought I should tell you. I realized – I realized I don't really know what happened.'

'I don't want to chat about *that.*' The memories fade into the black. These Walkers can't leave him alone. 'Like mother like daughter,' he mutters.

'What was that?'

He doesn't answer.

'I'm sorry, it's hard,' Ann-Marie replies.

'I'm not being funny, like, but – I don't know. Coming into my truck and chatting about that?' A bitterness overtakes him. 'You'd better mind I don't tell your parents about your sneaky wee drink habit.' The road stretches ahead. 'Wouldn't be so perfect to them then, would you? Jeez.' They drive some way in silence before he starts to talk again. 'You're just like – you're just like your mother. Ask any more of those questions and you can . . . piss off back to Edinburgh.' The last phrase comes out as a mumble.

He glances over and sees Ann-Marie looking resolutely out of the window. He starts up again. 'I'm not talking about that, OK? She's gone. *Gone.* Nothing is "conclusive". It was all fucked up and she's gone.'

'OK. I'm sorry,' Ann-Marie says.

He indicates and the clicking noise soothes the silence. They turn off the main road and drive down the forest track. The uneven stones and potholes make the ride bumpier. The pines are dark and dense. No other cars are about. Niall dips the head-lamps to a half-beam that spreads into a yellow pool of light in front of them.

'You all right, Niall?' she asks again.

He grunts.

Ann-Marie crosses her legs in the tight space. 'You sure?'

'I'm *fine*!' He swerves the truck into the road and Ann-Marie jolts to one side, clinging to the door handle. 'Jeez.' Niall carries on looking ahead but he can see her out of the corner of his eye.

'OK. Niall? I'm fine just here. *Here.*' When he looks over properly she is pressed against the door.

'Sorry about that,' he murmurs. One hand reaches about for a can or a hip flask in the space near her legs but finds nothing.

'Look,' she says. 'Please. This is nearly me home. Just drop me in the passing place. I can walk the rest of the way, no bother.'

'No, no, I have to get you home.' The truck bumps against the roadside and drifts closer to the stony verge.

'Niall, please.'

'Can't have you walking.' He says it almost sarcastically.

'*Niall.* I don't feel well. Please. Please. Stop right here. Stop here in the passing place. It's almost . . . We're almost at our house.'

'*Fine.*' He jerks the vehicle into the lay-by and they lurch in their seats again. 'Ann-Marie. You're a young girl. I canna . . . let you out.'

'What?' She curls back into the corner of the seat and the curve of the door.

'I canna.' He touches her on the shoulder, his fingers clumsily brushing her lapel. 'I canna have you walking that way. On your own. In the trees and that.'

Ann-Marie looks at him and he sees then that she is scared. The trees are better than he is.

17

In a camp bed in the downstairs study of Billy's house, Lauren wonders what's happened to her father. If he is with Sandy, she can't understand why he hasn't texted her or phoned. She has to go to school tomorrow. Maybe he's drunk. Maybe he had an accident. She tries to remember what he said he was doing that day, but it doesn't come to her. She tries to think hard, to pick up psychic signals of some kind, but there is nothing. Before she went to bed, she looked out of the ground-floor window to see if she could catch sight of the pickup, but the road was empty.

Lauren is woken in the night by the Mathesons' home telephone. She can hear Kirsty padding downstairs, her soft speech, her intake of breath. She jogs upstairs again. Some time later, Lauren hears a rumble of discussion in the kitchen next door. Kirsty is standing on the other side of the wall. She sounds upset. 'We should.'

Lauren listens hard.

'I know. I know. But we should.'

Then there is quiet, followed by a soft tap on her door. 'Hi,' Kirsty whispers. 'Are you awake?'

'Uh-huh,' Lauren whispers back.

Kirsty crouches by the camp bed, her face close. 'I was just wondering. When's the last time you saw Ann-Marie?'

'When she was babysitting.' Lauren looks out of the door, as if Ann-Marie might be there.

'Did she tell you anything? Say that she might be going somewhere?'

'No, why?' Something is sinking inside her.

'OK. Don't worry. You try and get back to sleep.' She walks out, more quickly than usual.

Lauren lies very still in bed, barely breathing to try and hear more. Craig is pacing the room and Kirsty is talking on the phone again. Their discussion grows a little louder. Lauren tilts her head towards the wall.

'We'll do what we can,' Kirsty says.

'We can't both—'

'Why not?' Kirsty says.

'Now is not the time to be a smart alec. You stay here. We've got work tomorrow. The kids need you. Your phone working OK?' Craig says.

'Fine. But don't – don't talk to me like that,' says Kirsty.

He sighs. 'I'm *knackered*. This is *odd*. Not just her, it's Niall. Eh?'

Lauren squeezes her eyes closed.

'We don't know,' Craig continues. 'Need to be safe.'

Their voices dip, and Lauren moves closer to the wall but can't catch the words. Soon she hears Craig ask for the keys, close the door and speed away in his car. The house ebbs back into silence and Lauren pulls the bobbled duvet over her head to think. Under the padding she hears the shrill call of the phone again and pokes her head out to listen.

'Yes, that's right. He's away out. Don't worry, Angela, we'll do all we can. No, no, she hasn't heard anything. Oh, right, I see. Diane. OK, well, like I say, Craig'll have a wee look around.'

Lauren wonders what Diane might have to do with things. She tries to imagine a situation in which her father and Ann-Marie have ended up spending time together, but it's such an odd idea, like a rabbit eating a dog, instead of the other way around. Billy's walkie-talkie is lying by the side of her bed. She takes it under the covers. 'Billy,' she whispers. 'Are you there, Billy?'

Only static answers as she puts the radio down on her bedside table.

She tries to sleep, but her body is too alert. Impulsively, she reaches for the radio again. 'Bill—'

A young woman's voice replies, 'Go to sleep, Lauren. Stay in bed.'

Lauren jumps and pushes the device off the table. She looks around, as if the young woman might be in the room with her, but she isn't. The radio bounces on to the floor and the battery flap springs open. The static stops and the room is silent, except for the ticking of the clock.

There is a gentle knock on the door again and Kirsty peers her head around the side. 'Everything OK? You made a noise.'

'Oh, did I? I'm fine.'

'You mustn't worry.' She begins to close the door, her head tilted to one side.

Lauren looks down at the floor. She feels a little silly, because the woman doesn't seem real any more. 'Kirsty?'

'Mmm-hmm?'

'Where's Ann-Marie?'

'Ann-Marie is being a silly teenager . . .' Kirsty tightens her grip on the door. 'She'll be with friends or something. She's on holiday at the moment, isn't she? Craig's out and I might . . . nip out too, so you'll sit tight here, won't you? You'll try and get some sleep now? I can give you one of Billy's school jumpers for tomorrow. Or we can drive past by your house.'

Lauren nods and pulls the duvet over her head. She wishes she had her worry dolls to talk to or her knife to flick. She thinks of her father and imagines him falling into a ditch or getting lost on the single-track lane. She texts him again and hears the front door slip shut and realizes she is alone with Billy and Lewis.

She slips in and out of sleep for a while, but when she wakes up it is after midnight and the house is still empty. Anxiety twists around her like ivy. She lies there, remembering what Craig and Kirsty said, how they mentioned Diane. They should have been back by now. *Your mum and now your dad and now Ann-Marie*, a voice inside her is saying. She can't think, only feel what it would be like without them, as though they had all been swept away by a wave.

The dark outside is huge and cold, but she knows she should be out there. It's no good trying to sleep. She feels as if she could run a mile. The grown-ups drive everywhere in their cars. They don't know the fields like she does. She could walk the Loop through the woods blind.

She thinks of her dad and how he walks Jameson in the dark at Cowrie Point. Perhaps he'll be OK. But perhaps he has been drinking again. Perhaps he came home and is so fast asleep, he didn't hear Craig ring the doorbell. Ann-Marie, on the other hand, doesn't really live here and is used to the city. It's easy to imagine her losing her way.

She creeps upstairs and softly knocks on Billy's bedroom door. When there's no answer she goes in, making out her friend's sleeping body on a bed along one wall. Out of his window, she sees a couple of cars parked at the side of the road at the front of the house and three spots of light in the fields to the right. The night is clear and still; snow gleams. The neighbours must be searching. The realization stings her like ice.

She hurries downstairs and puts her wellies on, leaving a note for Kirsty. She stops still, remembering the woman's voice over the radio. Outside looks dark, but there are people with torches and if she were to scream they would hear her. She knows she has to be brave. Then she realizes she is the only one with the key to her house and decides that is where she should start looking. If her father is home, she'll text them. She makes her way back over the dark field towards her home. She doesn't feel scared if she stands still and lets her eyes open up to the dark night around her, remembering it is the same place it was in the sunlight. The neighbours' torches are bright specks behind her, but when she stands still, she can hear the voices of Malcolm and Angela calling: 'Ann-Marie! Ann-Marie!'

Back at her house she peers into the front drive and sees the pickup there, frosted over, like a dark block of ice.

She runs up to her father's bedroom. 'Dad! Dad?' The house is still chilly and dark. She hears Jameson behind her, barking, excited she is home. She ignores him and, switching the lights on as she goes, creeps into her empty bedroom and then the bathroom. Nothing. She yanks back the mildewed shower curtain. The bath is empty too. She picks up the torch from the landing cupboard on her way back downstairs.

He is not sitting on the sofa or cooking in the kitchen. The house is vacant, yet she still calls his name, hoping she's made a mistake. He wouldn't go far without his pickup.

The only room she has not checked is the one she is not allowed to go into. She tries the door and finds it unlocked. (Has it always been unlocked?) Inside, cardboard boxes are heaped in a corner. A woman's dress is draped in a dry-cleaning bag over the yellow sofa and a pair of women's boots stand by the mantelpiece. Extinguished candles are sitting in a line. Lauren leaves quickly and calls out for her father once again. She opens the sliding door and peers around the garden. *It's only the dark*, she tells herself. *The dark can't hurt you.* Her body feels skittish.

A buzzard is sitting on the fence post, watching her. It takes off into the sky, towards the woods. 'Dad?' She doesn't know why she is calling for him. She takes her mountain bike from under a tarp, clicks on the front light and wheels it along the back way, where the edge of her garden meets the fields and a track runs in between. She can see lights bobbing at the edge of a distant field.

She drags her bike over the snowy field, then hauls it over the paddock fence to the start of the

Loop. The track is almost too dark to see, but she has walked it so many times, and ridden her bike here too, it should seem easy. Before she can scare herself, she tears up the track into the acres of woodland ahead, away from the lights of the search party. The bike throws a shaky beam in front of her and then the old water tanks. She doesn't dare to look inside, this time. The trees start to close in around her. She wonders if Ann-Marie or her father have headed along the Loop and fallen somehow on the way. It doesn't lead anywhere, so it doesn't make sense. She is sure for a moment that she hears Diane's voice in the fields shouting too, far away, but it's hard to hear over the tyres whipping the stony track and the noise of her own breath. Just a little further along the path, she gets to their usual spot by the hut. In the dark, it's just a faint shape among the trees. The sight is familiar yet unnerving. She closes her eyes and hears the flapping of wings.

She carries on further along the Loop, as the trees thicken and the forest deepens. She thinks if she rides along here, calling, maybe she'll get an answer. The path seems to go on for hours. She can't ride very fast in the dark, but she rides fast enough not to feel scared at the prospect of cycling into a black hole.

After what could have been two hours or five, her adrenaline is running out. The path she is on becomes narrower until grass is brushing her legs. She looks around, hard. It dawns on her that she is not on the Loop any more, but a narrowed animal track. Suddenly she is moving fast, downhill, unable to stop.

A rock looms in the darkness and she turns sharply and then pounds to the ground with a clatter of metal. The bike light goes out. The breath has been knocked from her lungs. She lies there as the damp from the slushy grass seeps through her trousers and chills her tired body. At that moment she is too tired to cry and too angry with herself. Part of her wants to sleep. She has never been so aware of her childishness.

In a patch where the moon is big, she spots an old saucepan in the undergrowth and a rusty beer can. These objects are strange. The only signs of life she has seen before are from a very long time ago: the stone foundations of a croft, an old bridge. She wonders how long she will have to walk to try and find a way out.

When she looks up she realizes that hidden among the trees is a tumbledown house, without a roof. Lauren stands her ground, feeling fear curl around her arms and legs. She begins to walk away, her steps turning into a run. After at least a mile, when she can't run any longer, she finds a gorse bush and crawls beneath it.

* * *

Niall is walking through pitch black, the crunch of ice and rocks beneath his feet, the smell of the pine fresh and frosty, heavy with snow. He knows he is getting closer to the centre of the forest and he knows he shouldn't be there. All at once, a small, dark-haired man steps out from behind a tree, dressed in a cloak of moss and dead bracken. 'I'm looking after the lost girl,' says the man. 'Come with me.'

Niall can see bugs crawling in the man's cloak, earwigs and brown lacewings, crane flies and iridescent leaf beetles.

They start walking along narrow, shadowy paths. 'She's just around the corner,' says the man. 'I found her.'

The dense ferns brush against Niall, their leaves as high as his chest. He has to wade through, pushing against the undergrowth, feeling bugs crawl under his sleeves. Moonbeams light the path as he follows the small, shaggy-cloaked man with a shining lantern and staff. 'I live alone,' the man says. Niall notices they are among birches now and he has a strange feeling he is at his grandfather's cottage in Gairloch and he's telling him the myth of the Ghillie Dhu. The cloaked man begins to turn around as a cold dread seeps into Niall's bones and he springs awake in the dark, then passes out again.

18

Some hours pass. Lauren stops herself from falling asleep completely in the bushes. Her dad once told her of mountaineers who went to sleep in the snow and never woke up. She sings songs to herself in her head. 'Bat Out Of Hell' and 'Stairway To Heaven'. She closes her eyes for minutes at a time, dazed with cold, and then opens them. At last, the forest begins to get a little lighter. She realizes she is far away from any path and the trees look identical around her. In the distance, she can see spots of light. They are not torches exactly, but more like fireflies, if those existed in Scotland. Something ephemeral, she has heard told in stories. She follows them, over the mossy forest floor, past boulders and banks of ferns for a couple of miles. The birds are starting to call. Her legs are about to give out when she realizes she is walking alongside the edge of the forest, glimpsing the fields between the trees. The early morning is still dark, but deep grey rather than black. It will not be light for hours.

By the time her whole body is nearly numb with cold, she hears her name being called. This time there is a strong light growing out of the main path. 'Is that you, Lauren?'

She freezes. It's a woman's voice. Diane, scruffy and confused, walking up from the fields.

Lauren calls out and Diane shines the torch towards her, then runs, her army jacket flapping. Lauren looks down in the waving light at her own clothes for streaks of blood. As Diane runs, Lauren notices she is looking past her, into the tall trees. When she arrives, she hugs Lauren close, taking them both by surprise.

'I couldn't get any sleep, so thought I might as well try looking for her,' Diane says.

Lauren realizes her friend is wearing a heavy backpack. She smells like stale peaches and smoke. She hugs Lauren closer and rubs her back methodically. 'You're freezing. Thank God I found you.' Her face is a mask of ivory-crème foundation that has sunken overnight into the uneven acne it was trying to hide, making her skin look as if it is cracking.

'Thank you,' Lauren says, her teeth chattering involuntarily. 'What time is it?'

'Five thirty,' Diane says absently. She stays next to Lauren, but shines her torch into the trees around them, and then looks back over her shoulder. Lauren is so close she can see Diane's eyes are scared under their dark, clumpy lids; she sees how young she really is.

Diane is paying attention again. 'How'd you even get here? *God.*' Her tongue piercing clicks against her teeth as she talks. She unzips her bag and digs out a woollen jumper and bobble hat that Lauren pulls on.

'I was looking for—' Lauren's ribcage is cold and tight, like the icy bonnet of a car. She tries to catch her breath.

'That was really dangerous.' Diane's voice is faint and her eyes keep flicking sideways and up ahead. 'I just need to see something.' She leaves Lauren and sprints a little further into the black, her backpack jostling against her shoulders.

'What are you doing?' Lauren's voice is starting to sound as hoarse as Diane's. The early morning is still and silent and her words carry.

She hears a murmur from the dark trees and trudges up towards it. She finds Diane crouching on top of a huge tree trunk. Diane puts her pinkies in her mouth and whistles. There is a leaf-rustling and twig-snapping behind her and a dog leaps out over the snowy bracken. It's Lola, Diane's grey and white lurcher, who bounds up to Lauren and pants stinky warm breath in her face. Diane coughs into the icy air and pulls out a creased packet of Richmonds from her pocket. Her hands are red with the cold and her nails flake purple glitter.

'Are you up here looking for Ann-Marie?' Lauren asks cautiously.

Diane blows smoke into the deep-grey air, from atop the tree trunk. 'Yep. Uh-huh. Everything's fucked.'

Rooks croak back at her.

'I need to go home. Which way is it?' Lauren feels as though she has been on a roundabout too fast. She is faint with hunger.

'I'm not letting you go by yourself. It probably isn't safe.' Diane unscrews a thermos and hands the cup down to Lauren. 'Here. Tea. Put your hands round it.'

Lauren holds it under her face and feels as though the steam is thawing her out. 'Thanks.' She takes a gulp.

'This was for Ann-Marie. But you need warmed up. Climb up. Come on,' Diane says, pulling on Lauren's arm.

Lauren wishes she could smoke like Diane. School says it kills people if you do it too much. It's Monday. The dread of school seeps into her stomach.

'I'm waiting just a little. I want to see if she comes out. We sometimes meet here, though not this early. She said she'd see me later, but then wasn't answering her phone. I just have a bad feeling about all this.'

Though she could turn up back at her house. I don't know. Angela was on the phone to me—' She stops and looks around as the trees creak. 'We have to be quiet.' She sees Lauren's puzzlement. 'There are bad people. A man did something bad.' Diane starts lighting a cigarette, looking around furtively. Between clenched teeth she says, as if talking to herself, 'Wouldn't it be nice to be the person everyone's scared of?'

Lauren looks at her and guesses she probably won't tell her what she is really talking about. She thinks back to Halloween and making herself scary. Imagining, as she put on her make-up, that she could drink someone's blood. 'I wish sometimes I was a vampire. I could just fly over this whole forest and find them.'

Diane laughs, blowing air through her nose. 'I wish you were too. Do you want another cup? I'm trying not to think the worst. It's like a dream. You and me, sitting here. Barely morning. We heard stories, me and her, or rather I heard a story about these woods. It's better not to tell you. But that was the start of it.'

She takes out something wrapped in foil, and opens it up. A stack of cheese sandwiches. Lauren takes one gingerly and realizes she has never been so pleased to see flimsy white bread.

'The start of it?' she asks Diane. 'It's OK. I was told something like that. The story about the dog in the woods and the human leg?'

'Someone told you, aye?' Diane looks surprised. 'That's the one. I heard it a few times. Down at the Black Horse. Whether it's true or just one of those stories.' She resettles herself on the trunk, stretching out her legs as though they are cramping up. 'Well, this guy – this bad manny we're talking about – he hears that story in the pub the other month, his friend's telling him it, and when he hears the ending, he doesn't look right. Everyone who hears it gets a bit freaked out by that story, you know, but his face. It was different. He looked like he had seen a ghost, or whatever it is they say. He started sweating. He was worried. He wasn't scared. He was worried. Like he was gonna be sick. That was what I thought anyway. The man telling the story, he was drunk, and he saw his friend's reaction and he started saying, *Don't worry, I was having a laugh. It wasna my dog, it was my friend's.* It's always somebody's friend's. Didn't hear much more, but he left quickly. So I was telling this to Ann-Marie on the phone and she got all wound up about it. She wanted to start looking in the woods, questioning the guy. All sorts. Had all these plans. She said, *This proves it*, meaning his reaction, *I knew he did it.* She kept saying, *I knew he did it.* Then she got that tattoo and she got, you know, suspended. And I wouldn't be surprised if she did all that stuff to get sent back here.'

Lauren looks around her. 'The man. You think – he . . . killed someone?'

'Yeah, that's what we were thinking. And we know him.' She raises her eyebrows. 'We all know him. She wanted to talk to him. Get a confession, get proof, I don't know what. Get to the bottom of it. That story, his reaction, it's not going convict someone on its own, is it?'

Lauren looks at her. She doesn't understand.

'Never mind. So she had this plan. And she got carried away. We had an argument. But this is where we usually meet. Here.'

'You should tell the police.'

'Yeah . . . I think I will.'

'I saw this house, way up the track. It was weird,' Lauren says.

'Yeah? Where? I only know the Loop.'

'I'm too tired to go. It's cold. Maybe I won't be able to find my way back.'

'Another walk'll soon warm you up. C'mon. You want to find her, don't you?'

It takes some time, fumbling through the pre-dawn grey. Everything looks the same to Lauren at first; then she recognizes the way the ferns make an 'S' shape and starts on the right track. 'It's up here. Come on.'

They walk for half an hour in the snow, keeping to the deer tracks. This time around, Lauren notices how close they are to a bigger track, through the trees, its tarmac overgrown. She sees the shape of a parked car. She looks again and tugs Diane's sleeve. 'Look. Isn't that *yours*?'

'What the hell?' Diane sprints over the snowy undergrowth. Together they call Ann-Marie's name. Lola circles the area like a wolf.

When Diane comes panting back, Lauren asks, 'Can't we drive home?'

Diane whispers her reply, 'No. Better not. The keys aren't in the ignition. We need to keep it there.'

'But who—'

'*They* did. This bad guy and Ann-Marie. I'm telling the police as soon as we get back. Let's just try and find her first. At least try.'

Lauren can hear the fear in her voice. Her eyes are wide and white.

After another few miles of trudging in the cold through the trees, they reach the dilapidated house. It looks jagged under the torch beam. Diane switches the torch off and darkness drops. When they're close, Lauren stops in her tracks; then she edges a little further. 'Are you sure you want to go in?'

Lola makes a noise that is half a whine and half a whimper, pulling back on her lead.

'Well, no,' says Diane, 'but she could be in danger. Lola. Stay outside.' She drops the lead. 'We'll only be a few minutes.'

'We?'

'Yes.' She grabs Lauren's coat sleeve. 'I need to know where you are. I'm not letting you out of my sight.'

Lauren's stomach lurches. She creeps to the entrance, telling Lola to stay behind, and cranes her head inside the gloomy hallway.

The wooden floor has been ripped up in places with splinters spiking up here and there like tufts of grass. In the dark, Lauren makes out peeling wallpaper and a rotten staircase. Beyond that is dark. Outside the wind rustles the trees.

'Ann . . . Ann-Marie?' she calls.

There is a creak and then a crash in the room next door.

Before the girls have a chance to react, the ground beneath them rumbles like a small earthquake and they freeze. There is the sound of crockery clattering from another room and they lose their balance, falling hard on the floor. As Lauren tries to scramble up in the dark, the heavy front door to their left creaks wide open and then bangs shut. A sound rattles through the house like a train passing. Diane shines the torch on the front door. It is covered in scratches, as if an animal has been at it. On the back of the door, there hangs a white dressing gown, blanketed in mould.

Lauren stays as still as she can. She feels a sense of dread creep into her bones and wants to whisper *We need to leave*, but her voice is stuck in her throat, the way that can often happen in a bad dream.

She looks down. They are standing in a perfect circle of broken crockery.

Diane grabs Lauren's arm and pulls her close, switching off the torch.

'Do you feel all that?' she says, her voice shaky in the dark. 'Something is here with us.'

'I wanna go,' Lauren whines. 'It wants us to leave.'

'But Ann-Marie,' whispers Diane. 'If she's somewhere in here, I have to . . .' She jumps as a blast of air makes the door slam again.

Tentatively they make their way around two ground-floor rooms with the torch, pausing now and again as the wind slams through the house, but all they can find are piles of debris, broken crockery and mouldering curtains.

'Maybe we should try upstairs,' whispers Diane in the darkened hallway. The staircase has been built side-on from the front door.

Lauren clutches Diane's arm as she points the torch up the staircase, but the floorboards are rotten and begin to disappear, further towards the first floor. Then the staircase stops altogether. Still at the foot of the stairs, Diane shines a light in a hole in the roof above, catching the flutter of wings. The two girls jump. They flatten themselves against the staircase wall, facing the door. Lauren needs the bathroom.

'Bats,' Diane whispers. She stops and moves her hand around the wall of the wooden staircase. 'There's a . . .' Lauren sees Diane is tracing her hand over a join in the wall. 'There's a hinge!' hisses Diane.

Lauren touches Diane's arm. 'We should go home. Don't—' she whispers, shaking her head. 'I don't—' She can't finish the sentence.

'She could be . . .' Diane's eyes are wide. 'In the wall?' She traces the outline of a door. Placing her fingers by the skirting board, she feels it starting to open.

It is much thicker and heavier than expected, with some kind of foam padding lining the inside. The space is like a small broom cupboard, with nothing inside except an ancient bucket, a mouldy rug and a pair of old work boots that look oddly familiar.

'This is weird,' says Diane, shining the torch along its bare walls.

They notice a dripping sound and the air feels damp inside. Diane points to the bare ground. The wind whistles low. Lauren looks closer and sees the rug is partially covering an outline of a square. When they lift it up, there is a handle in the middle. Diane pulls at it, and Lauren tells her to stop, but she opens it up and shines the torch into the black pit below.

A deep fear passes through Lauren as the beam lands on more stairs, leading downwards to nothing. 'Ann-Marie?' Diane shouts into the hole, blocking Lauren from the pit with her arm. 'ANN-MARIE?'

They wait and listen. 'Did you hear something?' asks Diane.

'No,' Lauren whispers, looking out of the cupboard door. They need to leave, get help. Lauren can hear their breath in the quiet.

'I can hear something rustling down there,' says Diane. She grabs Lauren by the arms. 'You stay up here.' Her voice quavers in the silence. 'She's my best friend. And we had this plan. And something has gone very, very wrong. It's my fault.' Diane starts to climb down, her torch light disappearing. The cupboard is dark now. Lauren props the door open with one of the work boots. She lingers, listening, looking out of the doorway. She is too terrified to pee.

There is a low thud from the basement, and a clatter, Diane's voice calling out.

'Diane! Are you OK?' Lauren's voice is reedy. Perhaps Diane doesn't hear her, because she doesn't call back up.

'Diane?' Now she's scared.

'Lauren,' Diane says from below, out of breath. 'The torch. I fell and dropped the torch. I think it . . .' She sounds as though she is scrabbling around.

Lauren hesitates, making sure the cupboard and the trapdoor are securely open, then starts to make her way down the stairs slowly, sick with fear and vertigo, running her hands along one wall to steady herself. Then she sits down, as she did when she was younger, and moves down the stairs on her bum. In the basement she crawls on her hands and knees towards Diane's voice.

'I'm here,' Diane says blindly. 'I'm here. I've found my car keys.'

Lauren's hand touches something round and rubbery. The torch. She breathes out, wanting to cry with relief. The beam of the torch scans a mess of papers, dirt, boxes, sacking, and a bare, soiled mattress in one corner. Then she sees Diane, in front of a branch she presumably tripped over. Diane makes her way back to Lauren and puts her arm around her shoulders. 'Hold my hand,' Diane says, taking the torch. Lauren moves round so her back is against Diane's. She swivels her head to watch the torch beam. Black grime and a fetid, meaty stink coat the walls. Something lacy is lying among the paper. There are long freezers and a washing machine. Metal loops are built into the wall by the mattress. Mounted on the wall is a thin, curved sword, encased in a black sheath.

The sword. *The Ace of Swords signifies clarity, raw power, triumph.*

They move over to the wall and press themselves against it, back to back. Lauren can feel her breath in the dark. It's easy to be scared now.

'I think I imagined it,' whispers Diane. 'I don't think she's—'

There is a rustling in the corner in front of Diane, towards the back of the room. Maybe a rat, Lauren thinks. Maybe.

Diane swivels the torch towards the sound and lands on a pair of feet lying upwards. She jumps backwards, jolting Lauren forward. By turning her head, Lauren can see the feet are large, male. Diane clutches Lauren's arm tightly, as if to say *Don't*. Diane has pulled her sleeve over her hand, and Lauren feels the bulk of the car keys pushing against her skin.

Diane flicks the torch around the room again, checking for signs of anyone else. She is breathing hard now. They stand stock-still, listening. The rustling sounds again, from the corner. When Diane moves the torch back, the feet are gone.

Diane nudges Lauren towards the sword on the wall. They are nearly there when Diane screams and almost falls, the torch light vaulting. Lauren springs back, grasping at the brick wall behind her. Someone, the owner of the feet, is crawling on the floor.

'Get off me!' Diane yells.

It dawns on Lauren that the person has a hold of Diane's leg and is trying to pull her to the ground. There is a deep groaning sound. Something between strength and pain.

Lauren tries to take Diane's arm, but misses in the dark. Diane is shuffling forward, trying to get closer to the wall. There is a thick rattle from above them and Lauren realizes Diane is trying to grab the Japanese sword from the wall. It is just beyond her grasp. Struggling and kicking against the man on the floor, she reaches again. Lauren tries to help, but she is too short. Finally, Diane manages to ease it off with her fingertips. It falls. Diane catches it. Lauren hears the whack of metal on bone, followed by another moan. Dropping the sword with a clang, Diane springs away, pushing Lauren ahead of her. They are running towards the staircase, the torch in Diane's hand throwing a shaking light ahead of them. When she reaches the stairs, Lauren looks back to see if the man is following them. She hears a strange sound: a freezer rushing its way across the concrete all by itself, behind her, pinning him to the wall. Lauren's body won't move up the stairs as fast as she wants it to. She runs as carefully as she can in the thin beam out of the house.

Fear streams through her burning muscles as she runs back into the forest. Diane is close behind. They race in the direction they came from and eventually Lauren feels she can't run any further. They both walk without speaking, in shock. Diane stops suddenly and doubles over, her hands on her knees, retching. She wipes her mouth with her sleeve.

Lauren's throat burns with bile and she remembers she is dying to pee. 'Look the other way,' she says to Diane and crouches by a tree. As she does so, she sees part of a path up ahead that looks familiar. The best option they have is to try and retrace their steps. Lauren is so alert, she feels animal.

She shows Diane, who looks deep in thought. As they begin the long walk back in the dawn light, Diane says, 'There was a plan. And it was all about finding out what happened to your mum.'

'What do you mean?' asks Lauren, but Diane walks ahead, silently. As Lauren walks, she thinks of the hermit, the sword.

Some time later, they are standing in front of Vairi's front door. 'Why?' Lauren asks.

'I don't know, Lauren.' Diane's voice is hushed by the wind. After two hours walking in the heavy snow, they have found their way back to the village. It's now after ten o'clock and she is ravenous and exhausted. Lauren can't imagine what her teacher might think, or Kirsty for that matter. She feels a pang of shame.

Diane is speaking quickly and conspiratorially. 'I don't know what's going on right now. That guy's still alive back there. What's he done with Ann-Marie? I'm telling the police. Show them that secret door. I'm going on Twitter with this. Everyone has to know. Vairi's a better person for you to stay with. I mean, Kirsty's off her head. Like I say. Angela's gonna be absolutely ragin'.' She touches Lauren's shoulder. 'I'll tell them all you're safe though.' She goes to the doorstep to ring the bell and stops. 'One more thing.'

Lauren's aching head feels light. 'Huh?'

'D'you remember, you know – Ann-Marie says she was talking to you about . . . your mum? Do you remember that? Your mum? How it happened? Anything?' Diane looks panicked.

Lauren searches for the answer Diane wants to hear, but nothing comes and she shakes her head. Diane sighs and rings the doorbell. Vairi appears, looking flustered behind the glass. Her dogs bustle at her feet.

'You found her!' Vairi chirps as the dogs burst out on to the crazy paving and start growling at Lola. 'Get inside, girl,' Vairi says to Lauren. 'You've had us worried sick.' She turns to Diane. 'Kirsty's having kittens. She feels terrible. I have to say I gave her a good talking to.' Lauren feels enveloped by guilt. 'So,' Vairi continues, 'how'd you find her?'

'I was looking for Ann-Marie. In the woods at the back of mine.'

'Is that right? She might have gone back to Edinburgh, do you think?'

'No, she couldna've. Listen, I've got to get away and talk to the police.' Diane has half her body turned to the gate. Now the day is getting lighter, Lauren can see how pale she looks.

'How – how's she not in Edinburgh?'

Diane sighs impatiently. 'I'd know. She said she'd meet me.'

'Well. Girls will be girls. She's maybe got some fella down there.'

Diane takes a few steps to the gate. '*No.* Well, maybe, but no. I do know.' She pushes back her clammy hair and looks at Vairi straight on. 'I do know. I mean – she couldna've. Also, we've been friends since we were six years old. It doesn't make sense. Now, if you don't mind . . .'

'OK, look, keep your hair on. I know we're all worried here. Are you not coming inside?'

Diane tips her head back and gives the lead a tug. 'No, I've got to tell the police and other people and I've got Lola.' The dog looks tired.

'Right, yes. OK. And you've got school and all. Well, I can take care of this one. Thank you, my dear. Get yourself warm. You've done a good thing. If you need to come back, come back.'

'OK.' Diane begins to walk away, but before she reaches the garden gate, Lauren runs to give her a hug. She knows Diane won't be leaving for school.

'C'mon, now. They'll find him.' Vairi leads Lauren up the musty staircase to a spare bedroom with flowery brown wallpaper.

'Who?'

'Your dad. Who else?'

Lauren sits down on a flouncy bed and dips her fingers in a pink bowl of dried petals on the bedside cabinet. The smell of the basement comes swirling back to her.

'Where is he?' she asks.

Vairi shakes her head. 'I'm telling you, I'm about to try and find out, if you're patient. Leave that. You're freezing,' she says. 'Take off your socks and give your feet a rub, so you don't get chilblains, eh? Get under the covers too.' She finds Lauren a towel and runs her a hot bath in the kelp-green bathroom. 'Look there,' Vairi jokes, trying to raise a smile. 'You're using all my hot water!'

19

When Niall wakes up he can barely open his eyes. His head is rusty with pain. It takes him a moment to realize he is still strapped into the frozen pickup. Someone is battering his window. He stays where he is. There is a muffled, female voice on the other side of the glass. 'Niall. Niall.' Groggily, he opens the truck door and staggers out into the sharp morning sun.

Kirsty is bundled in her bumblebee ski jacket. Her eyes are watery and pale and her breath comes out in clouds as she speaks. 'Niall. The hell. Lauren had to come to ours last night. And she got lost. It's been terrible. Now she's at Vairi's. Come inside, come on.' She guides him into his house and piles a heavy tartan blanket over his shoulders. Niall coughs violently, doubling over on the sofa by the dinner table when he thinks he might be sick. He gets up and begins to stoke the boiler.

Kirsty keeps talking breathlessly through the kitchen hatch. 'Lauren didn't know what was going on and she went looking for you. Something awful's happened.'

'What?' Niall coughs again. 'Fuck. Is Lauren OK? I'm a piece of shit.'

'Look. She's at Vairi's. I went to check on her, but Vairi says she's sleeping. Sit down and I'll get some food ready. Diane found her in the goddamn woods up there. She's fine. I'm sure she's fine. Have you got any Lemsip?'

'No.' He feels relief knowing Lauren is safe and wishes he weren't in such a state. Guilt crashes down around him.

'Tea, then. Paracetamol.' She calls through and he hears her open the cupboard. 'Porridge. Whatever.' There is the sound of running water, a pan clanking.

When it's ready, she scoops the steaming porridge into two bowls and joins Niall at the dinner table in the living room. After a couple of mouthfuls, she looks him straight in the eyes and says, 'The thing is, we can't find Ann-Marie.'

'How d'you mean?' His mouth feels dry.

'I *mean*, we can't find her. She's done a runner. She's not at home.'

'Fuck me.' He pushes the bowl aside and sinks his head into the crook of his elbow. 'Fuck *me*.'

'What?'

'Have you tried calling her?' Niall replies. This doesn't feel real.

'Not me personally. Has anyone tried calling you?'

He takes out his phone. 'Missed calls from Lauren. *Fuck*.'

'Never mind, she's fine now. Safe in her bed. The state of you, Niall. What the hell happened?'

He pushes the remaining porridge into a clump. 'I fell asleep in the car.'

'How'd that happen?' He can't tell if she looks worried or suspicious.

'Tired. Drank too much, if I'm honest.' He tries to change the subject, but flounders. 'So Lauren's with Vairi then. What the hell happened?' He feels as though Kirsty isn't telling him something.

'It's a long story,' Kirsty says and looks over at Jameson whining. 'If he's not been fed, then I'll feed him.' She doesn't wait for a reply and gets up to find the dog food, looking around the darkened room as she goes back to the kitchen.

Any normal parent would go and take care of their child. He feels powerless, seeing the room as it must look to her, the layer of dust on the rose quartz, the crystals by the window and the empty bottles by the fireplace. The squashed daddy long-legs on the glass doors that he has never washed off.

'Jeez,' he says. 'I canna take all this in. How did you let Lauren go looking for me? How could you?'

'I was out till all hours looking for Ann-Marie, you know, Niall.' There's a sharper tone to her voice; he can tell she's been hiding it. 'I'm not a full-time childminder. We need to talk. When all this is over. The search, I mean. Because you're not well.'

Niall shakes his head. Kirsty sounds like someone from Christine's family. He eats a little more of the hot porridge, which tastes smoother than he makes it. His stomach roils. He wants to go to bed, pull the covers over his head and start again. Jameson barks at something outside. The day is bright and dry. The clouds are moving fast.

He hears her set the dog food on the kitchen floor and Jameson scampers over.

'She'll be with Diane or those lot.' He speaks loudly with his mouth full, trying to find the best way to reassure her, ignoring the dread in his bones. 'Thank you for this, by the way.' His hand is shaking, holding the spoon.

'No, she's not, Niall. She's not with Diane.'

'She'll be fine.' *Who are you trying to kid*, he thinks to himself. He can't deal with this before he has had some more sleep. Then he'll pick up Lauren. His shoulder aches where he has been hunched asleep in the cold pickup.

Kirsty comes out of the kitchen and picks up her jacket.

'But I'll give you a hand trying to find her if you want,' Niall continues. 'Once my head clears. *Fuck.*'

She looks at him for a second too long and says goodbye.

20

At noon, Lauren wakes up from a dead sleep. Vairi is sitting neatly on the edge of the bed, picking a stray thread from her tartan skirt. Lauren can smell talcum powder mixed with the old lavender smell of the sheets.

'Kirsty's found your dad,' Vairi says. 'But he's not in the best state.'

Relief pours through Lauren like the opening of a canal lock. 'Where was he?'

'They found him in his car.'

She feels exhausted all over again.

'Man needs to look after himself. What a carry-on. Never, ever, go out like that again. Kirsty is going to give you some talking-to, let me tell you.

'I'm thinking, if you're up to it, Craig'll give you a lift to school. They'll be wondering where you are.'

Lauren is bleary, but scared too. She murmurs, 'When we were in the woods, we found a house. And there was a manny inside. Hidden. Diane's telling the police. '

Vairi stops what she is about to say and her face crinkles with shrewd curiosity. 'What did he look like?'

'It was too dark.' Lauren shakes her head at the images that fly in. When she talks, she tries to describe a photograph of the place. Still and far away from her. 'It was old. Run-down. There was no glass in the windows. Everything was broken.'

'A manny, eh? A manny. Those woods. Ten miles wide they are. Used to ride my bike round the Loop all the time as a girl. That must cover less than a quarter of that whole area, you know. Lived in the house next to Diane's. That was where my parents were. I know that track like the back of my hand, but I can't say I know about a house, no.'

'It was a different bit. Further up. Much further.'

'You should have stayed away from the likes of that.'

She remembers the sound Diane made when the man grabbed her. She focuses on a picture on the wall: a basket of puppies with a blue bow. She wants something familiar, not this strange room, with this strange woman. Eyes like the High Priestess. The classroom, with her teacher, suddenly feels safe. She remembers when they left the basement. Diane was close behind. They ran in the direction they had come from until Diane stopped and heaved up sick.

'And what's that on your thumb there?'

'Nothing,' Lauren says, covering the ring with her other hand. It's private. 'Just something I found in the woods. Jameson dug it up. It's mine.'

'Let me see that now!' Vairi's frail hand grabs Lauren's wrist with surprising strength.

'Let go!' She needs to get out of here.

'Give that. Give that here.' She yanks Lauren's arm again.

Lauren squeals as the muscles pull tight and she is in the basement again, the man's hand around Diane's leg. She twists away and the little dogs start to yap on the landing.

'Stop that. Come on now.' Vairi picks up the ring in her dainty hand and holds it close to one eye.

'I didn't find this at the house,' Lauren says. 'It was yesterday. In the snow, in the woods. A ring. Lady's ring.' She wishes the lady were here now. The way she had sat on the edge of her bed.

'Mmm. Mmm-hmm.' Vairi is silent for a while. 'You got this from the woods, you say?'

'Yes.'

'You've never seen it before?'

Lauren stays silent. It belongs to the young woman who visited.

Vairi says briskly, 'You can wait downstairs in the lounge, before Craig comes to pick you up. I've put the fire on.'

Lauren does as she is told. She sits with a heavy cardigan wrapped around her in the living room, warmed by imitation flames. She wants to go to school. Vairi is in the kitchen, clattering through the drawers and cupboards. 'I've been up all night, you know,' she says in too loud a voice. Then she says something else that Lauren can't quite hear. It sounds as though she says, 'I was talking to the wind.' In the living room Lauren picks up the binoculars on the windowsill and looks out to the forest. She can see the figures of a few people in the field. Two are laying a thin white tape across the trees. Others are getting out of a white van.

At the doily-covered dining table, Lauren eats a fried tattie scone that Vairi has laid out for her. She realizes how hungry she is, and thirsty, taking a sip of orange squash in a glass printed with the Pepsi logo. Scuttling, the rustling of the basement, comes back to her, and Diane hitting the man on the floor, the noise he made. It was as though he was already in pain; he couldn't stand up. She takes another sip. Vairi's mug also sits on the table, a miniature painting of a hedgehog and a dandelion printed on its side. Lauren touches a lily leaf in the middle of the table and realizes it is made of fabric.

Vairi fetches a large, leather-bound photo album. 'Here we go,' she says. 'Craig'll be here in a few minutes. He'll call when he's outside. He's come out of work. Let's take a look through this while we're waiting.' She goes carefully, page by page, the stiff, cellophane leaves unpeeling from each other. 'There.' She opens the album wide.

There is a picture of Lauren's father, much younger, and the woman, the woman from Ann-Marie's bathroom, her mother, glowing healthier and smiling in a white dress, cutting a tiered cake. Lauren's face feels hot. She starts to cry. Her mother's absence is always a quiet hum of sadness, but now it is so loud.

Vairi looks concerned. 'Now, now, you're a brave girl. Look on her finger, Lauren.' There it is, the blurred silver band of a ring. Lauren can make out a shape that looks like a heart.

'That's . . .' Lauren begins. 'That's my mum.'

'Oh, for heaven's sake. Have you not seen a picture of your parents' wedding? Doesn't she look like you?' Vairi's voice is dreamy. 'Anyway, anyway.' She taps her hands lightly together and pats her neatly curled hair, as if checking it's still there. 'She was always wearing that ring.'

'She's been visiting me. My mum's visiting me.'

'What did I tell you then? What did I tell you?' There is a twinkle in Vairi's eye. 'She wanted to protect you. She could tell something bad was on its way.'

The dogs bark from behind the bathroom door.

'Right, that'll be Craig, get your things ready. I've got to make a phone call.'

As Lauren pulls on her coat, Vairi picks up the phone, gesturing goodbye. Lauren watches Billy's father's car pull up in the driveway as she listens in to the phone call. 'Oh, hello, Vairi Grant here. Well, I'm calling because I have found a small ring. Ah, no. No. Now listen, I'm not calling about lost property. I think this could be a useful piece of evidence. No, I know about all that. But I'm talking about the disappearance of Christine Mackay.'

In the first days of baby Lauren's arrival, Niall was a blissful fool. People from the village dropped by. Their newborn was a wrinkled thing. He didn't always like to remember that sleepless time. It was too happy. In fact, he only really remembers when he drinks. It frees him and it traps him. If Lauren is around he will hug her tightly and kiss the top of her head.

The doorbell rings and he staggers up. Two policemen are standing on his doorstep, saying they would like to ask him a few questions. He invites them in. They do not want any tea.

'We're here to ask you about Ann-Marie,' one man says. He is large and nearly bald, with an uncertain expression.

'Ann-Marie?' He makes himself sound surprised, then realizes it's a bad idea.

'She's been reported missing.'

'Yeah. I heard. I'm very sorry to hear that.' Niall pulls his mouth tight in sympathy. 'And thank you for finding my kid.' He is mumbling.

'We didn't, sir. She was found by a Diane Armstrong and then brought to Vairi Grant, I believe.'

Of course he knows that. Craig phoned him to say he had taken her to school. He wishes he had had a better sleep and was a better parent.

'Regarding Ann-Marie, we understand that last night you gave her a lift. Is that right?'

So they know. 'I did.'

'Had this been planned in advance?'

'No . . . not at all . . . I bumped into her in the shop.'

'Which one?'

'Spar.' He feels sick.

'Feeling a bit forgetful this morning?' the other policeman says, raising a faint eyebrow. He is small and red-haired with freckly skin. Niall wonders if he is the son of someone he has worked for.

'No,' says Niall. 'Yes, I had forgotten actually. When I first woke up, not long ago. But then it came back to me. My memory isn't what it was, these days. Like a sieve.' He doesn't bother to attempt a smile.

'*Uh*-huh,' the smaller policeman says and writes diligently on a notepad. Niall does not remember their names, but he knows that they do not believe him. He doesn't want to feel like a small animal in a trap.

'Aye,' the bald one continues. 'And?'

'And that's about it, really. I took her home. To her parents.' His voice is even, matter-of-fact. He tries to stay calm, but panic is rising.

'Her parents didna see her last night.'

Niall lets out a long, shaky breath. 'Well, that's about it, as I say.'

'Thank you, Niall. So, to the best of your ability, please tell us in full what happened last night.'

'I'm so sorry. Can you remind me of your names, officers?'

The bald man exchanges a quick look with his colleague and says, 'Officer Cameron.'

'Officer Cameron,' repeats Niall with a nod.

'Officer Morrison,' says the red-haired man.

'Officer Morrison. Officer Cameron. Thank you. Well. I was at the Spar.'

'Yup.'

'And she was there. Ann-Marie.'

'Whereabouts in the Spar did you see her?'

'The drinks aisle.'

'The *alcoholic* section?' says Cameron. He glances at his colleague, who is writing.

'Yes.'

'And you knew she was under age?'

'Yeah. I wasn't expecting to see her. Didn't notice her at first.'

The conversation lapses and the red-haired policeman jots something else down on his pad. 'And what were you buying?'

'She was trying to buy wine, I think.'

'What were you buying?'

'Some food and a few bottles, like.'

He nods and writes. 'A few bottles. And, if you don't mind us asking, Niall, did you buy her any alcohol?'

'No, no, I didn't. I told her that she was too young, and she shouldn't be buying that stuff. Kids grow up too early these days.' He wets his lips. Why does he sound guilty, even when he tells the truth? 'Sorry.'

'Right,' says the red-haired policeman. Niall has forgotten his name already.

He stares at his hands and hears the sound of pencils scratching. He scrapes his chair back a little.

'And so,' says Morrison or Cameron, 'you took her back.'

'No, wait. Sorry. I remember more clearly now. She said she was meeting her dad when I offered her a lift. Then I left her in the shop. I don't know if she had alcohol in her backpack. I saw her on her own. Outside at the bus stop. And gave her a lift in the end.' Inside his boot, the toes of his left foot curl.

'Right, so you don't know if she had any alcohol?'

'No, that's right, I don't.'

'OK. And what was she wearing, when you saw her?'

'I . . . I canna mind. Light jacket, I think. Her hair is shorter now. She – was wearing a hat. I—' He runs a hand over his head. 'Couldn't see her hair.'

'Uh-huh. What kind of hat then?'

When Niall tries to think back there are blank spaces. Ann-Marie is now missing. A blank space. 'A woolly hat.'

'We are searching the woods to see if we can find her. A bit about you then. What is your relationship with Ann-Marie?'

'Relationship? How do you mean?' The room feels unsteady.

'Describe your relationship with Ann-Marie.'

'She's my neighbour's kid.' Again, he makes sure to sound reasonable, helpful.

'OK. And did you see her often?'

'No.' He looks towards the window like some kind of escape route.

'When was the last time you saw her? Before the supermarket.'

'It was just the Spar. I canna mind, y'know. Maybe in the summer.'

'She's your neighbour's kid and that was the last time you saw her?'

'She's at that school in Edinburgh. No. Hang on. I last seen her when she was looking after my kid, Lauren, and Ann-Marie took her back to hers. I was playing a ceilidh that night.'

'When did Ann-Marie babysit your daughter?' Their eyes are so trained on him that they stop his own gaze from wandering.

'The other night,' Niall says.

'Specifically.'

'I'll have to check. Last Tuesday I think it was. Ceilidh up at the castle.' He scratches the hair on his forearm.

'So, back to last night, she got into your car and then what?'

'I dropped her off home.'

'Did you see her parents?'

Niall feels an itch of impatience. 'No.' The truth is he can't remember the events in sequence very well. He stopped earlier than he should have. He got angry.

He goes through as many details as he can, all the time wondering how he sounds to them. They thank him for his time, without emotion, and when they shut the door, he remembers he did not drive her all the way home. There was the passing place. He remembers watching the ice blue of her anorak disappear in the rear-view mirror. He has failed, again. He goes to the cupboard and pours himself a large vodka, and then another.

Back when Christine lived in the house, his friends would tell him privately, when they were drunk enough, that she was out of her tree. Her strange, bright clothes and hair that frequently changed colour. Silver rings and a bar in her ear. A nose stud. She may well have been beamed in from the Starship *Enterprise*. There were men who fancied her too; he knew that. Fascinated by her, or the idea of her, at least. Thought she was up to something kinky in the bedroom and they were almost right.

After she left he had the word *Forever* tattooed on the left side of his ribcage. In recent years, the boys have often told him that he needs to move on. He would reply, 'But who is there? But who *is* there?' and they would leave him be. Who was there? Not the GP Catriona, he's decided, sick with guilt. She doesn't even come close.

After Christine disappeared he flew into rages, real rages, and saw how, in all their years together, he had only pretended to be angry. Shaking, he would have to pull over into a lay-by. Or sit down on one of the chairs by the supermarket checkout while the world turned white. One time, when Lauren was at school, he took an axe to a fence post. Another time he took his axe into the woods at dusk and swung it hard against a tree and birds exploded into flight from the branches above. He drove the pickup out to the woods and built a bonfire as big as he could make it. He burnt junk and tyres. He burnt a guy. He played metal. He felt as though he was turning into a werewolf.

A doctor came to visit and recommended counselling, but he refused. By that time his father was beginning to show signs of illness. Niall would drive forty minutes to visit him and watch daytime TV in silence. He remembers talking to his father once about Christine's disappearance. They preferred not to mention these things.

These days, he doesn't want any more reminders. His work is erasure. He has his own medicine. He is OK. But occasionally still he finds himself on his knees.

At one o'clock Lauren's class form a queue by the door to say grace. Lauren has arrived just in time, red-faced and tired. Their teacher starts the prayer in a hushed tone while the children stay silent until the final line.

> 'Some hae meat and canna eat,
> And some wad eat that want it,
> But we hae meat and we can eat,
> Sae let the Lord be Thankit!'

When Lauren opens her eyes, she notices the tip of Mrs Gray's nose is pink and her eye make-up a little smudged. The word about Ann-Marie has spread fast.

The class walks in a crocodile across the car park to the shiny new high-school canteen. She and Billy usually queue up at the hot counter, but she doesn't see him today. She sits next to Jenny and her friends who let her eat with them but don't pay her much attention. Jenny is talking about a boy band on the talent show the night before.

Lauren sighs and picks at her pizza slice. Her eyes feel red raw. The adrenaline has not quite gone. She feels too alert.

'Did you not like them, Lauren? It was honestly so good. But the judges coulda been nicer, I thought. Especially Simon.'

'No, she's upset because it's, you know . . . that girl,' one says.

Lauren shrugs and takes another bite of her pizza. She doesn't know if she wants to be like them, and wear their clothes, or if they are idiots. 'Yeah. Kinda. My neighbour.'

'She went to the high school?' Jenny asks.

Lauren shakes her head. 'No, she *goes* to school down in Edinburgh, but she's pals with Diane Armstrong?'

The girls nod uncertainly and Lauren shifts in her seat. She can see they are dying to talk about it, but not in front of her. She finishes her pizza and gets to her feet, a little unsteady. 'See you guys later.'

The light outside is turning dusky as she makes her way along the walkway back to the primary school. Something hits the back of her head. She doesn't look round or slow her pace but sees a bread roll bounce to the grass verge. She is about to turn into the car park when she hears running footsteps. Someone behind her covers her eyes with their hands. A child, but a strong child. Another twists her arms back.

'Hey!' Maisie's bright voice is close to her ear. 'Do you know what a Chinese burn is?'

She feels Maisie's cold hands wrap around her wrist and twist the skin in opposite directions. She struggles for the knife in her pocket, using her whole body to lunge away, but they pull harder and her body bends back.

'Want a shower?' she hears Maisie say, while another girl crows. The edge of a thermos appears in the corner of her eye. Something warm and viscous gloops over her face and into her nostrils. Little chunks settle in the hollows of her eyes and ears.

'We found that rabbit by your house. Your dad cut its head off.'

'Is it true you eat them?'

'He better watch out. The police'll be on to him this time. Everyone's saying it.'

'Rabbit killer,' Maisie says.

'You know those girls tell stories about your mum,' the other girl chips in. 'They're trying not to let you hear.'

Lauren coughs up carrot chunks and tries to twist away blind, her face stinging.

'We all know he did it, Lauren. Everybody knows.' They have stopped pinning her arms back and are standing close behind her, explaining matter-of-factly. 'You know it, don't you? Tell your dad we know.'

Lauren jams her hand in her right coat pocket for her knife, but it's empty, the same as the left. She feels the nub of a shoe close to her heel and stomps on it, hard, feeling the ridges of toes crunch flat. She turns around and wipes soup off her face with one hand while the other shoots out and rips out a small hank of Maisie's hair. She begins to run fast down the open walkway, away from the howling. Her footsteps reverberate and her breath comes out in gulps. Her fists are hot with sticky soup and hair.

'*I'm gonna curse you. I'm gonna curse you,*' she repeats breathlessly until she reaches the cloakroom entrance.

'Hie, Lauren!' Billy walks out of the double doors with another boy, David. They are wrapped up in football scarves and hats. He runs to her. 'What's happened?'

'Maisie.' Rage is pulsing through her. Her own hair, thick with green gunk, could crawl off her head like an animal.

'Honestly, enough's enough.' He looks over at his friend.

'We'll find them. I don't hit girls, but you know. We're gonna bloody find them,' David says.

Lauren's anger flickers at his tone, this other boy, repeating something he has heard, something he ought to say. She smiles a fake smile, driving down anger and embarrassment and freezing it. She can feel the clump of Maisie's hair growing sticky in her hand. 'My dad's gonna go mental,' she says. She can see excitement flare in David's eyes.

Billy looks at her a second and says, 'Here.' He pulls off his Aberdeen beanie and thrusts it at her.

'What?'

'Just till you get to the toilets, so they don't see. Go on.'

She beams at him, scrunching the soup out of her hair. 'Thanks. I'll wash it for you.'

'Go,' Billy says.

On her way to the cloakrooms, in the hot hat, Lauren checks her pockets again, but her knife is gone. She tries to remember the last time she used it.

By the time Niall leaves the house at lunchtime, the sky is darkening and the air has a sharp bite. He stops at the Spar and walks past the cereal to the top of the booze aisle in a daze, staring at the labels.

'Niall.' Jill, the woman who served him last night, comes out of the back room behind him, pushing aside heavy strips of clear plastic that hang in the doorway. He hadn't realized she knows his name. He nods.

'Y'allright?' she says as one startled syllable.

'Yes, thank you. You?'

'Have you heard about wee Ann-Marie?' She jerks her chin to the door, the outside.

'Aye.'

'I was telling Aileen, who's at the till the now, mind when you were in here? Mind . . . she was in here too.'

'Aye.'

'And you left together.' She is serious now, giving space to the words.

'Sorry?' Was she the one who reported him to the police? He remembers how he left the shop and got into his car. He was alone. His heart is beating fast. He left the shop alone.

'Mind yesterday evening. Yous left together.'

'We didna . . . Jill. Yes, I bumped into her in the shop.' He needs to sound calm and show none of the fury he feels. Treat it as a joke. 'We didn't *leave together*.' He tries to laugh.

'Ah. Did you not?' She turns and walks into the next aisle, where he hears her voice. 'Are you wanting any vodka?'

'What?'

'Ah. OK then.'

'Fuckssake,' Niall says and leaves the shop.

21

As they eat their mince and tatties that night Lauren feels so exhausted she could drop head first on to her plate. This afternoon was a struggle. She almost fell asleep at her desk. The thought of Ann-Marie has kept her awake. She says to Niall, 'Maybe I could make some posters? Do they have a photo of Ann-Marie or I could draw a picture?'

'No.' Niall shakes his head. 'Don't worry. No, no. They're doing posters.' He doesn't know this for certain yet, but he is sure someone will soon. 'I think, love, just between you and me, it's best we don't get too involved.'

'Dad?'

'Look. You know what they're like round here, they're all at it, gabbing away about us—'

'Dad! She could be . . . she could be . . .' She looks down at her plate, willing the tears to shrink back into her eyes, wanting to knock it to the floor.

'The police know what they're doing, love, OK? I'm just thinking about us as a family, what's best for us. What's best for you. C'mon, toots, eh? C'mon.

You look like you're about to pass out and it's only half past six.'

Lauren's head swims as she looks at the peas embedded in the hill of mince. She remembers Maisie's words and the way that woman sat on their sofa close to where she is sitting now, and the way she has vanished. Like a ghost. She remembers Vairi said Christine would come back to protect her. She remembers the circle of stones she made for Ann-Marie on the beach when she was little. Lauren tries to imagine the woman as Christine, even though she looks both too young and too haggard, and it's hard. She steals a long look at her father, watching his jaw work the meat. Then she gets up to go to bed. She feels sick with exhaustion.

'That's it. You did well to go to school today. You need to keep warm. I'll put some more coal in the boiler.'

As she gets up, her legs feel wobbly. 'Have people told her boyfriend?' she asks at the foot of the stairs.

'She's got a boyfriend?' Niall calls back from the table.

'Yeah. I can't remember his name, but I saw this photo of them, on a beach.' Could he hurt a person?

Niall comes to help her up to bed. 'Where does he stay?'

'He's called Rory, I think, and he's maybe at Ann-Marie's school. I'm not sure. She didn't want anyone to know.'

'Don't worry about all that now,' he says, handing her her pyjamas. 'I'll take care of it.'

Once he's sure Lauren has fallen asleep, Niall, having second thoughts, drives back to the shop and buys a bottle of Glenfiddich, two packets of crisps and a new Disney magazine for his daughter. It's just gone eight. He is a methodical shopper. Sometimes he catches himself tracing a thumb over the drink label. Luckily Jill and Aileen are no longer on their shift.

Back at home, he checks on Lauren and puts the magazine by her bedside, pouring himself a dram downstairs. He can't face talking to Angela so he phones Kirsty. She tells him that Cherie at the petrol station has told her the police have interviewed two girls in the village. They mentioned this boyfriend but don't know much about him.

'They're working fast, aren't they?' he says.

Lauren sleeps for a while, then wakes up needing the bathroom, in a strange state of exhaustion and anxiety. She turns on the light, realizing only a couple of hours have passed. For a moment, the magazine on her bedside table makes her smile, then the sense of helplessness slides back. The day runs through her head, relentlessly, as the murmur of her father on the living-room phone drifts up from downstairs. She remembers Maisie, shoving her, then the strands of hair she grabbed as she fled.

She locks herself in the bathroom with the spae-wife's book and lights a candle for Ann-Marie, carving her wish for her return into the wax before she burns it.

She shivers when she thinks of Ann-Marie out there, somewhere, and wishes over and over again that someone or something will keep her safe.

Next, her anger still raw, she washes the clump of Maisie's hair under the tap, and, wringing it dry, drops it into one of the Ziploc bags her father uses for guitar strings and screws. Lauren leaves the hair carefully by the soap dish and writes sleepily on a piece of paper: *I hereby freeze Maisie and her friends to bind them from causing me harm.* She folds the paper, puts it next to the hair and fills the pouch with water.

Her heart starts to beat fast as she creeps down to the living room and sees her father passed out on the sofa, his mouth open, snoring. She thinks about making a spell for her father, but decides against it. This evening has been enough.

She makes her way through to the utility room and sees that the dripping has stopped. She opens the chest freezer and its light shines out into the dingy room, illuminating frozen rabbit meat and polythene bags of vegetables. She slides the Ziploc bag behind an old box of raspberry ripple ice cream, something her father does not enjoy, and closes the freezer lid. She promises herself that when the bullying stops, she will take the bag out to thaw and bury it with a releasing spell. In the meantime, the freezing must happen.

Close to ten o' clock, long after Lauren has fallen fast asleep once more, the doorbell rings, startling Niall on the sofa. It's the police again. Today, they searched the woods and are examining a dilapidated house, after a tip-off from a young member of the public who came across a secret annexe. Diane, Kirsty told him, has put something on social media that has been shared thousands of times. Niall only has a vague idea of what this really means. The police are interviewing a man found on the premises and have found *human remains*. The words don't click into place. He clings on to fragments of sentences. *Female.* They were *fast-tracked to a lab.* He wonders if Angela and Malcolm know.

The police pause. 'And we're sorry to bother you so late, but we're working against the clock and wanted to talk to you before anyone else, reporters and the like, do.' Their voices are smoothed out, softened.

'OK, sure,' says Niall, trying to figure out what they are getting at.

They tell him that the DNA does not match Ann-Marie's DNA and the search for Ann-Marie must continue. He breathes out.

The DNA, they continue, matches with Christine Mackay, his wife. He tries to understand but his brain has slowed. He goes to the kitchen and eyes four fingers of whisky in the bottle under the sink. He pours a glass.

'Niall, if we may . . .' The policeman's voice reminds him of laminate flooring, flat and colourless. 'Our forensic team found the remains – bones, to be precise – of your wife Christine, deep underground. We had her DNA on file and it is an exact match. Therefore, her status has changed from that of a missing person to deceased. We are sorry to tell you that her skull suffered trauma.'

'She was wearing a blue dress that day.'

'We have not yet found evidence of clothing in the basement. There was a dressing gown near the door. We have to tell you that while we have taken in a man for questioning, you remain a suspect in this case and we are going through your interviews on file. If you want to say anything else, now is the time. We will set up another interview with you at a later date. We're currently running tests. And we have this ring now as potential evidence.' They put a silver Claddagh ring on the table in a clear plastic wallet. 'It was handed in by your daughter today. But she says she found it earlier and didn't tell anyone. Can you tell us, Niall, if this belongs to your late wife, Christine?'

'Yes,' says Niall. 'My daughter. Why didn't she tell me?'

'Are you sure?'

Niall's muscles are contracting. 'And any other DNA?' he says flatly. 'Any other DNA. You found that? Someone else?'

'We've found separate DNA evidence, yes, but it is inconclusive. At this moment in time. We'd like to take a fresh sample of your DNA.'

He holds his emotions on a tight leash. 'You don't still have me on file?'

'I'm sure we have. It's just to make sure everything's as up to date as it can be. We offer our sincere condolences, Mr Mackay, but we hope that you can find solace in this information, however small.'

She had not gone far. She had not deserted him.

'We'll keep you updated with more details as soon as we have confirmation. The press are already getting wind of this, as we say, because of social media, and you may see them about – but we would ask you not to speak to them at this stage. We'll be preparing an official statement and will keep you updated. We wanted to tell you as soon as we could.'

He coughs like a wretch. 'Just so . . . Excuse me, this is a lot to take in. The annexe?'

'We cannot say much about the annexe we described as we want to interview you about it later. But we have reason to suspect . . . that she had been held there. Against her will.'

Niall stays motionless, the words sloshing through his head like blood. 'I don't know anything about it, I can tell you that now.'

'We appreciate you may need a moment. We hope you can understand that we need to see . . . if there's some kind of link between Ann-Marie's disappearance' – the policeman raises his eyebrows – 'and Christine's. Have you any idea?'

'No, as I said before, I don't, officer.'

'Then we would like you to describe the nature of your relationship with your wife.'

'We loved each other,' he says. 'I loved her, so much.' His eyes are warm and wet. 'I want you to know that.'

'Who, can you remember, was the last person to see Christine alive?'

A woman who lived by the beach, Clarice Egbert, had seen Christine for a therapy appointment. Christine would sit facing her clients in plastic doctor's chairs in a windowless room. The room was part of an old building in the square above a gift shop that sold toys wrapped in cellophane. In this room she would make them go through a process of tapping. The room was mauve. Niall painted it a shade called 'Recuperate' and built the shelves around the edge for candles and a cabinet for the CD player. The man who rented the room was a friend of Sandy's and let her use it for next to nothing.

'Thank you for your answers, Niall. We know you would have been asked this before, but did you ever argue?'

He looks over at the sliding door. He wants it to open. He wants her to walk through. 'No. Well, you know, only the usual.' Somehow any disagreement they had now seems significant.

It is true that Christine was distant sometimes and they'd gone through periods in the four years they were together, not of arguments, but of silence. It would happen after his worst moments, the times he called her a whacko, a quack and once – and he winced at this – that she was exploiting vulnerable people. He didn't think she ever forgave him for that one.

He remembers a book about wolves she owned and loved. A book about wolves and wild women. She could spend whole days walking in the woods without him. Or she would hold Lauren and say, 'I want her to be wild.' She used to build bonfires.

Before this, when she was heavily pregnant, she argued with him about birthing methods. She wanted to be 'free' of the hospital. He knew it scared her. She tried to eat natural foods and talked about 'chemicals' as if they were poison. She had a fear of her body being pushed into certain positions on the hospital bed. Of not being in control. She insisted on a home birth. He invoked God and the Lord Jesus Christ. 'You realize, don't you, you nutter, they'll have to helicopter you to the hospital if anything goes wrong?' he said.

There was so much testing of each other, pushing each other, so much that was fierce. So much shouting. He thinks of it now as passion rising from their words. He never admitted he loved that she was crazy. She didn't care about anyone's opinion of her, let alone his.

'And, just so we're clear, Christine was the mother of your daughter Lauren?' A voice comes out of the ether. He nods.

In the course of the conversation he answers some of their questions with a few words, and in answer to others a story comes pouring out of somewhere, bringing details he thought he had forgotten about, like driftwood.

He remembers that, as a baby, Lauren liked looking at the therapy CD covers. One had a picture of dolphins, another was a picture of a sunset and a third was the Tibetan mountains. Lauren's favourite was the clàrsach album, an instrument Christine said she would learn one day. Niall remembers berating her: 'Whatever you play, for God's sake lay off the pan pipes.' There could be times when he felt as though all they did was pretend to hate each other. Secretly he dreamt that she would play the clàrsach for him.

When there were not enough massage or alternative-therapy appointments, Christine started to read palms and tarot cards. The pack she used was battered. She kept it in a blue velvet pouch decorated with gold stars. It must be knocking around the house somewhere now. All these things she used must be. Niall had refused to let her work from their home. He suspects she used her crystal ball too, and black obelisks, but didn't tell him. She worked from the therapy room and at the castle sometimes to entertain guests, and at fairs. He hated seeing her dress up for the occasion in her strange clothes and jewellery. It is easy to remember what annoyed him about her. She used to say, *The lungs hold grief.* He called her Mystic Meg and Rafiki. She called him Ozzy and Nigel, after the front man from *Spinal Tap*.

'And can you tell us a bit about the type of therapy Christine practised?' the bald policeman asks. Niall isn't fully aware of how much he has answered aloud and how much he has kept silent.

He has some understanding of her therapy techniques. She was nineteen then. Niall used to worry that male tourists would pick up her card and think she offered more than a massage. Yet her only clients seemed to be retired women with flowery scarves who kept their grey hair long. Christine would say that there was trauma inside them. Her therapy took their trauma into her and cleansed them of it. Whenever she spoke about this to Niall they argued.

First she would tap the top of the client's head, then under their eyes, then above their mouth, under their mouth, under their breast bone and below their armpits (*The lungs hold grief*). These were points that caused 'energy blockages'. The client all the while would be saying words that came to mind, words connected to what was troubling them. It was called Emotional Freedom Technique.

In their early days, she showed him this. She told him how it was unhealthy to bottle up memories and pretend that painful things didn't exist. He needed to let his emotions out into the air, otherwise they would rot inside him, making him sick. She asked him to mirror her, tap his own head, before moving down his face to his ribcage. *The lungs hold grief.* It was some kind of mad ritual. He felt like an ape, scratching itself under the armpits, and he remembers doing an impression: *Is this* The Jungle Book *now, love?* He rugby-tackled her on to the bed and she pushed him back, saying that if he couldn't take things seriously, she would stop showing him.

When she found there were not enough traumatized tourists to keep her in the black, she bought a therapy bed and increased the massages. Niall tried to stop her, saying he could support them. He didn't want her touching other men. She said she wanted to help people. She would rather massage an attractive young man, she said, but she had yet to meet one. She was still spending her time helping old ladies with their back problems.

'And,' says Morrison, whose name is starting to stick, 'do you remember anything more about the day she went missing?'

He can't remember the day. The white day. Absolute white. The day he'd tried his best to describe to the police once before. The day that felt as if there was no colour and the significance of things became untethered in fog. He'd felt as though he was floating somewhere frozen and blanched, while she evaporated. There was nothing truly surrounding him. This world showed its true self: not a place for him after all and not a place of any kindness. Any kindness in the sort of quantity that could ever match her absence: the horror and the cruelty of it. If it wasn't for Lauren, he would be dead by now.

Phone calls on that day, the day she disappeared, and the days following, lit up like lightning against cloud. The sound of a phone sent electric currents up his white spine. Always the doorbell, never the key in the lock. And she never came home and she never came home. White days, like being high in the mountains without oxygen, without breath, a tightness in the lungs and baby Lauren in her cot.

Angela Walker was so distant in the days after the disappearance. Kirsty and Craig rallied round to take care of the baby. Angela never spoke to Niall about Christine's disappearance and yet he overheard her once when she was queuing in front of him at the bakery, gossiping with another woman. 'It's been simply awful,' she said to the lady, as if Niall's grief somehow belonged to her. 'She was my best friend.'

Niall wanted to spit in her face for such a pile of shite. He carried on doing odd jobs for the family, unable to turn down work, but her braying voice on that day stayed with him.

Seemingly satisfied, the police leave into the night, thanking him for his time. He barely registers their departure. He straightens himself on the chair and, for the first time, he tries Christine's technique now at the kitchen table, hitting his ribs. He is glad he can't see himself in the mirror. To his surprise, his face screws up of its own accord.

If you do this long enough, you might find you laugh, yawn or cry . . .

Something strange is happening. He feels his mouth opening. His expression changes to that of a howling baby, a silent scream. Something starts to open up and things come flooding back. He keeps hitting his sides, relentlessly, the grief coming through his face, until he feels exhausted. He takes a deep breath and steadies himself at the table. The tea is cold now; his face is wet. He remembers the night he saw Christine again.

She was so close by. The softness of the headlights flood back to him and he saw her body emerging from the passing place. He remembers how beautiful she looked, how alive. He remembers what she smelled like when he saw her again, how he thought himself mad. How bruised she was and how cold. The thought of it makes him weep some more. When he gently washed her hair with the shower. Her beautiful hair. The curls of it through his fingers. How he held her and washed her and how he washed away blood and teeth fell out, and he was crying. Her bones as thin as a rabbit's. Her sad blue eyes looking at him again. He can think this without questioning any of it. The *how*. Just the anxious joy of being with her again. The way he tried to make her safe again. He never wanted to stop holding her. This shivering woman was different from the one who had grown in his memory.

In her dream that night, Lauren makes her way downstairs again in blinding sunlight. It shines through her hair and she wonders if she is in heaven. She notices a strange smell coming from the utility room and opens the chest freezer, leaking mist.

Inside are frosted flowers, tulips, roses and mari-
golds growing out of glittering crushed ice. She
pushes back their icy stems and sees Ann-Marie,
curled in a ball underneath, her head tilted up, her
skin faintly blue like a Smurf. She is wearing the
crown of the High Priestess as she sleeps.

Niall lies awake, the edges of his eyes raw, his heart
beating like a trapped bat.

He heaves himself out of the bed and takes the
key to the living room that is always kept locked. It
is so neat in there: a yellow sofa and a circular coffee
table, facing a stone fireplace he installed himself.
There is a framed poster from an Edinburgh art
exhibition they went to; a tie-dye dress draped over
the sofa. In the middle of the floor are two cardboard
boxes. He touches the dress, entwining his fingers
around its thin spaghetti straps, and holds it to his
chest in a bundle. He buries his face in the fabric
and whispers, 'Christine, I'm here, Christine. Come
and see me.' He looks around, then places the dress
carefully back on the sofa, as if it is frail.

From the next box he takes out her crystals and
midnight-blue candles and lights them. *Christine.*
I'm here, Christine. I want to see you. He lets the
candles flicker in the dark room. He slides out a
photo album and peels through the pages. All his
pictures of Christine are in this room and Lauren
has never seen them. He used to tell himself she

was too young. That she would only miss her if she saw her smiling face. Her face and her Claddagh ring on her slender hand.

He stares deep into one flame and holds the glassy stones in purple, amber and green. 'I know,' he breathes, 'I know somewhere you'll be laughing at me. But for the love of God come to me. I'm ready for you. Come to me.'

He crouches like a lump of rock until his shins and spine ache. There is a rustle outside the window, but it passes. A full moon shines fit to bust in the black.

He sinks into the armchair that she used to love to read in. He takes a deep breath and shuts his eyes. Once again he tries to feel her here, with all his concentration. *Please*. But when he opens his eyes he is alone. The dress does not smell of her. It hasn't for years.

Back in bed, he holds the duvet tightly, twisting it in his hands, and tries to remember that what he has been desperate for has in fact happened. He tries to maintain a new feeling, that mortality can be traded, that death is finite and part of a circle.

22

When Lauren comes down for breakfast, her father is sitting with his back to her. Shiny photographs are spread all over the table. Some have fallen on the floor. When she gets close, she sees her mother. He looks up at her, tear-streaked, as if she is a strange girl in his house.

'Your mum's not coming back, Lauren, she's not coming back. Christine, your lovely mum.'

From his tone, she feels as though she has been thrown into freezing water. She pats him on the shoulder. 'Don't worry. Don't worry.' It is all she can think to say amid a world that is breaking like a huge wave around her, its force crushing.

'Why don't you stay at home today?' His voice is wobbly, unnerving.

She can't face the idea of spending the rest of the day in the house with him, so gets ready for school again. He kisses her cheek as she leaves.

She boards the bus under a faded sky, finding a place in one of the unpopular seats, close to the front. Today there is a cold, unhappy silence below the rumble of the engine. She spends the journey scanning the passing farmland, trying not to think about the basement and looking for something that could be a clue. Miniature bodies of moles hang in lines from the wire fence that runs parallel to the road. Lauren wonders at their lack of eyes. She wonders whether they smelled death if they were not able to see it. When the bus passes the brown hillside, she sees a young wildcat hidden in the broom like a gift.

The silence of the bus creeps into the classroom like a haar and, after interval, the deputy head visits the classrooms one by one. Everyone must now know about the sad disappearance of Ann-Marie Walker, she says. Who was local but not a pupil at the high school. It has been over twenty-four hours, but this does not mean they won't find her soon. Lauren struggles with the double negative, pushing her pencil lead hard into the corner of her jotter until it pierces the paper. She blots out the teacher's voice by watching the seagulls swooping and jeering outside in the clammy, dreich sky. She doodles a scraggly flower of life in the margin. Her mother's never coming back. Absences have hewn huge chunks out of the space she lives in, making it harder to breathe.

The teacher's speech interrupts her train of thought. If pupils have any questions, or information, she is saying, they can come to her office at any time. They must not attempt to try and find Ann-Marie for themselves, she warns in a tone one would use for a pixie in a glen. Lauren thinks of hands in the dark. They must stay safe and let an adult know where they are at all times. An email is going out to all parents today. And if anyone has seen anything strange on the way to Raven's Rock or near Evelix Gorge, they must let her know.

Lauren scribbles out the flower doodle and tries to draw the moon crown of the High Priestess and star lamp of the old hermit on his lonely, secretive path.

The deputy head is still speaking. There will be a community search party for Ann-Marie with posters and leaflets. If the children meet anyone who says they are a journalist, they should talk to a trusted adult first.

Lauren is one of the first to return to the classroom after break time. A white bakery box is sitting on her desk. As she gets closer she sees it is printed with the pink logo of the local bread shop. She looks around as two other pupils take their seats and lifts the lid cautiously. One black, bulging eye looks up at her in the lumpen mass of a head. She springs back. Its tawny fur is half eaten away and matted with blood. Things squirm at its neck. She slams the flimsy lid back down and looks around again, her body shaking. She opens her mouth to tell the teacher, but then freezes as Maisie and her friends enter the room. Their heads are bowed towards each other as they talk in whispers. She puts her school bag on top of the box and puts them under the table together. She feels as though she is crawling with mites. For the rest of the lesson she imagines the eyes of the rabbit, watching her feet through a crack in the box.

Niall sits motionless at the worn table. The house feels sunken. He notices how the ceiling slopes, how it needs more paint. A damp patch discolours one corner. He has flooring to fit at Catriona's: seven square metres of bathroom tiles in 'sea mist' now that he has finished up in the living room. Another job building kitchen cabinets at the high school's janitor's house will have to wait. Sandy always says Niall is too slow and too picky with his jobs. Too scattergun. If he worked more efficiently, like he does, he'd be rich by now. Niall knows it helps that Sandy is always able to get out of bed in the mornings with a clean spring in his step. Sandy says Niall has a face on him like a wounded stag.

Niall wonders now if he has been putting off doing the bathroom. White tiles always remind him. That day seemed to happen to a different, younger man, with a growing business, a future. He was laying hexagonal tiles, kneeling next to sacks of grout in the kitchen of a local family. He painted the room 'absolute white'. He remembers the day Christine went missing that way, absolute white.

He remembers, too, Ann-Marie's dark, short hair and the way she was holding the bag of bottles. Alcohol. He scrapes his hand along one side of his arm and grabs the empty cereal bowl, clattering the spoon against the cold edge. He pushes himself up and looks out of the patio doors, past the dark fields. There are lines of people walking shoulder to shoulder, combing the undergrowth. Some are wearing white hooded suits. Three police vans and a Jeep are parked along the edge of one field. He has looked at this land every day for the best part of a decade. Now people are looking. Closer than he ever has.

He puts his work bag together and goes out to the pickup. There are more cars in the road at the front of the house and Niall realizes he is almost hemmed in as he tries to back out. A balding man gets out of a blue car and scowls. Niall tries to place him.

He edges close to a four-wheel drive by the gate. A woman in the passenger seat beckons to him as she winds down her window. 'Are you coming to help us with the search?' Her make-up is too bright.

'Well,' he begins, 'I'm away to work the now, but I'll, yes, I'm coming back, for sure.'

'Uh-huh. You're Niall Mackay?' she continues as he reverses carefully. He recognizes her from around the town, but doesn't know her name.

'Aye?'

'Thought if anyone knew about where to look, it would be you.' Her expression is judgemental.

'Heh?'

'On you go,' she says, waving him on sternly.

As he drives to the town his fists are clamped to the steering wheel. People need new bathrooms and he has to put food on the table. He has to carry on for Lauren, even when it kills him inside. He stops in Catriona's drive, his head in his hands. When he closes his eyes, he sees Ann-Marie looking up at him, startled, clutching the door handle, trying to escape.

Catriona answers the door in a boxy jumper that touches the thighs of her neat trousers. He wants to hug her, just for the comfort of another human being. She seems distracted and does not ask whether he wants a cup of tea.

He tries to act like someone who hasn't just found out their wife is dead. 'So how was Sandy then, the other night?'

'Oh, fine.' She looks flushed with happiness. 'We had dinner, then, you know, he went on his way.'

Sure he did, thinks Niall, but nods with what he hopes is a plausible smile. *I'm not here to judge.*

His wife Christine is all around him now, and while his body goes through the motions part of his mind is separate, with her.

On the radio in the kitchen, hosts Dan and Grace are playing 'Win It Minute' with a land surveyor to the sound of a heavily ticking clock. Catriona starts to put her coat on for work and asks him if he knows the missing girl. Her question sounds forced as she pretends to answer an email on her phone.

'Aye, I knew her,' he says. The past tense spooks him and he shakes his head. 'I know her.'

She looks up, genuinely surprised. 'So, you stay out there?' she says.

'Uh-huh.'

'Out by that forest?'

'Yup.'

He can feel her examining him with her big brown eyes. Maybe this is the first time she has really looked.

'She's at boarding school, isn't she?' she says, sliding her phone into her pocket. 'People are saying she was expelled.'

'People?'

'Some kids online – this Diane Armstrong? – apparently she's gone "viral".' Her voice adds quotation marks. 'And lots of people are talking about it, especially her friends in Edinburgh. Saying she's lying somewhere in a field. Twitter. The local news, you know.' She looks at him more intently.

He tries to imagine her now as a doctor, talking to a patient about a serious illness.

She pauses. 'As I've said before, people talk a lot here, Niall. A lot. Not just the internet, it's wherever you go. They've been telling me you knew her. And people seem to know a lot about you too. Your past.' She's nodding as she talks, as if she has pieced something together, something they both have to accept.

'Right.' He turns towards the bathroom.

'I'm sorry,' she says. 'I just wanted you to know.'

He ignores her, puts down his bag on the cement floor and hears her come in behind him. He switches on his radio. She begins to ask a question but stops herself. When he looks up, she is eyeing the white splatters of paint like bird shit on the radio, trying to choose her words.

'Here's a question for you: where does the rock for the Carlin Stones originate from?' says Grace, the radio presenter.

'Ballachulish?' asks Dan, her colleague.

'No, well, you're not far off: Ailsa Craig.'

'I don't think she's out in the fields. I think she's in the forest,' he says. 'If it's no bother to you, I'll be helping them out this afternoon.'

'Oh, of course,' she says in a faraway tone. 'Go now, if you'd like.'

23

He arrives at the search party, a group of people standing on the track, in the dry air. A woman, a secretary at the primary school, is handing out sausage rolls from a Tupperware box in the open boot of a Vauxhall Astra. She's saying, 'The thing is, all that snow is thawing.'

'What can I do to help here?' asks Niall.

She thrusts the box towards him. 'Join us, by all means, Niall, by all means.' Then she says, more softly, 'I know it must be hard for you.' He's grateful for the sympathy and the food.

A man, a shopkeeper from the village, comes out of the field with ruddy cheeks and takes a sausage roll that is burnt around the edges. 'We're all here to help. Awful, i'n't it?' The afternoon is almost dark now, but Niall can see the outline of a little old lady walking up into the forest.

'Here's a torch,' says the shopkeeper, taking one from the back of the van. 'Come on. We've pretty much covered the fields here today, I think. But we are going to try the forest. Is there really any point,

Andy was saying to me, back there, but I said yes – of course there's a point. Of course there's a point. We don't want to miss a minute.'

'It's not been too long, has it?' asks the secretary. Her voice is hoarse as she looks at each of them glumly.

Niall lags behind as they trudge into the dense, gloomy trees. When he was a boy, Niall lived on the other side of the town, away from the forest, but he still felt it at the edges of his life like a stretching shadow. He is with five other people: two tall men, a woman and a couple of teenagers Niall thinks must be friends of Diane. He wonders why they aren't at school, or if they've left.

The group wave their torch beams in the fern banks and ditches, but it is still difficult to reach every corner of the forest. Some thickets of gorse simply grow too densely to walk through. It's so cold out here. His nose is running. At any moment, Niall worries torch light might fall on the girl's dead body. Images pass through his mind's eye, of her matted hair, the whites of her rolled-back eyes, her naked, pale skin, her sliced throat. Maybe they'll just find a body part: a hand, a leg carried away and eaten by wild animals, predatory birds. He doesn't know how he'll be able to live with himself. They cross the soft mossy floor, wet with melting snow. The phone signal has long gone and after a while all the trees begin to look the same: thin, tall towers.

The quiet is broken now and again with someone shouting 'ANN-MARIE,' and then another, calling into the gloom, occasionally overlapping like church bells. Their line spreads deeper into the forest and crosses paths with other small groups searching as the sun is slowly swallowed by the hillside. A fluorescent tape is strung tautly between the trees like a macabre ribbon to mark their pathways.

'ANN-MARIE.'

'ANN-MARIE.'

'AAAAAANN-MARIE.'

'ANN-MARIE.'

'ANN-MARIE!'

Her name takes on an importance each time it is called. There are now eight of them walking through the blossoming dark. Now and again their identities are exposed brightly in the questioning beam of a torch.

'ANN-MARIE.'

'ANN-MARIE!'

Niall takes his turn to shout, deep from his lungs: 'ANN-MARIE.' He looks all around as he goes. The shouting has opened something up in him and he shouts again, over another calling voice: 'AAAAAANN-MARIE.'

'Ann-Marie.'

Niall whips round and strains his ears to catch the voice again. He counts the search party. There are still eight of them, but they don't match the voice that spoke. It is becoming hard to see without his beam. A male tawny owl hoots deeply like a gym teacher blowing on a whistle. A female screeches back. Niall shifts the torch to his left hand and sees Vairi standing small and frail by his side.

'Gave me a fright,' he says, breathing out.

'I'm listening,' Vairi says. 'Did you hear her too? I know you did.'

Niall doesn't answer as the rest of the group plough on.

'It is Christine,' she says. 'Yes? Christine.'

'What . . . ?' He starts to walk away to catch up and trips over a root.

'She comes to say hello sometimes. She's been here.'

He looks back over his shoulder. 'What?' His voice is a growl. 'Don't be daft. What are you on about? You're—'

'Shhh.' The sound comes from someone else. His torch falls on another member of the search party, their finger to their lips. He walks on in silence.

He thinks he hears a woman singing faintly through the forest.

'*Ann-Marie.*'

When the children leave the school building at three thirty, hundreds of white helium balloons wait for them in the playground, provided by a local radio station. A food van is serving hot teas and coffees as surprised parents begin to gather. Dinner ladies bring out a trestle table with free squash for the children.

Another TV presenter is talking into a big black camera in the weakening daylight. 'If you see anything at all, please phone us, or the police. Help is at hand. We warn you not to approach anyone suspicious. This is a town historically hit by tragedy. Nearly a decade ago, it saw the disappearance of Christine Mackay, an event that shook this tight-knit community to its core, and now there are fears of history repeating itself. Could Ann-Marie be out there with Christine, the woman she knew as a child? Certainly, many people round here can only hope' – here he pauses for effect – 'that she is safe. Back to you in the studio.'

Diane is interviewed on TV, wearing black lipstick and a dog collar. People bundled up in hats and coats walk past as she talks about why she decided to use social media. 'She's my best friend,' Diane says, her hoarse voice cracking. 'If you're out there, watching this, please come home. We need you.'

Ann-Marie's parents arrive to a small group of press, shaken and gaunt, nodding at the camera while pleading for their daughter to come home.

Lauren looks around for her father; then she remembers he texted to say he's searching in the woods already.

'You all right, Lauren?' asks Diane, sidling up to her from the cameras when it's over.

'No. It's . . . I don't know how I'm meant to feel.'

'How d'you mean? We know she's out there. We do. She'll be back.'

'But that's not true. My mum's never coming back.'

'You poor wee soul. I know it's all very mixed up at the moment, but we've gotta think positive for Ann-Marie, you know?' Diane doesn't look very positive. Her face is pale and anxious.

'My mum.' The images of death are involuntary and relentless: crushed snail shells, veins in meat, vampire teeth, soil filling a mouth. She remembers how, in the spring, one of Angela's hens hatched chicks and she put them in a rabbit run. A polecat snuck under the run and ate all the chicks, leaving their heads in the grass. They didn't know how it had entered at first until they saw a single scratch in the ground.

'Police gave me my car back,' says Diane. 'C'mon.'

They leave the crowd of people with their dogs and crying children in buggies. Diane drives them through the dark lanes to her home, speaking too quickly. 'People think I'm cool because I have my own car, you know. You don't know. No. You're too young. But it's my mum's car and I do all her shopping. I'm just trying to get my grades. I'm trying to take my mind off this.' They drive past Lauren's house and into the pines. 'You don't mind if I smoke, then we'll go and meet your dad, shall we?'

Without waiting for an answer, she jerks the car to a halt in the muddy mound of her driveway, overshadowed by hazel and holly trees. 'I'm smoking way too much now, but it's all that's helping. I'll just be a minute, then I can drop you off at the field.'

Lauren knows that they will not be going into Diane's house, because Diane's mother is ill and has been ill as long as Lauren can remember. For most of her life, Diane has looked after her mother. In recent years she has worked shifts at the Black Horse, and for a while did cleaning at the Castle Hotel in a black dress and white apron that she hated. For this reason, Lauren has hardly ever been to Diane's house. The times she has, it felt sad. An over-stuffed-cushion, lots-of-teddy-bears kind of sad, rather than the sparser sadness that could leak from the walls at her own home.

'It's nice we got to know each other better,' says Diane forlornly, dragging on her joint and tapping the ash out of the window. Lauren watches it fly away in the biting wind. 'Well. That was the only good thing to happen. I'm having these fucked-up nightmares.'

She looks over at Lauren, who wants to go home. 'Can you read the cards again, and maybe we can find out if Ann-Marie's coming back?' Diane's voice is soaked in desperation. 'There might be some cards in the car somewhere.' The back seat is littered with clothes, old food wrappers and a make-up bag.

'No.' Lauren draws herself up. 'My *mum*'s not coming back.' Her voice is even. 'I never even knew her.' These words have been going through her mind on a loop until she is compelled to say them out loud. She sighs and looks down at Diane's nails, black-purple like hard berries.

Without a word Diane rolls up the window and carries on smoking against the windscreen. 'It's on the radio,' she says with a drawl, turning it down. 'Whenever I switch on the radio, they're talking about her, wherever she is. It's the least I could do, really. They've got to find her soon. I've told the police everything.' She starts rolling another joint.

Lauren knows there is something else that Diane is not telling her. She can smell the strange smoke strongly in her nostrils. She smiles without wanting to.

Diane says, 'There is this show I watched, called *The Dark Net*, where some girl found this cult online and she just kept listening to these podcasts all the time, I'm serious, about like twenty times a day. Then she did this thing where she wrote her parents a letter saying that she was gone and if she ever felt like seeing them again, she'd get in touch.' She laughs a high, infectious laugh. 'How about that? Fuck. I mean, I'm never going to leave my fucking mum, no matter how bad things are. I mean . . .' She pauses, sighing, breathing out smoke that is infusing the front seats. 'Sorry, Lauren, sorry, but I sometimes think about it. I sometimes look at that long road there stretching out to wherever. But that's the thing about here, where we live. Where do you go?'

'Sometimes,' says Lauren slowly, 'I think the same thing.' *What about the man in the basement?* she is thinking. *Are we never going to talk about that?*

'Oh my God,' Diane says, looking down at her phone. 'Oh my God. I'm not reading this straight. That girl that you hate, whatshername. Who's got the farm.'

'Maisie.'

'Aye. My friend just text me, saying that girl found Ann-Marie's hat. The black one.' She looks straight ahead of her, then reads another message that has flashed up on-screen. 'Apparently she won't stop crying about it. They say "she's had a shock". She tried to cross that frozen lake in the field and fell through? Lucky someone in the search team rescued her.'

Lauren tips her head back and laughs, a round, generous laugh, as she watches white balloons float across the sky beyond the sunroof.

24

They are driving home from the search party when they see her. The trees are coarse and tall in the winter light, standing like men.

They see her, a slight figure, stumble out into the road at the bottom of the hill. She is bent over, her arms tightly folded. The sun is low between the trees but strong and Niall squints, keeping his hands steady on the walnut patches of the wheel, slowing his speed. He brings the truck to a halt by the trees.

Lauren opens her mouth to speak in the quiet space the engine has left. She makes an 'Aa' sound. Most of the name is still lodged in her throat.

'Yeah,' he whispers.

She is still wearing the same black jeans and her padded blue anorak, a ragged blanket over her shoulders. He remembers the anorak as she walked up the side of the road and he called after her to come back. He breathes hard. 'Don't get out of the car.'

A twin memory overwhelms him. How he had held her. Christine.

As she walks unsteadily up the middle of the steep road, there is no mistaking Ann-Marie or the fact that under the blanket she is covered in dark stains, the colour of rust.

Lauren is already unbuckling her seatbelt and wrenching open the door.

'Don't leave the—' Niall barks. He watches Lauren run down the edge of the road in her battered black Clarks.

Ann-Marie doesn't quicken her pace, nor does she turn her head. He can see it is an effort for her to walk up the hill, her eyes trained on some spot in the distance. Lauren catches up with her and throws herself into a hug. Ann-Marie stiffens and tries gently to push her away. Then she seems to register the truck and she sinks towards the tarmac. Lauren tries to haul her up with her small body. Ann-Marie nods her head slowly, staring blankly. Lauren says something. Niall stays still in his seat as fear begins to knot around him like a creeping plant. There is a wide streak of blood on the girl's forehead. Her hair is crusty and there are dark patches on her frail denim knees. A small, selfish part of him wants to grab Lauren, swivel the truck around and go. He can already see how the situation will look if they bring her back. Nobody trusts him. He peers through the gloomy trees on either side, checks his rear-view mirror and sees nothing. Ann-Marie doubles over and retches bile on to the road.

He watches Lauren run back towards him and his body wakes up.

'Dad!'

He stumbles down from the truck and squeezes Lauren's hot hand, before bundling her into the passenger seat. He hesitates, looking around one more time for any traffic. He yanks off his coat and puts it around the teenager's shoulders. Ann-Marie flinches and wipes her mouth. She looks behind her with wild eyes and gestures *Go* towards the pickup; her other hand is tightly clenched. As she moves, Niall notices her baggy, bloodstained T-shirt is ripped open at one side. He tries to find the wound and then realizes he is looking at something dark and inky tattooed on her skin. She sways again and Niall lifts her up over his shoulder. Her limp body weighs almost the same as Lauren's as he tucks her next to his daughter in the front. Lauren shifts half off the seat, one foot by the gear stick.

'Dad.'

He sees she is terrified. 'Do you want to sit on my knee again?'

'*Dad.*'

He leaves her where she is and jogs over to his side of the truck, slamming himself into the seat and pushing back against the headrest, chin raised, eyes screwed shut. 'I need to think.'

'What? She's bleeding.'

'I need to *think*.' He says this too loud and Lauren starts to cry. He tries to pull her over to sit on his lap, but she pushes him off.

'Why can't you do anything?' She turns to Ann-Marie. 'Where were you?'

Ann-Marie shakes her head in reply, her eyes on the messy truck floor.

Lauren reaches out to touch the blood on Ann-Marie's T-shirt and Niall pulls her hand away.

'*Dad*. We need to go.' She looks up at the trees again. 'There could be someone.'

'Well, I'm not driving with you like that. Come over here.' Lauren reluctantly scoots over on to his lap. She is getting too big for this now and it feels uncomfortable, bony. Her ponytail obscures his view as he starts the engine. 'Move over further, I can't see, come on.'

'Fine. Ann-Marie, what's wrong?' Lauren says. 'Speak to me. We need to know.'

Niall's hands are shaking as he grabs the steering wheel. As he pulls back into the road he looks over and sees Ann-Marie's hand is still clenched. There is a corner of something poking out of the side of her fist.

'Right,' he says and drives fast through the forest to where it breaks into ghost-white birches. Lauren sniffs with wet eyes.

'Is she still bleeding?' he asks.

'I can't see from here,' Lauren replies.

He glances over and sees Ann-Marie sitting still, crusted blood on her face, in her hair, her hands, her skin. 'Christ. Where the fuck were you?'

There is a long silence. Niall tries to watch the road.

'I got lost, but I found an old shed to sleep in. There were strange fires. All around me. Burning in a circle. Like a dream.'

He sighs, glad she is alive, still breathing, still speaking, yet he isn't sure where he is driving. Something like shame courses through him as he tries to picture Angela and Malcolm's reaction. He left her by the woods that night. He drove away. She is alive, though, she is alive.

As they come to the fork in the road between the village and the town, he turns towards the Elms instinctively. They could call 999 from there, her house, with her parents. The shock begins to ebb a little. He starts to wonder what could have happened to her. He almost can't bear to think. How injured is she? He glances over again and sees she is shivering. He turns up the heating. The windows start to mist, and Niall's brain feels clouded. All of this is not happening. Not all of this is happening.

Niall stops the truck in the long driveway of the Elms. 'Look,' Niall says to Lauren. 'I need some fresh air, just for a minute. You try and talk to her.' He climbs out and rests his gloved palm on the frosty window. In the distance, at the top of the drive, dogs begin to bark.

He takes a deep breath and gets back into the pickup.

'Well?' says Lauren to Ann-Marie. The other girl looks down at her feet and closes her eyes.

Niall leans over to touch her shoulder. 'What? What happened? We need to know, c'mon.'

Ann-Marie's face changes. 'There was meant to be a plan. Diane was going to meet me after. We invited him to her house first. It all went wrong.'

Not knowing what else to say, he shakes his head and says, 'I'm so sorry. C'mon now.'

She is quiet. Her fist tightens around what she is holding in her hand.

The two Irish wolfhounds stand at the top of the drive, looking down towards them.

'Ann-Marie, if you can, tell me. Who is it? Be clear. Nothing bad is going to happen to you.'

Ann-Marie nods her head. 'There was this story. About a dog with a leg in its mouth. I drove him away. It was . . . him. The guy I was looking for.'

'Take your time,' Niall says, trying to encourage her, sitting back in his seat to give her space.

'Uh-huh,' she says, still nodding her head. She swallows. 'It's hard to talk about.'

'Look, I'm not following. You went to Diane's after I left you that night and . . . Who did this to you? Tell me.'

'He wasn't like I thought. Diane knew him better, at the Black Horse. I had this idea that he would meet us for a drink and a smoke and we would record him talking. Secretly. Diane said he liked to talk. Show off. She thought he was arrogant, so I was nervous. But he was so *nice*. I was convinced we had something wrong. We started talking about his band; he wouldn't stop talking about it. He said we should go and see him some time, at a ceilidh that was happening. He liked that we were interested in Christine and said he had his own theories, about his old PE teacher – you know, Alan Mackie. He told me how he really admired me. For caring about Christine. He said he thought Alan Mackie was guilty. And that he used to know her really well too, like I did. I felt sorry for him. And that – I'm sorry, Niall – that *you* were his friend and you didn't know how well he and Christine knew each other. He got his friend to rent her a room, for her therapy.'

He slams the heels of his hands against the steering wheel, making the truck shudder. 'Sandy Ross. Are you telling me it was *him*?' It is too much to take in. 'She didn't know him.' The few times they met flash through his mind. He remembers how he and Sandy became friends in the years after she went missing.

Her voice is low. 'He said he could show me where he *thought* she was buried.'

For a few minutes he is paralysed, his brain working too fast and then too slowly. Violent thoughts crawl over him.

She carries on speaking, as if unable to stop. 'There was *something* about the way he said it. He was so confident and he seemed kind too. I know this sounds like I'm crazy, but I thought it would be OK. Diane and I had a conversation when he was in the toilet and she tried to make me stay. The thing is, I thought I'd read him wrong. I was recording our conversation on my phone, that was the idea, but I began to feel safe. I thought we were going in his car, but he didn't have his car. That was a bit strange, I admit. I asked why he didn't have his car. I should have known something was up. He said he had cycled from the lochans, but his bike wasn't outside. No fishing stuff. He said we could use Diane's car. Looking back, he wasn't taking any chances.' She coughs, and Niall can see tears rolling down her face. 'I was such an idiot. I left him outside and asked Diane again if she wanted to come too, but before I could mention the car, she dingied me. Told me she wanted to stay at home. I said I'd text her and if anything happened we could meet. This place in the woods we go to smoke. I nicked the keys from her coat pocket.

'To be safe, I insisted on driving.'

Niall looks at her, surprised.

'I learned from my dad out here. I remember, when we first got into the car, he put his gloves on. He had been standing around in the cold, waiting for me, with bare hands, but to get in the car, he put his gloves on. Inside the car, he then zipped up his jacket and put his hat on. I just thought he was warming himself up, or something. But the car was warm, so it didn't really make sense. Then when I was driving up a track in the forest, several miles away from Diane's, I didn't really know where we were. It was then he told me he knew. Christine was killed in a hidden basement.' She starts to shake but no more tears come. 'Kept saying that Alan Mackie had done it. I went to check my phone was still recording, to get all this, but it wasn't there . . . I looked over and he had tied a scarf tight over his face. It was just his eyes looking at me. I stopped the car. We were deep in the woods. I didn't really know where. He took the car keys, then made me get out and walk. I must have walked for miles.' She starts to cry again, holding herself tightly.

Niall feels almost scared to be near the girls. His body wants only to destroy something. Destroy as he is being destroyed, piece by piece. He thinks of Sandy, in his house, talking to his daughter. Catriona and the fishing trip.

Ann-Marie speaks again, in a low voice. 'We got to this house and he made me go down into the basement. It was so dark. There was a Samurai sword on the wall. His. I wanted to take it when he was looking for something in one of the boxes, but it was too far away. I got so lost in the woods afterwards. I was so tired, I couldn't think any more. Started to hear things. I thought someone was following me. A bird. I found a stone shed – too far in the other direction. I had seen small fires in the distance. The lights. I felt warm, when it was so cold. In the shed I could hear a fire crackling outside. The fires, I told you. I was scared they would burn the whole place down. The next morning, there was nothing, just the snow melting.'

Niall reaches over and yanks open the glove box. The girls flinch. He snatches his flask of vodka and gulps it. The burn feels soothing. He stays still until he can trust himself. Two thoughts swim to the surface. One is the axe in the boot. The other he speaks aloud. 'You've been bleeding. You've been bleeding everywhere.'

The barking is getting closer. Niall sees the two black dogs bounding towards them at the top of the drive.

Ann-Marie's closed eyes tighten. 'I'm OK. I feel so dizzy in here,' she whispers. 'In the basement, he stopped rummaging about and came towards me. But as he came, the air screamed. Like a woman's voice. Things in the room started to move. I thought I was seeing things. I didn't know what to do.'

PINE

Niall turns to her again and puts a hand on her shoulder. He swallows. 'You've been badly hurt.'

'No. I've not.' She is hunched, barely moving with exhaustion.

'The blood. It's all over you.'

She takes a deep breath and opens her eyes. 'It's not my blood.'

Her fist is still tightly clenched, but he can see the end of something, a glint of metal.

Lauren says, 'Is that my knife?'

He can hear the dogs panting outside the door, circling the truck, still barking.

Ann-Marie looks at Niall, a current of adrenaline running through her expression.

'Can I have it?' Lauren strokes Ann-Marie's shoulder in a way that breaks Niall's heart. 'I lost it.'

'It was in my pocket,' Ann-Marie says, staring out of the window. 'I don't remember why it was there. I just remember I felt something made of antler. Then there was something soft, like fruit splitting open. I don't know how it came to me.'

'I lost it. And I think she found it. She took it,' says Lauren.

'I didn't,' says Ann-Marie.

'No, I meant the other woman. My mum. Christine.'

A dog jumps up at the window, its paws on the glass, a hairy, sharp-toothed grin.

Ann-Marie starts and sinks her head in her hands. 'If I didn't. This. Wouldn't be here. I wouldn't. Be here.' She looks at Lauren and hugs her and cries. 'Thank you.'

Niall can see the figures of Angela, Malcolm and a teenage boy at the top of the drive. At first, he thinks it must be Fraser, home from university, but as they walk closer he sees he has blond hair under his hat and looks completely different.

Lauren looks out of the window too, then carries on, her hand on Ann-Marie's shoulder. 'I lost it. But I think she took it from me and gave it to you. You needed it. You can keep it. What happened?'

'It's not my blood,' she says.

25

Some nights Lauren wakes as Oren, her new old name, and is called to the window by a silent language. She does not know when these nights will announce themselves but knows they are connected to the shape of the moon and the movements of the planets. She is learning the constellations she sees from her window and carving animals into wood.

When the blue-moon nights arrive, Lauren smells summer flowers. She might see a cast of hawks or a scattering of herons. A knot of toads or a richesse of pine martens. One night there is a destruction of wildcats. And when she sees them from her window she knows she goes out into the garden, because the next morning the soles of her feet are muddy. Yet she only remembers Christine, her mother, in her dreams and in the stories her father tells, now he is ready to talk. He tells her he wants to talk as much as he can, to her and other people, like Kirsty. He needs to practise for Sandy's trial. With Diane's help the police found him, stabbed in the face with a pocketknife. They had to treat Ann-Marie at a different facility to him, for her dehydration and hypothermia. There was a news story about it and one when Ann-Marie recovered, and was being taught at home by a tutor. The story showed a photo of her grinning with Diane, who sometimes joins her to study. The paper said Sandy will never get his sight back. His eyes are gone.

Lauren enjoys it when her father tells her about all the things her mum used to like. The colour lilac, red apples, sea anemones, blood oranges. This way, she has a sense of how she might have laughed or the tone of her voice. Lauren and her father have made a photo album together, from the box of old pictures in the living room. The room is always open now and catches the sun in the afternoon. Lauren lies on its yellow sofa after school, to read a book and let the light settle on her face. Her father goes to a group at the doctor's every Wednesday. Sometimes he is very sad afterwards, but on the whole he is happier. Some nights Lauren wears her mother's jewellery to bed: long necklaces made from moonstone and tiger's eye. She turns the silver ring on her finger, snuffs out her candles and watches crystals wink in the moonlight.

ACKNOWLEDGEMENTS

Writing a book with a full-time job was always going to take a while. Over the past four years, I have been grateful to many people who have helped me through the process.

A big thank-you to my fantastic agent Emma Paterson for her wisdom, belief and shared taste for the macabre. Special thanks to Aitken Alexander.

Many thanks also to my insightful editor Fiona Murphy for her warmth, understanding and shared love of forests. A big thanks to my amazing publicist Alison Barrow, the lovely Antonia Whitton, the eagle-eyed Sophie Wilson, Richenda Todd, Beci Kelly, Fíodhna Ni Ghríofa, Orla King and the rest of the team at Doubleday, who have buoyed me with their enthusiasm.

Thank you to my own lovely authors and colleagues at Sceptre for your support. I feel very lucky.

Thank you to Glynn Powell, from the Scottish Parliament Police Unit, for his insight into a typical missing person's case. All inaccuracies are squarely my own.

Huge thanks to Lorna and Graham, for letting me stay with them in Sutherland on Halloween, when I had an inkling of an idea for this novel (even though I was keeping it secret!). Thank you to Alice for putting my questions to the residents of Inverness. I will always remember our hut-building and pebble competitions at Newton Point. Even though all the characters are self-consciously fictional, the novel wouldn't be the same without the best neighbours we could have asked for, the Sawyers and the Richardsons, and our walks around the Loop in Clashmore Wood.

Thanks to Karl Smith for the conversation that started me on the path to writing this book, and to Dominic Esler for suggesting it take a super-natural turn.

A big thank-you to May-Lan Tan for her own Laurens and telling me where to end this novel. Her reading meant the world.

Love to my personal coven – Kate Loftus O'Brien, Cecily Davey, Livia Franchini and G Bowie – for their endless support and witchiness. Kate and Cecily's words have kept me going at difficult times. Thank you to Audry Bowie for her Caithness knowledge of whin bushes.

I was lucky to have two incredible friends who read multiple drafts from the beginning: Nick

Cole-Hamilton and Christiana Spens. Their time, humour and kindness has been invaluable to me. Thank you.

Love to my wonderful parents, Annie and Steve, who decided to move to the Highlands when I was nine years old. Thank you for giving me some magical experiences. Their reading and continued support has meant everything to me.

Thank you to my amazing sister Charlotte, with all her positive energy. I'm so lucky to have her in my life.

Last, to Yassine, whom I can't thank enough for navigating this journey with me, always having time to chat at any hour of day or night, cooking for me, putting up with my strange routines and questions, taking me off to a cottage on the west coast to finish the first draft and being there for me in every other way possible. I'm dedicating this book to you because it wouldn't have been possible otherwise. Lots of love.

Francine Toon grew up in Sutherland and Fife, Scotland. Her poetry, written as Francine Elena, has appeared in the *Sunday Times*, the *Best British Poetry* 2013 and 2015 anthologies (Salt) and *Poetry London*, among other places. *Pine* was longlisted for the Deborah Rogers Foundation Writers Award. She lives in London and works in publishing.